Redbriar

by Jack Hemphill

Published by
Willow Oak Publishing

Library of Congress Control Number: 2013952447
ISBN: 978-0-9899516-0-9
Printed in the United States of America

Acknowledgements:

I would like to thank some of the people who patiently helped me through the long process of writing this book.

I am very grateful for my editor Patrick LoBrutto for his infinite understanding of how novels work, Judge Hugh Campbell for legal background, Jerri McCloud for literary guidance, Carole King for her insight, and Ashley Bird for graphic design.

I would like to mention the dozens of sheriffs and all the honest, brave, unsung law enforcement heroes I had the privilege of working with over the years.

Most of all I want to thank my dear wife, who not only is my best friend, but also is my most severe critic, without whose help, I could never have written anything.

CHAPTER ONE

TAD

I was only fourteen when I was taken away from my Dad. It was impossible for me to get over losing both my parents at the same time. What does a fourteen year old know about anything? I knew how much Dad wanted to see me, but I was afraid. There are some things that just can't be forgiven.

My name is Kathleen Remington Burns. Kathleen was Mom's grandmother's name, but nobody ever knew me by any name other than the one Dad gave me—*Tad*. Believe it or not, Tad was short for *Tadpole*. Yes, Tadpole, the baby frog thing. I loved it when I was kid, but when I grew up, I couldn't get rid of it and I never told anyone where the name came from.

My childhood ended early. I can tell you the exact time and place when it happened. It came with a single word—"guilty." I saw Dad's face as he stood alone in front of the judge. For that one moment, he seemed like he was the child and I the adult. No one before or after the trial, questioned me about what I knew, and I promised myself never to tell. In spite of the verdict, in spite of the storm caused by the trial, Dad's cadre of attorneys managed to get him set free.

I was sent to live with my grandma, but when she died, I

ran away. My cousins let me stay with them on the other side of the river as long as I wanted. They never told anyone I was there.

All my cousins in that little cabin were boys. Some of them thought they were men, but they were more like a pack of puppies escaped from the kennels. I did my part around there, but much of the time I just sketched or looked out the window toward the river.

I never had a brother and the truth is, before I moved in, I wasn't really all that close to my cousins. I never knew what guys were like. I knew nothing about their inexhaustible energy, their insatiable appetite for anything solid or liquid—anything the stomach would hold down. I didn't understand their unrelenting competitions over everything from who would get the soft chair by the TV to who could piss the farthest off the back porch. My conclusion then, and I still half believe it, was that boys, as well as men, are funny, fascinating, lovable, inexplicable pigs, or—in the case of my cousins—*piglets*. But, they were good to me and took care of me.

They liked to laugh more than talk and, except for Silas, they had no use for serious discussions. Silas was the only one in the family who served in the military and had recently returned from active duty in Vietnam.

I loved living in the woods—especially in winter with its white blanket shrouding us. Every morning I looked out my window for fresh tracks left in the night by critters that crept by our little cabin. Some of them traveled in pairs or in small groups—especially deer. Sometimes, I followed the tracks until they disappeared into the stream or over the hill. I always wondered where the animals hid during the day, but I never followed them beyond my cousin's property. That's as far as I ever went except when I walked up the long gravel drive to get their mail. Even then, I was careful not to let anyone see me. But, I knew sooner or later Dad would find me.

More than three years after the trial, on the coldest day I

can remember, all the window panes were glazed over. Through a hole in the frost about the size of a pie plate, I watched gray snowflakes fall from the sky. A gust of white blew across the window. When it cleared, a face was peering in. I don't think he saw me at first. His eyes were cast toward the fire, but I saw him jump when I screamed. I almost didn't recognize him, wearing a wool knit hat pulled to his eyebrows and a stubbly beard half covered in snow, but still it was my Dad. I couldn't look at him even then.

I ran to the back of the house, stood still against the wall between two windows and closed my eyes. The silence was broken by the sound of steps stomping through snow to the back deck. When he reached the landing, I ran through the house, out the front door, and up the drive. I was wearing only a sweater, blue jeans, and sneakers, but I didn't even notice the cold. By the time I got to the first curve in the drive, I turned long enough to see him kicking his way toward me through the snowdrift by the house. I think he called my name, but I shot off again climbing the steep slippery roadway. Another hundred yards. I was exhausted. I looked back again.

"What the hell you doin', Tad?' a voice blasted at me.

Four of my cousins, returning home, were suddenly around me.

"What are you doing?" Scott asked again.

"He found me."

"Who, your Dad?"

I shook my head then blurted, "Hide me!"

"The car's right up there. We couldn't get it any closer."

Without another thought, I plowed up the remainder of the hill, jumped into the back seat and locked the door. Lying flat on my back, my head throbbed in rhythm with my chest. In spite of the cold outside, I felt a trickle of sweat cross my forehead and past my ear. The windows quickly steamed over and the world

3

disappeared until I grew cold again. *Did they find him? What were they doing?* I flew back down the drive. The cold bit into me like a hungry animal. The door of the cabin was still open. Nobody was there. I found my coat and ran out the back door just as my cousins marched toward me around the frozen laurel below. I couldn't move.

Billy motioned at me with both hands as if to say "It's taken care of." That's when I saw the tracks like something had been dragged through the snow by the cabin and around the laurel toward the river.

All four of the guys were wearing a half smile, almost a sneer.

"Where is he?"

"Don't worry about him no more."

"Where is he?" My hands gripped the railing.

"We threw the murdering bastard into the river."

I must have collapsed or something after that. All I remember was the feeling of my knees colliding with the snow on the deck. Scott and Ralph picked me up and carried me to a spot on the rug by the fire.

CHAPTER TWO

STUART

The cold had already frozen parts of my wet clothes—my sleeves, the wool jacket across my back, and the bottom of my pants. I weighed a ton as I climbed out of the river and up the stone gully behind my house. Sergeant was waiting for me in the studio by the door. He saw the blood trickling from my lip and the condition of my clothes. As all dogs instinctively do, he comforted me immediately, and I wallowed in it for a moment before throwing my frozen coat on the floor. With a rag I knocked ice from my hair and blotted my lip. From a vertical bin beside the couch, I pulled three or four sketch pads and a box of charcoal drawing sticks. My frozen fingers refused to grasp the charcoal. I replenished the logs in the fire and thawed both hands, then with a small pad on my lap, I started sketching. Her eyes first. Carefully. Over and over I caressed them onto the paper. Then her nose and lips. As soon as one drawing was finished I tore it out and let it fall to the floor to start another. Eventually I drew her whole face—straight on, profile, looking up, glancing over her shoulder.

As I have done all my life, each line was drawn slowly with soft charcoal, then with my fingers and hands I stroked and rubbed the black powdery lines into tones and shadows carving the gentle curves in her face.

Sergeant tiptoed around me, careful not to step on the piles of paper scattered across the floor.

Night came and I finally grew drowsy. I could no longer distinguish the images in my memory of Tad from my imagination. By then I wasn't sure I was drawing what I actually saw or what I had hoped to see. After re-feeding the fire one more time, I stretched out on the rug and fell asleep. Sergeant nestled against my back.

Only official cars in Jefferson County wear chains on their tires. It's an ominous sound and not something anyone wants to hear first thing in the morning. I had already stoked the fire, and nursed my swollen lip. My left leg was stiff as I moved as fast as I could to the window. The bright morning sun on the snow was blinding. I saw a brown sheriff's car making his way up my drive. I knew it wouldn't take the sheriff's crew long to figure out I was home again in violation of my court order. With Sergeant running beside me I hobbled to the den at the back of the house and closed the blinds. The deputy pounded on the front door. Deputies never ring door bells they just pound with their meaty fists. I put Sergeant out the back door. Sergeant had the heart and killer instinct of a bunny rabbit, but he was a great actor. From the dining room window I watched him play out his role as I knew he would. There is nothing particularly frightening about a barking dog, but the same 85 pound animal half crouched, head fixed in straight line with his shoulders, eyes set, and a full-toothed growl will back a 250 pound deputy all the way into his car. The thumping of snow chains was much faster as the car disappeared down the driveway and turned west toward Redbriar.

It was nearly Christmas. I had looked for Tad four months, ever since my mother died. I finally found her and I had to leave. It only took me a half hour to gather everything I needed and load my Ranch Wagon which I kept tucked away in the barn. At the end of the drive, I turned east toward Tom's Creek. If the wooden bridge was open, I would get out of the county without going through town. It took me nearly twenty minutes to drive the four and a half miles to the river. Nobody knew exactly how old the bridge was or who built it. I think the only reason it had never been replaced is because the dividing line between Jefferson and Madison County goes right down the middle of the river and each county was hoping the other would fix the sagging structure.

The moment I crested the last hill and started my descent toward the river I saw the blaze of hoar frost igniting the entire valley. Hoar frost doesn't look at all like snow. Snow changes everything into a nebulous soft-white landscape, but in sunlight, hoar frost exaggerates everything it touches with a shine ten times brighter than snow.

Each plank on Tom's Creek Bridge stood out like it had been carefully extruded from a baker's funnel. Sergeant gave out a high pitched whine as he looked up and down the river. We slowed to about five miles an hour as we inched across the bridge. The frost, frozen in layers on the wood floor, shattered like delicate glass under our tires. By the time we reached the center, I heard chunks of ice breaking from the underside and splashing into the flowing steam below us. The old timber was bending under the load of my station wagon and the extra weight of built-up ice over every square inch of the bridge. I tried to speed up, but that only caused the car to drift closer to the rail. Slowly, keeping my speed steady, I managed to ease my way to the other side where we stopped about twenty-five feet up the road. I got out and walked back to the bridge. The slow moving stream was black and the sun-lit, glistening trees looked like frozen flames of white fire. I followed the stream with my eyes all the way to the bend fifty yards to the south. I sketched every detail into my memory.

Looking toward Redbriar, just beyond the hoar frost, a flash of light caught my attention. I shuffled my way back to the bridge. About sixty yards up the road, a deputy was standing beside his car watching me. We both knew he wouldn't cross the bridge and I wasn't going to give him the pleasure of seeing me run away, so I ignored him and drank in the scenery for another few minutes.

Sheriff Hodges never personally came after me, but he liked nothing more than to harass me by sending his deputies instead. I had known him my whole life, but spent most of that time trying to avoid him and most of the last decade trying to forget him. I couldn't. I was never ashamed of the fact that I was afraid of him and I never knew whether he feared me in return or just hated me. The very sight of me caused him to boil.

I walked back to my car and drove away.

It only took three more hours to get to my home in Charlotte. When Tad was ten, I moved her and Sarah, my wife, to a house in Myers Park on the south-east side of town. I did it partly because I wanted my daughter to go to one of the private schools there and partly because I would be closer to the main gallery promoting my work. Sarah hated Charlotte and returned to my Redbriar home every chance she got.

The first thing I saw when I pulled up to my house was a large white note taped to my garage door. I knew right away it was from Pierce, my agent, who put notes on the garage when she wanted to get my attention. I never told her I was leaving town, or where I would be, but she knew.

Still exhausted and sore, I went to bed early that night. When the doorbell rang at 7:30 the next morning, I slipped on some socks, sweat pants, and a jersey. I wasn't surprised to see Pierce's face at the front door.

"How did you know I was home" I asked.

"The note on the garage was gone."

"Have you been driving by every day?'

"Yes. Where did you go?"

I didn't reply. She already knew the answer.

"Did you see her?" she asked.

"I did."

"Did you talk to her?"

"Not exactly."

"What does that mean?"

"I saw her face. Let's start some coffee." She followed me back to the kitchen.

"Breakfast?" I asked.

"Just coffee. What happened to your lip?"

"I banged it on a rock."

'Where?"

"In the river," I said with a deadpan voice. She tossed her head back knowing I wasn't going to talk about it anymore.

I put on some hot water and poured myself a bowl of cornflakes.

"You know why I'm here, don't you," she said.

"You want some paintings."

"No, I want *lots* of paintings."

"You've *got* lots of my paintings."

"Not anymore."

"What do you mean?"

"Everything's finally gone nuts—in Charlotte, Charleston, and Atlanta. Its all gone. Sold out. Even some of the old ones we've had around a while. I got calls from people looking for more. Even a gallery in New York is interested in you—in your work."

"Why now?"

"It doesn't matter."

"Of course it matters. What you're saying is they're finally becoming interested in my work because I'm a murderer."

"No, Stu...Well, okay, the trial got their attention, then they discovered you—they discovered you as an artist, I mean. It's your paintings they want. It has nothing to do with your wife's death. Anyway, in the art world, it doesn't matter whether you're famous or notorious. If your name is known, your stuff sells."

"But why now?"

"It might have something to do with the articles I wrote."

"Pierce! What articles?"

"Well." She stopped to take off her long coat and sit down at my kitchen table. "I wrote some articles about how Sarah was your inspiration and what it must have been like for you to be put on trial for her death."

"You've got to be shitting me!"

"I would have told you, but I couldn't find you. Anyway it's done some good. Everything's selling."

I walked to the window for a minute.

"I can't believe it," I finally muttered.

"So, I need more," she said.

"What about all the paintings I gave you a few months ago"

"All gone. What are you working on now?"

I ducked into my garage and pulled the stack of sketches I had done two days before in Redbriar from the back seat.

"What are these?"

"Tad. Tad's face"

"Stu. I can't sell portraits of your daughter."

"These are for me."

"Okay, but you can't hold back on me, Stu. You can't stop your work."

"Stop? You know damn well I'm not going to stop, but I need for you to leave me alone right now. At least for a while."

"If you can't stop, then get me some paintings, and I don't mean of Tad's face. Now is the time to do it, and besides, I'm sure

10

Tad's not going anywhere. There will be time for her."

"She ran away."

"When?"

"Last summer."

"When your mom died?"

"Yes. I've been looking for her."

"And you found her."

"Yes, only a mile and a half from the Stone House."

"The Stone House?"

"My mother's house, my house. I found Tad living in a cabin across the river with her cousins. But, she won't talk to me."

"Then let her be."

"I can't."

"You can. You've got to. "You know what the judge told you. Do you think he was joking? Tad's what, seventeen now? One more year, Stu. One more year and you'll be allowed to see her."

I flipped through my sketches for a minute, then said, "I need to be with my daughter. I can't wait another year."

Pierce exhaled in exasperation. "You don't need her in your life right now and she doesn't need you. *I* need you! I need you to paint, God-damn it!"

She got up from the table, walked to the cabinets, poured two cups of coffee, and placed one cup in front of me. She then took a long sip from her cup, placed it on the table, walked behind me, and then laid her hand on my back.

"You know we've worked and waited a long time for this day," she said. "You know I'm counting on you." She stroked the back of my neck. I choked on her perfume which had an overwhelming cedar-trunk-in-a-wet-basement smell.

"Pierce," I said with no emotion. She kissed my neck then walked to other side of the table. I bolted to my feet. My chair flipped over. With the back of my arm, I swept the two cups of coffee off the table so hard they shattered against the cabinet doors by the sink. I reached for her hand, pulled her close. She opened her lips and tilted her head. I slammed her palm on the shiny granite table top in front of me. In the slick stone surface she saw her own face.

"This is the spot, Pierce. This is the exact spot where they found Sarah. Face down. I was at the gallery with you that night— our big show—and my wife was here, right here, vomiting her life away, alone."

Pierce stared at her image, stunned. As soon as I let her go she moved to another chair, planted her elbows on the table and placed her fists just below her eyes. She sat in silence while I caught my breath and continued in a more controlled voice, "Two days ago I was three feet from my daughter. It was the first time I'd seen her in years. She's changed. The little face I knew was gone."

Pierce closed her eyes.

"What do you expect me to do?" I said in a whisper barely holding back the avalanche inside. She walked to the closet and found a broom and dust pan and started cleaning up the broken china. I wiped up coffee from the cabinets and floor with a towel.

"You're going back to Redbriar aren't you?"

I didn't answer—didn't need to.

CHAPTER THREE

STUART

There is no quick route to Redbriar. The mountainous county is almost entirely surrounded by national forests which meant the world would never beat a path to its doorstep, but the town considered isolation its most valuable asset.

I waited four full months before returning. Sergeant loved the scent of the farm, the cedar forests and newly thawed clay. The moment I opened the car door he shot into the fields that grew in the shadow of Mt. Tsula. Ankle-deep wild onions spotted the yard and a wash of pale spring green covered the mountains. I stepped into the empty house and listened to its silent echo. No arms greeted me and no soft kiss blew against my cheek. The vase on the side table in the foyer sat empty, waiting for spring flowers.

Within the shadow of the big house and across stone pavers directly to its rear, the old carriage house smiled at me. Looking through its windows, I pictured Cleo, the family cook, bending over her stove. Cleo had been one of my few channels of comfort against the extreme isolation into which I was born—an isolation caused by my family's suffocating wealth in the middle of one of the poorest counties in North Carolina.

I heard an engine sputter in the distance. As I rounded the

corner of the barn, Possum, the caretaker, drove a tractor past me. He stared straight ahead as if he didn't see me. When I waved him down, he shut off the engine and sat for a moment. Then he said, "Why'd ya come back, Stuart?"

"You *know* why I'm here, Possum."

Possum climbed to the ground and stomped about ten paces away from me, pointed upriver and said, "She ain't comin' back."

"She'll come back."

"You killed her god-damned mother."

"That's what she's been told, but she'll change her mind."

"If you'd talked to her anytime over the last three years, you wouldn't say that." Possum returned to the tractor, scraped red clay off his boot, folded his arms, and glanced at me as if he were daring me to reply.

I put both hands in my pockets lowered my head and said, "You think I killed Sarah?" Possum looked back over the mountains, tightened his lips around a cigarette, and took a deep draw. The crackling ember left a three quarter inch ash.

"They found you guilty."

"What the hell does that prove?" I said, as I kicked a stone past him, barely missing his head.

He took in another long drag. "Does the sheriff know you're back?"

"No. Not yet."

"How long you gonna be here?"

"I'm not going back to Charlotte for a long time."

"How long?"

"Help me get her back, Possum."

Possum climbed into the tractor seat. A puff of black smoke shot from the back end as he drove into the garden.

I emptied my car and carried everything in. After putting my bags in the loft above the kitchen, I laid my painting supplies and canvasses on Cleo's wooden bread table. I remember how her powerful arms pounded and kneaded her dough on that table with such strength the house shook. But those same strong hands once brushed my hair, wiped my nose, and patted my back as affectionately as if she were my own grandmother. As I sat on the hearth and rested my head against the brick fireplace, I heard Possum plowing the garden. For a moment, it seemed like nothing had changed, but everything had changed. My mother had left all of it to me. I'm sure Possum must have known it. It's not the kind of thing he would talk about, but he knew he was working for the lanky kid he watched grow up on the farm. The kid he probably didn't think would amount to anything—now a convicted felon.

For the next year, Sergeant and I took a daily walk up the riverbank. Looking across the shallow stream, through briars and thick bushes, the Remington cabin peeked back at us from the north side—the Weavertown side of the river. I saw clothes flapping on the line, but no sign of Tad. I took comfort in knowing she was there and believing that the sheriff was clueless about her hiding place.

As I threw stones in the river, I was ripped somewhere between relief and frustration, connection and separation, hopefulness and helplessness, but it was the helplessness that boiled inside me. That was the one thing for which nothing in my life prepared me. I was born knowing my family could fix anything broken, but for me, this was unfixable. On my best days that year, I contained the steam swelling my gut knowing how much I needed to stay calm and find a way to convince Tad of my innocence, but also knowing how much I still feared my own guilt.

Spring easily melted into summer and summer finally gave way to fall, but fall ends in the mountains of North Carolina like the slam of a door. The first snow came in mid-November and left a chill so thick and heavy that it covered the river banks with an impassable glaze of ice that lasted until spring.

Redbriar is a small town. It only took a few weeks for rumors to sweep across the little village that I was back in the old house. I'm sure the sheriff knew.

A year is forever when you are alone. Sitting in my usual spot by the fireplace, I closed my eyes and ran my fingers across the rough brick beneath me. The last glow from the night's embers floated up the chimney. It was Tad's eighteenth birthday—four years, twelve days, and two hours after the last day of my trial—an event permanently branded on the thin skin of my memory.

"Stand and face the jury," they said to me just before they spit out their one word verdict. I looked at Tad. From the pain in her eyes, I saw she believed the decision. My team of attorneys was able to get the charge reduced from first degree murder to reckless homicide. The judge tightened his eyes, peered over the top of his glasses, and gave me my sentence of ten years in prison, but he suspended the sentence on the condition I pay a heavy fine and accept a complete ban on seeing my daughter or even living in the same county with her until her eighteenth birthday.

The sheriff was still the most feared man in Jefferson County, but I was probably the most hated for what they thought I did to Sarah. Even before the trial, half the people in Jefferson County despised me because of my family, but since the trial, almost all hated me. I had talked with no one that year except Possum and a few of his workers, and the boy who delivered groceries.

I was surprised to find how fast my beard grew and how much it changed my appearance in just twelve months—especially with its new dusting of gray. Before I started to town, I took one last look in the mirror. I doubted if anyone would recognize me, at least not right away. From the jingle in my pocket, Sergeant knew we were going for a ride and he was already scratching at the front door. To avoid the usual courthouse crowd, I took the back way into town to a little café on Main St. It was the only place in the little village I knew I would be welcome.

Jack Hemphill

CHAPTER FOUR

Every law enforcement vehicle in Jefferson County was lined along River Street that morning from two blocks north of the courthouse all the way to the old jail two blocks south. The superior courtroom couldn't hold half the people who showed up for the trial. The murder was the latest chapter in an old family feud that erupted with increasing violence every five to ten years for almost a century. The conflict lasted so long that, in one way or another, every family in Jefferson County was affected by it. Most of the people on one side of the argument lived north of the Redbriar River in Weavertown or deep in forgotten parts of the mountains, and most of the families on the other side of the feud lived either in the town of Redbriar or on the south side of the county. The two camps agreed on only one thing—they hated each other more than they hated Yankees. Constant anonymous threats against county officials and witnesses caused continuous delays to the trial.

Emily Budd shivered in the morning sun as she studied the front of the courthouse. She ran her fingers across a stone in the old building's massive granite foundation, quarried not two miles away. The stone was laced throughout with veins of deep red matching the color of the brick façade. This was her first opportunity to renovate such a beautiful example of turn-of-the-century architecture, and the first time her business partners let her manage a project like this on her own.

Before starting her drawings, she needed to measure and record everything that had been changed over the years, but because of the trial she was told to limit her efforts that day to the exterior. After working for several hours measuring the side of the structure and recording the places where new windows had been added and old ones had been bricked over, she sat cross legged on the ground and spread the original blueprints across her lap. She rested her head against the wall and closed her eyes for a moment. As she opened them, a man in silhouette, partially covered by a parapet, appeared on a roof across the street, then another man in uniform popped up on top of an adjacent building. Both men scanned their territory, back and forth, with their faces fused into the hammer end of their long black rifles. Emily scrambled to her feet, put her sun glasses on, picked up her measuring tape, and moved further down the wall towards the rear of the building.

Near the back of the courthouse, she kneeled and scribbled notes on the old blue prints. She heard the constant rush of the river a hundred yards away and the distinct whistle of bobwhites in the prickly thicket along the bank. Sweet fragrances, gathered by wind blowing through the grass and briers, came and disappeared with each breeze. Every few minutes she tilted her head to be sure she could still hear the soft moaning of the stream as it curved around the large knoll behind the courthouse. The rising sun had not yet burned off the morning chill. She zipped up her deep green, waist-length jacket. On her face, she felt the sun's heat reflecting off the old brick beside her, so she lingered there a little longer than she needed.

Like a gunshot, words rang out and echoed off the buildings. "Who are you?"

Emily jumped to her feet and looked toward the voice, but

saw only the shape of a man standing on the side portico with the sun directly behind his head. She attempted to answer, but her soft voice fell to the ground the moment it left her lips, as if it had frozen immediately in the chilled air.

"Who are you?" the officer yelled out again. Just as she started to reply, she saw the two marksmen on the roofs turn their aim toward her and heard the unmistakable double click of bullets being locked into the firing chambers of their high-powered weapons.

"I'm Emily!" she said again, as she stumbled closer to the platform, but by then her heart was beating so hard she was breathless and no one heard her faint reply. The man stepped down to the ground in front of her. In the cold, his breath billowed from his mouth and nostrils, leaving clouds in the air. That was when she realized it was Sheriff Hodges.

"I said 'Who the hell are you?'" he snorted, with steam and gravel in his voice.

"I'm Emily Budd, I'm an architect. I'm…I'm here to work on the courthouse."

The six-foot-five officer strutted straight toward her. His gaze cascaded from her red hair down to her brown shoes, then, without a word, he turned and disappeared into the courthouse. Two more pairs of double clicks echoed off the walls as the half-hidden deputies removed their bullets from the firing chambers.

Emily stood in silence a few moments until a light breeze rattled her unfurled blueprints. Wrapping them into a tight roll, she walked to a bench at the front of the building and dropped her drawings and clipboard on the seat. As she sat down, her red pencil fell into the grass. With one jerk of her foot, she smacked the pencil causing it to sail twelve feet then bounce off the sidewalk into the grass beyond. She unzipped her jacket and tightened her lips. From the bench, she saw straight down the middle of Main Street with its neat rhythm of small brick and wooden buildings.

All of them were late nineteenth century designs with white wood trim and white flower boxes under each window.

The old courthouse with its large front portico and towering Doric columns was, and always had been, the dominant building in town, sited so that Main Street literally terminated against the courthouse steps.

With drawings rolled under her arms, and a tote bag over her shoulder, Emily plodded through the little village for two and a half blocks until she found the only café in town, *The Briar Patch*. Since it was too late for breakfast and too early for lunch, she ordered a large cup of coffee.

Trying to shake the lingering feeling of what seemed a near death experience. Emily carefully poured cream into her coffee and watched its patterns slowly curl in the cup. A few sips, another dose of cream, and once again she was lost in her brew.

A vaguely familiar voice called her name.

"Emily?"

Without speaking she looked up at the man approaching her table, but saw nothing familiar about him except maybe his eyes— kind and gentle eyes in the middle of a sea of thick beard and half-gray hair pulled back and tied behind his head. He was wearing a sky blue shirt, navy blue sweater, and faded but well pressed jeans.

"Emily, it's me Stuart," he said. Remembering how much he had changed since the last time she had seen him.

"My God, Stuart. I hardly recognized you! Where've you been?"

"I've been up here over a year now."

He slid into a seat opposite her, facing the front of the cafe. They had met six years earlier through a mutual friend, but she hadn't seen him since his trial.

"It's nice to see you, but Stuart, nobody back in Charlotte knew where you went. You just kinda disappeared."

"I'm sorry about that. I inherited Mom's place here. I don't know if I actually intended to stay when I came, but here I am over a year later."

"You live alone?"

"Yep."

"Are you painting?"

"Of course… but, what brings *you* to this remote part of the world?"

Emily drew a long sip of coffee to give her a moment to answer. "My company was hired to design renovations of the old courthouse." She paused for another sip, not wanting him to know how pleased she was to find him. From her Scottish grandmother, she had inherited a fair complexion and blushed with the slightest embarrassment. She had also inherited her grandmother's mahogany hair—she did not yet know that it was a color that had fascinated Stuart from the first time he met her.

Without saying a word, the waitress placed a mug of coffee and a plate with four biscuits in front of Stuart; two were plain and two were sausage biscuits. She also placed a jar of homemade blueberry jam in the middle of the table, then gave him a little pat on his shoulder.

"Two of these are yours," he said to Emily pointing to the biscuits.

"Well, I'd love to have just a plain one."

"It's yours, but you have to try the jam with it. This place has the best homemade blueberry jam in the world."

A cow bell clanged on the back of the front door as it swung open. Stuart sat back and watched the deputy sheriff strut to the counter not six feet away. He mounted a stool swinging his right leg just high enough to bounce his black forty-five pistol above his waist.

Emily, oblivious to the distraction, examined the open jar

of jam.

Stuart continued, "We once had ten acres of blueberries on the farm."

He bit off a quarter of a sausage biscuit and washed it down with coffee, then watched her spread the sweet jam across half of her biscuit with measured, delicate strokes. She took a bite and gave him an approving nod.

"I thought your sheriff was going to have me shot earlier this morning," she said with a laugh.

After a hard swallow, he looked again at the brown overstuffed, starched shirt sitting at the bar, dunking a doughnut. The officer made a quarter swivel on his seat to scan the nine people in the café then returned to his snack.

Stuart, convinced the deputy had not recognized him, leaned on his elbow and placed his fist high against his cheek covering part of his face. In a slightly softer voice he asked, "You met our famous sheriff—what do you think?"

"Oh, I've heard about him, but Stuart, who is he, or better—what *the hell* is he?"

Stuart, without moving, flicked his eyes and head toward the deputy then back at Emily. She momentarily put her hand over her mouth and started over in a near whisper, "So, what's the deal with your sheriff?"

He spoke softly into his mug. "I wish I could have warned you about him. I almost hate to tell you this, but I've known him most of my life. He grew up about a half mile from my house. He was a great athlete, but a bully; he routinely beat the crud out of just about every kid I knew."

"Including you?" She said smiling before turning a brighter shade of red.

"Only once," he replied without returning the smile. "So tell me about your meeting."

"It wasn't exactly a meeting. It was more like… an execution that didn't quite happen."

"Yeah, that sounds like the 'High-Sheriff of Redbriar.'"

"So, you really know this guy?"

"To tell you the truth I can't think of anybody else in my life I wish I didn't know except him. He's been my living nightmare since I can remember."

"But he only beat you up once."

"Okay, more than once." Looking down, he shook his head slightly. "We're probably the most opposite two people in the world." Stuart looked out the window.

"I'm sorry about the way the trial worked out and everything," she said to change the subject.

"Thanks," he said, "It's been tough." He wanted to tell her more, but didn't know if she believed the DA's version or his attorney's account of how his wife died. "Of course, I miss my daughter; don't know when I'll see her again."

"When was the last time you saw her?"

"At the trial—well, actually only one other time, briefly."

"I remember she was sent here to live with her grandmother. Where is she now?"

"She's gone."

"When will you be allowed to see her?"

"Officially today, her eighteenth birthday."

"And you have no idea where she is?"

"Yeah. I pretty much do, but I can't go there now."

They looked at each other for an uncomfortable moment before the silence was broken by the clanging of her spoon as she stirred her coffee. He took another bite of biscuit then pushed the plate aside; he placed both hands on the table, intertwining his fingers, and looked straight at her. "Will you be coming here often?"

"I think so. This project will take a year or more."

"I know you aren't going to try to drive back to Charlotte every time you come. Where will you be staying?"

"There's a motel just this side of Asheville."

"That's at least forty-five minutes away!"

"I'm told it's the only motel within fifty miles of here."

"You're right. Jefferson County isn't exactly a tourist resort."

Well, I like what I've seen up here so far, except for your sheriff. I love the old buildings and little quaint houses."

"Let me show you my house. It's about a two-mile drive along the river. You got time?" He watched to see if she would hesitate.

"Sure," she said surprising herself. "I'm certain it's going to be more interesting than measuring up old courthouses in the cold." She laughed, A little embarrassed, excited, and flustered.

As they left, Stuart reached over the counter to pay. The officer sat three empty stools away. The waitress patted Stuart's arm again and said, "No. No charge. It's on me today, Stu." The deputy snapped his eyes toward them. Stuart nodded at him and left.

The road leaving Redbriar followed easy bends in the river until it reached the mountain just north of town where it began a slow upward spiral. Emily's ears popped halfway through the long turn. White and red oaks, maples, and tulip poplars were replaced with a landslide of thick, deep green plants clinging to every stone, hill, and rock. Cool, heavy air filled the car with the fragrance of wet earth. Emily glanced at Stuart who had stopped talking. He looked back at her.

A stream flickered two hundred feet below. At the ridge, a hairpin turn bent the road back to the right before it took a long winding descent to the river, then a slow, constant climb up the next mountain.

Stuart noticed she looked at her watch for the third time.

"Almost ...," his voice cracked a little. He started again,

"We're almost there, I promise."

She smiled.

The road straightened and he pushed down on the accelerator until they reached the next sharp turn. With each bend, new views across the county appeared in fading shades of blue.

After rising another fifty feet, he drove across a short, flat plateau. Directly ahead, a quarter mile away, the Stone House towered above the trees. Late morning sun reflecting off the reddish-gray stone house stood in sharp contrast with the deep green mountain beyond. Emily stretched forward, looked up, and squinted, too embarrassed to let him know that the structure was far more imposing than she had imagined.

"Almost home," he said. Lines of white oaks framed the long drive. Remnants of blueberry and apple orchards rolled off to the left. The front of the house looked down over miles of clouds hovering above the valley.

She slid forward in her seat. It was hard to picture Stuart living there alone with his dog, but Emily began to understand the seclusion into which he had been born and which he had now chosen.

Jack Hemphill

CHAPTER FIVE

Stuart drove to the end of the stone pavers. Sergeant, who was already standing on the seat made a full throttle victory lap around the yard the moment Stuart opened the door.

Emily gathered her nerves with a silent exhale as she climbed the steps soaking in details of the house with its tall slender dormers jutting out of the dark slate roof above the second floor, the massive cut- granite walls, and two rows of windows under stone jack arches.

"My grandfather built it," he said standing on the top step.

"Really- when?"

"1904."

"So your family's lived in Redbriar forever?"

"Since long before that. Granddad tore down the old family farm house to build it. The stone is from one of our quarries."

She walked across the porch for a closer look at the granite then said, "This looks like..."

"Yes," he said finishing her sentence, "It's just like the stone you saw at the courthouse. It's a rougher cut, but has the same red and black speckles."

She ran a finger down a ruddy vein in one of the blocks.

"How many quarries do you have?" she asked trying to sound like it was normal to own quarries.

29

"We had three, but we closed them all years ago. That particular color has never been found anywhere in the world except here in Jefferson County—in our quarries."

"Really?" She looked again at the wall. "Why did you close them?"

"Granddad mined most of the good stone out and then shut it down—put half the people in Weavertown out of work."

"So your granddad ticked off a whole town?"

"Yep. Most of them never forgave us. Even now, they'd just as soon shoot us as look at us."

"So why did he do it?"

"Because he was a stubborn, proud old goat. He had all the money he ever wanted, but wouldn't let anybody else have the quarries."

Stuart opened the door, stepped back, and motioned for Emily to enter the house ahead of him. She hesitated.

"Can I show you the inside?" he said lifting his eyebrows while lines furrowed across his forehead.

Emily's sneakers squeaked on the foyer floor. A grand stair penetrated through an opening in the center of the second floor. Rooms and corridors ran in all directions. He waited for her to speak.

"How do you take care of all this?" she asked looking around still trying not to appear impressed.

"I don't. I mean personally I don't. The family has always had help."

"Help?"

"Servants. When Mom died, I kept them on—some of them."

"Do they live here?"

"No. A long time ago they did, but they live in different parts of the county now.

I only let them work the first two days of the week. The rest of time I'm alone."

"Doesn't that bother you…being alone so much?" He didn't answer.

She looked at him and continued, "I mean isn't it hard, after a while?"

As if on cue, Sergeant tapped over to his side, sat down, and rested his head against Stuart's leg.

"Nope." He patted Sergeant's back, "Got my pal here."

"Yes, of course." She looked down at her sneakers scuffed with red clay.

"Let me show you something out back I think you'll like," he said.

Stuart motioned with his hand for her to follow him down a dim corridor through a rear door to an elevated porch with a row of round white columns. Sergeant ran down the steps and out of sight.

"Most of the time, I stay over there." he pointed to the old field stone structure 40 feet away with small rippled windows and a copper roof that had matured into its full dusty blue-green patina. The shadow of the Stone House stretched across the drive just far enough to kiss the base of the carriage house whose presence demanded respect like an old matriarch.

Thinking he was joking, and not knowing what to say, Emily laughed.

"No really," he said. "Carriages were once stored at the far end, but the cook's residence is at this end. That's where I stay at night."

"You sleep there?"

"Yes, that's where I sleep, but most of my waking hours are spent in my studio in the Stone House."

"It's actually a beautiful little house. How old is it?" she said.

"I don't know, but it's older than the Stone House. Our cook, Cleo, lived there since long before I can remember."

"You talked about her once. Didn't you say you did a painting of her?"

"Yes, several. I think I knew her better than my own parents. She couldn't read or write, but with a pencil she drew anything and everything she ever saw or imagined."

"Is that where you learned to draw?" Emily said as they walked along the porch.

"Yep. Cleo lived here until she died about five years ago."

"My God," Emily stopped to look at him, "Cleo worked for your family her whole life?"

"Yes. This was Cleo's home too—the carriage house was hers as long as she lived. She was born here."

Emily stopped and leaned against one of the columns at a spot where she could see down the gully all the way to the river. "So Cleo had other relatives in Redbriar?"

"She had a niece that lived downriver who had a son, Bakkuk, four years older than I, but we were good friends."

"What did you say was his name?"

"His full name was Habakkuk Key Oowatie."

"A bit of a mouthful," she said as her eyes widened.

"Well…he was half Negro and half American Indian, and when I was just a little boy, I was too young to say the name, 'Habakkuk'—so I named him 'Bakkuk.'"

"Oowatie sounds like an Indian name, but where did the name Habakkuk come from?"

"You're right. His Indian name was Oowatie which he got from his dad, but his mother named him Habakkuk. Cleo told me his mother thought it was the most Indian sounding name she ever heard of in the Bible. I don't think he ever knew what happened to his mother and father. He spent most of his time with me and

32

Cleo or in the woods trapping. I was his best—I guess, his only real friend. He earned money by doing little odd jobs for neighbors and farmers, jobs they didn't want to do for themselves."

"Like what?"

"Like getting skunks out of barns, or snakes and other pests out of the garden, and rodding out cesspool lines, but more than anything else he trapped raccoons and foxes that were raiding farmers' chicken coops."

"What could you two possibly have in common?"

"I know it's hard to imagine, but we had everything in common." He turned and touched her shoulder then walked toward the stairs. Following him, she noticed he was taller than she remembered. He was naturally strong, having grown up on a farm, but carried himself like a man born into wealth.

At the bottom of the stair, he hesitated slightly for Emily to catch up then continued talking, "Bakkuk was older, unusually large and very strong. My parents let me go on little adventures with him from early morning 'til well after dark."

"Little adventures?" She asked.

"They were great adventures, at least to a young boy. After each summer rain, for example, we combed every field morning 'til dark, from here to the reservoir, hunting arrowheads and pieces of Indian pottery and other things. We both had quite a collection."

They walked out of the shadow of the Stone House toward the door of the carriage house. "Would you like to see the inside of the old place?"

"Well...," she paused, "maybe next time." She was immediately embarrassed by her reluctance and even more embarrassed for suggesting that there would be a *next time.*

"Then let's sit on the bench a few minutes. Sergeant and I sun ourselves here on cold winter days."

They both sat on the bench facing the back of the Stone

House.

"I kept my Indian treasures in an old cigar box I got from my dad. Bakkuk sometimes kept his recent finds in a deer hide pouch tied around his neck. He actually sewed small beads on it in the image of a deer. He even made his own bows and arrows and took me hunting."

"Sorry, I can't quite picture you hunting with a bow," she laughed.

"I guess you could say that my boyhood was a little unusual, but there was a real price to pay to be his friend. He watched over me like a big brother. When I was a young boy, the kids I knew thought he was some kind of dark magic giant, but as we grew older, most of them wouldn't come near either one of us."

"That must have been tough," she said.

"Yeah. I never had a lot of friends, and the number got smaller over time."

Sergeant returned and nudged his nose against Emily's hands. It was her cue to pay him a little attention and a sign that she had officially been accepted into the pack. She stroked his head, but continued to look at Stuart.

"Where is Bakkuk now? Is he still around?"

"He left here a couple of decades ago after turning twenty. He never told me anything about it or warned me. He just left one day and nobody could tell me why. I figured he went into the army or something like that, and since he could barely write, I didn't expect to hear from him."

Stuart felt the warmth of her hand on his forearm. "You never heard *anything* about him again?" she asked.

"Nope." He tilted his head back against the granite wall. "He just left."

Emily admired the rows of windows marching in rhythm on each floor of the Stone House. In the middle of the second floor sat a large Palladian window with a full stone arch above it. "Did you say the servants—I mean the help—were gone today?"

"Yes, why?"

"I don't know, I thought I saw someone in that big window."

Stuart pushed his mouth to one side and said, "Nobody's home, but that old glass is full of ripples."

Noticing she was still staring at the house he said, "Sarah loved that spot. Some days she spent hours looking out that window to the other side of the river. Sometimes I think I see her standing there myself."

His thoughts drifted away for a moment, then he said, "I probably should tell you a little more about your favorite sheriff."

"Yes, of course, if you don't mind talking about him."

"Well, there's no way to avoid it. The truth is, there're parts of Lester I'll never understand."

"Lester!" she shouted. "You can't be serious! Sheriff Hodges first name is *Lester*?"

"Yes. Everybody knew him as "L.T. Hodges. That's even the way it was listed in the school yearbook. I never really thought about it, but I guess the name "Lester" doesn't exactly fit his image." He chuckled just enough for her to see how pleased he was that she saw something funny about Sheriff Hodges.

"I only wish I had known that an hour ago," she said, grinning.

"I don't know why, but Lester developed such a mean streak that the kids around here hid from him whenever they saw him coming."

"You said he picked on you sometimes."

"He never picked on me as long as Bakkuk was around. I never saw a mean side to Bakkuk, but Lester, for whatever reason, was scared to death of him and he wouldn't even so much as look at me when he thought Bakkuk was near. One day, right after Bakkuk left, I saw Lester creeping down the driveway. I didn't even recognize him at first. He was covered from the top of his head to his feet in a thick layer of red clay which had dried so hard all over his body, face, hair, hands, and clothes that he looked like a reptile with large red scales. The creature before me was so frightening, so far out of my sense of reality that I just froze—completely, hopelessly, motionless." Stuart pointed down the driveway. "He caught me right there—right by that gate. Grabbed me, bloodied my nose, and threw me over the split-rail fence into the scuppernong vines.

"He was eighteen by then and the strangest thing of all is, soon after that, even with the potential of an athletic scholarship, he quit school and disappeared. Just like Bakkuk. Nobody understood why.

"Bakkuk never returned, but Lester eventually did. That's when he started working for the sheriff's office."

"What could he possibly have against you?"

Shaking his head, Stuart replied, "I don't know, but you're right. He probably hated me more than anyone else. I don't have a clue why unless it was because of Bakkuk."

Stuart got up and walked a few steps up the drive and pulled a weed growing between the stone paves. Sergeant followed. Emily looked back at the window. After a few more steps, Stuart glanced at the bony scuppernong vines just beginning to sprout tiny green fingers along the fence. He turned around in a single motion and said, "Emily, next time you come...stay here."

"Here?" Feeling a blush flooding her face she placed her hand on her cheek and bent forward slightly then leaned back in her chair.

"Yes," Stuart answered, "It doesn't make sense to stay at a motel an hour away. Stay here. We've got... I've got all these rooms with no one using them. Just...make it your home and pay nothing, and be only a few minutes from your project."

"I'll have to think about it."

"Great, take my key. I have a spare. Just give me two hours notice when you're coming and I'll be sure you have clean sheets and everything you need."

"I'm afraid I'm causing work for you." She wanted to just say "yes," but knew she needed to make the decision when she was alone and away from him. She had become too comfortable with him too fast and she knew it.

Realizing he may have embarrassed her, he placed the key on the chair beside her and said, "You'll have almost the whole place to yourself—I won't bother you. I spend most of my time in my studio in the sunroom and the rest of my time over here in the carriage house."

He sat down beside her and moved the chair a little closer. Sergeant, realizing he was losing her attention, nudged Emily's hand once again. "The only person to visit me in the last year is the grocery guy who comes once a week." He drifted away again then continued, "If staying here is something you want to do, do it. You're not putting me out, and it'll give me something to do besides my work."

"I'll let you know," she said with a half-smile.

The sharpest curve in the road back to Redbriar was near the edge of town. Rounding the final turn, Emily and Stuart were jolted by pulsating lights in the middle of the street. A half dozen sheriff's vehicles blocked the road and two more had driven onto the courthouse lawn. Crowds of people lined both Main Street and River Street. From Stuart's car, Emily and Stuart spotted a cluster of activity on the courthouse steps, a squad of deputies ran toward the river past Ellie's Knoll, and town police barked at the crowd telling them to stay back. Two ambulances had driven across the lawn and backed up to the steps on the north portico. The sheriff, standing in the middle of the street, simultaneously commanded every activity. He had a natural bull horn voice, a demanding tone with a thunder that instilled both fear and obedience in everyone who could hear it—and everyone heard it.

"Hang tight a minute," Stuart said as he jumped out and ran to the police car in front of them. Emily couldn't hear what the officer said to him, but she saw that the officer's demeanor changed as soon as he recognized Stuart's face behind his beard.

Returning out of breath, Stuart blurted, "When court recessed and the defendant was being taken back to jail, he was shot to death on the steps."

"Oh, my God, who did it?"

"They don't know, they think it was someone down by the river. A deputy was also wounded, but he'll be okay."

For the next forty-five minutes all Emily and Stuart could do was watch the excitement churning from one side of the town to the other. When it was finally over, Stuart drove her back to her car. She promised again to let him know about staying at his house.

On the way back to Charlotte, Emily couldn't stop thinking about Stuart, Lester Hodges and the big stone house on top of the mountain. She wondered why Stuart preferred to stay in Cleo's little place rather than in the house where he grew up.

She wondered what made the sheriff such a horror show, but with time, Emily learned more about Lester Hodges. She learned about his teenage drinking problems and she was told about the warm afternoon late in May when he, stoned out of his mind, found Bakkuk asleep under a sycamore tree on Ellie's Knoll, picked up a limb, and smashed Bakkuk's head so hard it split open like an over-ripe melon killing him instantly, and she learned that Lester Hodges stuffed what was left of Bakkuk's body in a hole under that tree on Ellie's Knoll.

CHAPTER SIX

TAD

Mt. Tsula can be seen from all parts of Jefferson County. It always reminded me of Dad, even on days when I tried not to remember.

I don't know how many times I heard him talk about climbing it with his friend, Bakkuk, but he never thought I was old enough until my fourteenth birthday when he took me all the way to the top.

From the river side of the mountain, we pushed our way through thick laurel and hiked up the steep pine forest until we reached a rock that shot two hundred feet above us. After another hour of steady climbing, we arrived at a plateau, still fifty feet below the peak. We stopped there to catch our breath. He watched while I took a rubber band out of my jeans and pulled my hair back into a pony tail. I tried to keep him from seeing how my fingers trembled with excitement. He went first. Following him, I slid my feet along the narrow ledge and spiraled my way up the rock wall copying him as he clutched each stone handle and crevice like they were old friends. With his right hand, he lifted me the last five feet over the ridge to the summit. The view, the expanse, the relentless throbbing wind, and the sudden two hundred-foot drop, yanked out of me a scream of both joy and fear. The pure beauty of suddenly seeing fifty miles of blue Appalachian spine while I kicked pebbles off the rock into forever, ripped my emotions wide open. He clutched the side of my wind breaker to steady me while I squeezed his arm with both hands. I pressed my face against him and soaked his sleeve with my tears. I *loved* the summit, I *hated* it, I was *stunned* by it—I still am.

When we left, I made him promise to take me back to the top again as soon possible. Neither one of us knew that exactly three weeks from that day Mom would die and exactly nine weeks from that day, I would be permanently taken from him.

After Mom's death, her family kept me in the dark about what was going on—about how she died, about Dad being arrested, and the charges against him.

Granma did her best. She was supposed to take care of me, but it turned out to be the other way around—I took care of her. Everything that happened to the family weighed her down and each year after that she grew a little weaker. I dropped out of school.

Before long, she couldn't climb the stairs, so I made a bedroom for her in one of the servant's rooms near the pantry. It was only a short walk from there to the kitchen. To stay close to her, I did my drawings and paintings on the kitchen table.

Each evening, I put her to bed right after dinner. The night she died, she told me she was going to call Dad the next day and tell him to come home. "No one will know he's here," she said to me. "Wouldn't you like that?" she asked. Without answering, I smiled and kissed her goodnight. I held her hand and felt her grow cold, then, I cried.

After the ambulance guys took her off, I covered myself with a blanket in my bed where I lay all day until my aunt came for me.

Granma still had a few old friends around Redbriar who

came to the funeral. One of them was a retired preacher. He agreed to perform the short services—one ceremony in the living room and one at the family graveyard by the river. With Granma's friends, the servants, Possum, and me, we had twenty-five people there.

The big question around town was whether Dad would try to come to the funeral in violation of the court order. Patrol cars lined the road in front of our house. All but one deputy marched into the woods around our house. They made everybody so nervous that one or two of Granma's friends left without coming in. I couldn't believe it. I couldn't believe the sheriff would do this to me during my grandmother's funeral.

I don't remember a word the preacher said, but I know he did a good job and didn't say anything strange. After the services, everybody came back into the house for punch and cookies prepared by two of our cleaning ladies. I thanked everybody then let the crowd enjoy the food and each other while I slipped into to the pantry, up the back stairs, and into my room where I changed into slacks, pullover shirt, and a hooded sweatshirt. I returned down the rear stairs, picked up a wood handled ice pick from the utility sink, and crept out the service entrance. Once outside I then darted between parked cars in back, then through the orchard, and down the hill to a drainage pipe large enough to crawl under the road to the other side. Concealed by shrubs I slipped past the deputy sitting in his vehicle, and I ran all the way to the end of the row of sheriff's cars. All six of them were parked off the road onto our property leaving deep ruts in the ground. Banging with the heel of my palm on the wood handle I was able to drive the pick into the right rear tires of each car. By punching close to the rims, I made a hole just large enough to let out the air slowly and silently from each of the first five cars. The deputy sitting in the front car was watching both the driveway and the road toward town while I crawled to his rear tire. I tried puncturing a little further away from the rim thinking the air would seep out much slower and he wouldn't feel the tire deflating before I made my getaway. I'm sure he was as surprised as I was to hear the loud pop and the sudden crash of the rim on the ground.

I ran across the road no longer trying to hide myself. He flew after me faster than I thought he could. I almost made it into the culvert when he caught my foot and yanked me out upside down. With my hood tied tight around my face, I'm sure he didn't know who I was and couldn't tell if I was a boy or a girl. With one hand tight around my leg and one hand gripping the chest of my sweatshirt, he shook me until I dropped the ice pick, then he planted his fist into my stomach. My lungs collapsed. For a few seconds, face down on the ground, all I could do was try to restart my breathing. With his shoe, he turned me over exposing the crotch area of his pants while he stomped my side. I pulled both legs to my chest and kicked as hard as I could. My left foot missed, but with my right foot I scored a direct hit into command central of his macho pride. Whatever profanities he screamed were lost in the cries of his genuine pain. In no time I was through the pipe, back up the rear stairs, in my dress, and with the mourners. As soon as they left, I packed a few clothes, along with other items, in my bag and disappeared out the back without a word to anybody. I was the only one that wasn't surprised my dad hadn't come to the funeral, but I knew for certain he would come for me soon and I needed to get away.

CHAPTER SEVEN

TAD

My cousins took me in. Granma left me some money and I was glad to pay my share, but they would have taken me in even if I was flat broke. They let me live there in hiding almost two years until we were all arrested.

I'm one of those few people that would rather watch a sunrise than a sunset. I was always up hours before everybody else, even before Scott, who worked at a dairy farm and had to leave at 6:00 AM. Each morning I watched through the glass in the rear door the dawn turning the Redbriar River into a shiny stream snaking its way to the horizon.

We were all cousins—first cousins. All from dirt-poor parents—except me, but nobody cared. They enjoyed making fun of me, my snobbish background, and my inherent ignorance of the world—their world.

It was the seventies. Most all young people thought drugs were cool, even those who never used them. Every movie glorified them. All rock music was fueled by the stuff. I swear, except for once, I never touched anything stronger than pot and booze. As far as I know, that was true for my cousins also, except for Silas. We never knew exactly how he got into the junk, but it probably happened when he was a soldier in Vietnam. The guys did their best to keep an eye on him and keep him under control. But, that wasn't always enough. It was a family matter and we all knew we would figure out a way to fix it. Didn't want anybody else involved.

Silas stood a good four or five inches above the others. His deep voice had the sound of a perpetual yawn. In spite of his size, he had a soft but infectious laugh. Sometimes he liked to sit for hours by the river, silent like a mountain. I was the only one who ever laughed at his understated humor.

One Saturday morning in May, clouds spoiled the sunrise, so I started breakfast early. As I always did on Saturdays, I made pancakes for the guys. They were all asleep so I cooked the pancakes in batches and kept them warm in the oven. About 6:30, Silas popped his head around the corner. "What' cha doing?" he asked.

"Breakfast."

"Can I help?"

"Sure," I said, trying to remember the last time I saw him cooking.

"What' cha need me to do?"

"Which do you do better—stir or flip?"

"I want to flip."

I had second thoughts. "How about stirring?'

"Great!" he said with genuine enthusiasm.

"You ever put doughnuts on you pancakes?" he asked.

"Uh, no, that sounds a little too sweet."

"Damn right. Love 'em that way!"

He stirred and I flipped. Forty-eight pancakes in all. I sat at the table with my little pile of four flapjacks plus bacon and a pitcher of pure maple syrup. Still standing at the counter, Silas ate ten—no doughnuts.

"You eat pancakes grow'n up, Tad?" he asked.

"Of course, why?"

"Thought over at the Stone House you'd get egg omelets or fried prunes or somthin' like that for breakfast."

"Silas, I'm just a mountain girl."

"You're no mountain girl, Tad," he said laughing.

"What are you talking about?"

"I bet you don't even eat hominy grits."

"No, I eat real grits especially with ham."

"That's okay, if it's got red-eyed gravy sopped with cornbread."

"I grew up on cornbread."

"I bet you never plowed a mule."

"No, but I drove a tractor."

"You plowed a field with a tractor?"

"No, I was only nine and I sat on Possum's lap."

He dropped his head for a moment. "Moonshine," he said as he shot his hand, fingers extended, into the air. "I bet you never tried moonshine liquor."

"I've tasted the scuppernong wine you guys brew behind the water heater."

"Jesus! That's closer to cool-aide than moonshine."

"Silas, I bet you never actually had a still."

"Yeah, I did. But nobody knew about it but me. Three miles into the forest where no one would ever find it."

"Do you still have it?"

"No, I had to leave it years ago."

"Leave it? Why?"

"A black bear."

"My God," I exclaimed smelling a good story coming.

"He had me cornered standing by the still with my back against a big rock."

"What happened?"

"I should have known better. It's black bear territory. I had been there four days when a bear popped up on the hill above me roaring like I had invaded his sacred land or something. I don't know if he was attracted by the sweet smell of the still or by his desire to make lunch out of me. When he got within ten feet of me, I fired my pistol at his feet. You know, just to scare him away."

"Did he run?"

"No, it pissed him off so bad, he stood straight up, blasted me with his roar then lowered his head and charged. I put three bullets in his chest. He stopped and rose again on his back feet. Roared again. That's when I put two bullets into his head."

"Holy crap!"

"He fell, knocking me against the stone and spraining my ankle. I hobbled three miles home and never went back."

"You left all the moonshine and everything?"

"It belongs to the bears now."

If any of the other cousins had told me that story I wouldn't have believed it, but Silas had a way and a look that made you believe, or want to believe, whatever he said. He had a perfect Howdy Doody face complete with apple cheeks, stuck out ears, red hair, and a large gap-toothed smile. Except for his height, he hadn't changed since he was nine years old.

"That's the best story I've heard you tell."

"Every word the truth."

"I guess that makes you a certified *mountain man*."

"Naw, I'm a mountain man, but not because of that story or any other. I'm a mountain man just 'cause I'm a Remington."

"I'm a Remington too."

"How's that?"

"My middle name is Remington."

He pulled his lips into a serious face, then his boyish grin broke through as he said, "Then you are a mountain woman."

In a lot of ways, Silas was more like me than the others. When he was twelve years old, he lost both of his parents. I guess that made him kind of a loner even though the Remingtons took care of him. Unlike most people on drugs, he never flew out of his mind, but folded inside himself instead and watched the river go by.

Dying is irrational.

Grieving is personal. No one is born with the ability to understand or to accept death. That comes with experience.

I've heard people talk about the *dew of death*, but never knew exactly what it was until the morning before my eighteenth birthday. I found Silas on the couch. Shiny droplets sparkled across his cold face. I loved Silas and I'm not saying I wasn't shocked and upset, but I knew I had to keep those things buried inside me for a while. I closed his eyes and tried to close his mouth, but his jaw was already set. Over his face, I laid a soft blue towel someone left drying by the fire. I woke the other five guys (Billy, Scott, Ralph, and Fisher) one by one and together they all went berserk.

They didn't accept the obvious at first and screamed out half-garbled words like *hospital, mouth to mouth, revive,* and so on, but it didn't take long for the chaos to be replaced by guilt then by fear for they all knew he had overdosed.

"Jesus, were goin' to have the whole damn world down here checking this out," said Scott.

"We got to hide him," said Billy.

"What, get rid of him—the body? We'll go to jail, you idiot." said Ralph.

"No, just get him out of here," Billy answered.

"Call an ambulance, they'll take him away," said Scott.

"Yeah, then they'll diagnose him and then send the sheriff," Ralph shot back.

"What's our choice but get rid of him? We'll have to say he

just disappeared or something," said Billy.

"Stop this shit!" yelled Fisher.

I'm telling you guys right now, especially you, Billy, I'm not goin' to do that to him. He's going to get a burial."

"Don't worry, we're gonna bury him!"

"The hell you are. I'm goin' to see he gets a God-damned *Christian* burial."

"Christian burial?" Billy grabbed Fisher's shirt "You're dumber than a pine knot, you know that? There's no way they aren't goin' to somehow blame us for this."

Fisher knocked Billy's hand off his shirt. Instantly the two became a ball of legs and arms and fists knocking over a lamp and a small table. Scott managed to grab Billy's arm and drag him off, but before he could scramble free, Fisher bulldozed him from the side and both of them landed with their full weight on top of Silas's body bouncing him face down onto the floor.

Everybody stopped in place.

"Call an ambulance," said Scott, "they'll take him away."

Nobody moved.

"We gotta find his stuff and get rid of it," said Fisher.

"But," Billy said, "There's a lot more to get rid of than just his stuff," Said Billy.

"You're right. Any pot, liquor, pills without a prescription— dump it," said Ralph.

"Pile everything in the kitchen trashcan then bury it," said Scott.

"Does this include our junk behind the water heater?' asked Fisher.

"Everything that can be smoked, drunk, or swallowed that didn't come from the grocery store."

They all zoomed around me in different orbits as I sat still beside Silas. Every drawer, every closet, every dark corner under every bed was searched. Four sealed mason jars were found between the joists under the back deck. They mostly contained unknown pills and some kind of powder. Like pallbearers, two of the guys carried the kitchen trash can past me, piled high with bottles, bags, and other glop. They took it to the woods with two shovels. When they returned, I called the hospital.

Everything played out from that point exactly as predicted. One hour after they took Silas away, a deputy's car silently slinked down our driveway. The officer, already preparing a report, took his time getting out of his l car. I waited for him to bang twice on the front door before letting him in, as if we hadn't been watching for him. It was irritating the way he called everybody *sir* and *ma'am* with his scowling face and forty-five pistol riding too high on his belt that was fifty percent covered by his cascading gut. The next day four deputies and a crime nerd came, spent the day, and left the place a mess. They found nothing, but I knew it wouldn't be over.

We were all scared and all under liquor drinking age. It didn't matter. In less than two weeks, bottles reappeared in the cabin, within a month or so the fragrance of pot drifted out the windows and floated down the valley, and mash from scuppernong grapes was again fermenting behind the water heater.

After the questioning was over, after having every cranny of our house searched, after spotting deputies snooping through the woods around our cabin, and after a nervous quiet finally settled on our lives, I finally started my grieving process. A silent shock wave had been ricocheting inside me—a reverberating dull thud like the felling of a great tree. There was nothing more for me to do—Silas was gone. That was it. I would never see him again, but I wanted to remember him and I wanted to talk about him. It bothered the guys more deeply than they would ever admit to me or to themselves. They almost never talked about him.

The first deputy that came the day Silas died recorded each

of our names and other personal information on his official form. When I told him my full name, he stopped writing and took a long look at me. I gave back a glassy stare.

From the look on the deputy's face, we all knew Sheriff Hodges would soon be beating on our door.

We were right, but not for the stupid reasons we thought. We would eventually find out that Silas overdosed on a Colombian opiate that had never before been found in the United States until that day.

CHAPTER EIGHT

STUART

Crisp footprints in the morning dew followed my walk downhill toward the duck pond. My wooden bucket filled with dried corn rattled rhythmically with each step. Distant clouds began to reflect a soft glow silhouetted against a dark morning sky. A dozen mallards and wood ducks had already begun their flutter from the water, high weeds, and cattails onto the twenty seven-foot long earthen pier that penetrated the center of the pond.

The little flock had become accustomed to their morning corn and eagerly listened for the rattle of the bucket. It had all started ten years earlier when a pair of mallards stopped there during their usual September migration. When I discovered them hiding in the high weeds on the south side of the pond, I realized the male had been shot in his right wing and the injured bird's mate stayed close by his side. Although the wing finally healed, he was never able to fly again and they became permanent residents. Over a period of time more mallards and other types of ducks joined the pair.

As I spread the corn in a straight line down the center of the pier, the ducks waddled in file with an unhurried but determined pace—each to his own spot. A light breeze blew reflections of dark blue clouds across the pond. I watched the breakfast feast being devoured. Sitting on the wooden pail which I had placed upside-down on the ground, surrounded by tall marsh grass and cattails higher than my head, I quietly soaked in my own thoughts in a completely private world—a place I loved—a place where I spent fifteen or twenty minutes each morning letting my mind drift to wherever it wanted. Around me were the sounds, smells, and air uniquely Redbriar. I made myself a promise, that morning, not to think about Sarah, Tad, or the ordeal of being locked up in jail waiting for my attorneys to finish their legal gymnastics. I thought of how my daughter loved the early morning as much as I and often sat with me to watch the sunrise.

The first rays of sunshine caused the high grass around me to glow. A steady breeze drifted through the over-ripened fruit in the nearby orchard carrying with it a sharp medicinal scent which yanked my mind back to Sarah and the night she died. The fragrance engulfed me, covered me as it formed a picture in my mind of Sarah lying in front of me, draped in white while I watched all color fade from her face and lips. With frozen eyes and half-closed lids she glared at me. I knew the look on her face too well—a look that spoke louder than words. A silent testimony. A sculpture in white flesh portraying her final thought—her last message telling me she knew what I had done to her.

As dawn continued to warm the air, the breeze and fragrance stopped and thoughts of Sarah faded. I quickly filled the void.

Every creative person I have ever known has the ability to send his mind into a special world and take with it only the things and memories he chooses. I always do it when I'm painting, but every now and then I find myself doing it even when I'm with someone I love. Sarah always thought of my frequent retreats as a kind of rejection. I always thought of them as a kind of spiritual refreshment.

Redbriar

I sat by the pond until the clouds turned from peach to light gray. I then returned to the house, let Sergeant out and sat with him on the flat rock by the river for about a half hour. He knew that when we sat together on the rock in the morning he had to stay perfectly still and quiet. We spotted a small herd of deer drifting silently across the river about thirty yards away. Like ghosts, they disappeared the moment they reached the far bank. We then walked down stream several miles. At the flat rock, the river is deep and slow moving, but further downstream, it widens, and becomes shallow, rocky, and rapid. By jumping from stone to stone, we crossed the river and walked the far bank for another half mile or so. It was a familiar route that led to the old house where Bakkuk once lived. Passing by the unpainted clapboard structure, I saw a young man with an old-fashioned sickle, clearing waist high brush and weeds in an area about fifty feet from the house. It was, as I remember, a part of the yard where Bakkuk's family once had a clothes line and a large black kettle that they used for washing clothes. Since Bakkuk's family didn't have indoor plumbing, the laundry had to be boiled regularly in the kettle and hung out to dry. I didn't recognize the young man with the sickle but was sure from his size, build, and color that he must have been related to Bakkuk.

"Good spot for a garden," I said, to get his attention.

The man didn't recognize me either, and never stopped working, but smiled, pleased that a stranger had taken time to speak. Something on the roof of the house caught my eye. It was a canvas tarp held down by a half dozen hat-sized stones.

"Looks like your roof sprung a leak," I said.

"Yep, big storm end of February blew off half my shingles. Tarp's working okay for now."

As I left, I waved and received a strong nod from the young man. About another quarter of a mile from there, the river spreads out again and becomes shallow enough for me to hop across the stones back to the other bank. Sergeant and I pushed through the grassy fields, past two farms to a house belonging to Possum. My mother left the house and two acres to him when she died. He came from a family in Weavertown—mostly carpenters and farm hands. Possum could build a house from scratch, make furniture, work the fields and garden, fix the plumbing and do just about anything else that needed to be done. He was a chain smoker, had a deep raspy voice, was strong as a bear, and remained humorless as a pool of mud. I never really knew how old he was. He never changed. There was never a day that he didn't have a quarter inch gray stubble on his face. How he managed to keep it exactly that length is a permanent mystery, and I never dared ask. He lived alone and was as superstitious as anyone I ever knew. On a nail above his front door hung a horseshoe, a string with three cloves of garlic, a crucifix, and the skull of a cat. His wood shop was on the back of his house, facing the river. It was hot and dusty, with a shingled shed roof. The screaming of his saw could be heard a hundred yards away. I watched him for a while through the back window. He never looked up when working, never stopped except to get a fresh cigarette. The loud saw spooked Sergeant and I let him run off in a nearby field. Possum knew that I had entered the room, but didn't stop or acknowledge my presence until he finished a long cut through a piece of birch.

"Hand me that plank," he said, with only a glance out of the side of his eye. I picked up the wood and carried it to the business side of the table saw then returned to the open window. He never wore deodorant and never bathed before Sunday. It was Saturday. Possum enjoyed his own company and seldom started any conversations.

"I knew you was comin'."

"You did?"

"Yep, dreamed about you last night. You said you had a job for me to do."

"Well, that's why I'm here. I do have a job for you to do."

"I know. My dreams always come true. Sooner or later they always happen."

"So what job did I have for you in your dream?"

"Your paintings were piling up in the house 'cause nobody was buying 'em no more, so I had to build a big store room to put them in?"

"Why weren't they buying my paintings?"

"My dreams don't ever tell *why*, just *what*. For whatever reason, everybody stopped buying 'em and they piled up in the house."

"Well I've got some bad news for you Possum. Your dream was wrong; I want to take out one of the big closets adjacent to the two middle bedrooms on the second floor and convert it to a private bathroom. I also have a few other things I need to do in my old bedroom. I'll go over the work when you get there."

Once it was lit, Possum never touched his cigarette until it burned its way to his lips. He worked, talked, dragged in, and exhaled smoke, all with his weed permanently stuck in the corner of his mouth. When he bent forward to drill or run his saw, he always tilted his head to let the smoke drift by his closed left eye while using his right eye to work. "My dreams are never wrong, they jus' don't always happen right away," he muttered to himself then grunted, "Did you say one of the two middle bedrooms?"

"Yes, the left one."

"That's Tad's room."

"Right."

"You still think she's coming back?"

"Soon, I think, and I want it to be special for her."

"So what are you doing in the other room? Who is that

going to be for?"

"A friend."

"A lady friend?" Possum snapped back.

I avoided the question. "When can you come up?"

"I'll check my calendar."

"I'd like to get it started as soon as possible."

"I'll be up there day after tomorrow to take a look." Possum turned off his saw and straightened his back. "Is she pretty?"

I ignored him again.

"I'll bet she ain't nothing like Sarah."

"Why are you asking me these questions? She's just a friend who needs a place to stay when she's in Redbriar."

"It ain't right. She's not your mom, not Tad, not Sarah. She shouldn't be in there."

"Somebody needs to be in the house. Why not a woman?"

"It all has to do with getting' Tad to come back, don't it?" Possum asked.

"Someone besides me should be there." I changed the subject. "I've got another job for you too. On your way up there, how about stopping by Bakkuk's old place and look at the roof. It needs some attention, but don't tell them I sent you. Tell them you have some left over roofing materials from an old job and just thought they would like to have them. Buy all you need and I'll pay for it." Possum blew a puff of smoke straight up, which meant that he understood. He then exposed his dark gnarled teeth and removed the last quarter inch of cigarette.

I learned from Cleo long ago not to pay much attention to whatever Possum said, but I also knew that when he had something on his mind, it would come out when he was ready and not a moment before.

Possum cut three more pieces of wood, then said, "It's bad luck to talk about her, to talk about the deceased…but, Sarah still spends her summers at the Stone House. Don't matter if she's buried on the other side of the county. I still feel her there in the summertime."

I didn't answer, but turned and looked out the window. His comment about Sarah didn't surprise me a bit. I'd heard him talk about ghosts a hundred times before, and I knew better than to question him. Again I changed the subject.

"I know how much Tad will appreciate having her own private bath," I said.

Possum spit on the sawdust floor. "I told you she don't want to be there. She was real different after Sarah was gone, and she was real different all over again when your mother died. She hardly talked before the funeral and almost not at all for days after that."

"Days after that? *After* the funeral? I was told she disappeared that very day. When did you see her?"

"After her Granma's funeral, she left the Stone House and came straight here. Stayed two or three days."

"Two or three days! Here? Where?"

"Mostly just looked out the window, didn't talk much, took some walks, slept on the couch. She cried at night. Spooked the hell out of me."

"Why didn't you tell me about this back then?"

"You weren't here and you know I don't do letters and this is the first time you've asked about it."

I closed my eyes, pushed my hair back with both hands, and left.

It was still early enough in the morning for overhanging trees to create black shadows in the river. I paused a few times on my way home to look at the stream changing color in the muted light.

Being back on the farm again had given me a needed boost to my painting. I was back to producing two oil paintings a week plus numerous water color vignettes. My agent, Pierce, was calling me once a month to check on how I was doing.

By the time I got back to the carriage house, a streak of light penetrated the clouds in the eastern sky and exploded across the two houses. Crisp shadows outlined each rock in the Stone House while the sunshine, through rippled panes, wiggled its way across the brick floor and the fireplace of the old carriage house. Sergeant found his spot by the front door while I went inside to pick up a canvas I had placed on the bread table earlier that morning. It was an unfinished portrait of Tad that I hadn't worked on for a few years. It was a composition in shades of blue and green. In the painting my daughter knelt in the garden, picking hydrangeas behind the carriage house. Her eyes and dress matched the beautiful light blue that surrounded her. Her face was finished in more detail than any other part of the canvas, but I still found myself trying to picture how much she had changed since then.

Before returning to my studio, I found myself walking upstream along the river bank looking toward the Remington cabin. I must have gone two hundred yards before stopping myself. I threw a few rocks before I dragged myself back to the wood pile by the carriage house and chopped until sweat streaked my face.

Splinters and chips showered me and stuck in my hair and beard as my axe split each piece of dry wood. I chopped until I was breathless and dizzy then staggered back to the carriage house and picked up the painting.

I walked back to my sunroom studio and placed the canvas on the big wooden easel. After picking out my favorite brushes, I laid them in order from small to large on a work table beside the easel, and arranged the paint tubes beside them. From different parts of the room, I tried to get a fresh look at the canvas. Walked backward as far as the fireplace several times, then out to the deck. Watched the river flow a few minutes then returned to the easel. I propped up the portrait between two pillows on the couch.

I yelled at myself. *Start over!* I got out my drawing pad and placed it on the easel. From the storage bin under the windows, I pulled out my latest charcoal sketches of Tad and my wooden pencil box then selected several soft pencils. For an hour I walked back and forth in front of the easel and stared at the sketches. I picked up my stool and threw it through the window.

Glass and splinters crunched under my feet as I crossed the deck and down the stairs. Sergeant ran after me as I stomped downstream to add another assignment to Possum's list of things to do and fix at the Stone House.

Jack Hemphill

CHAPTER NINE

STUART

There are three ways to climb Mount Tsula. The easiest is along its rocky spine rising from the pine forest on the east to its final plateau 500 feet above the Redbriar River Valley. The hardest way to climb it is straight up the face on the river side. My favorite route up the mountain is hiking the sloped pine forest to a rock wall, scaling the wall another fifty feet to a lower plateau, and then spiraling up a narrow ledge just about the width of my foot around the stone knob all the way to the final summit.

It had been years since I was there, but early one morning I was compelled to go back. By the time I reached the stone wall, the morning sky radiated enough light to find handholds and crevices in the rock to pull myself to the lower plateau. After a quick rest and a little water, I was ready to shuffle my way to the top. I picked up one large stone about the size of my hand and two small stones and put them in my backpack then slid my way up the ledge.

The sky above was clear, but low black clouds covered the rising sun and rolled straight toward me.

I don't know how many dozen times I made that climb with Bakkuk or how many times I sat and sketched him standing there with the wind lifting his hair and a hawk's feather tied behind his ear spinning in the breeze. The last time I was there I was with Tad, just before her mother died. It was the only time Tad ever made it to the top.

From my back pack, I removed the three stones then a stack of twenty sheets of white paper. I place the paper on the rock floor and the large stone on the stack. I then put two boxes of pencils and a drawing pen beside the paper. I kept the pack of photos of Tad in the bag but removed two at a time and secured them with the two remaining stones.

I sat on the exact spot where I last saw Tad's eyes fill with excitement and the last time I heard her laugh and cry. With each piece of paper clipped to a board in my lap, I sketched every image of her, still floating through my mind. Twenty times on twenty pages I re-created her reaching for the wind and soaking in the sunshine. The rolling cloud surrounded me and whipped the edges of my paper so hard they flapped like butterfly wings, but I continued to sketch as fast as I could while the images were so clear. As I finished each drawing, I placed it under the stack of paper beneath the large rock. It took three hours before the images in my mind began to fade. I closed my eyes and waited for one more memory, but I was finished.

For three hours that morning, I felt closer to Tad, but at the end, I was still alone with nothing but the mountain and the wind rattling my coat the same way it did on that last day with her.

Carefully I placed the photos in my bag and lifted the rock off the drawings, but an unexpected gust exploded the whole stack and hurled them in a straight line across the rock and into the air like a flock of pigeons launching away from a thundering sky. Forgetting the two hundred foot drop off in front of me, I jumped to my feet and ran after the pages; if I hadn't fallen flat on my face, I would have been another pigeon in flight.

The twisting cloud moved straight up river and the little

white pages sailed several miles before released by the wind and allowed to fall. Tad's cabin was hidden somewhere in the trees below and I want to believe at least one found its way to her. I pictured Tad holding the sketch; it told her more than I ever had the words to say.

Jack Hemphill

CHAPTER TEN

Emily drove ten miles an hour slower than the speed limit all the way from Charlotte to Redbriar trying to tell herself that staying at the Stone House wasn't a big deal. For the umpteenth time, she looked down at the door key placed carefully on the seat beside her.

Arriving at the big house she drove to the back and parked beside Stuart's car. Nobody answered after knocking several times on the carriage house door so she drove to the front of the Stone House, unlocked the large front door, and tiptoed into the foyer. Stuart was absorbed at his easel and didn't see her come in. After putting her bags down, she crept through the living room toward the sun room studio, but the old planks under her feet squawked so loud it startled Sergeant who charged at her pretending to be in full attack. Emily froze in her tracks and pulled both hands under her chin. By the time Sergeant reached the far side of the study, he put on the brakes, and skidded to her feet.

The commotion brought Stuart back to reality. "Emily! Good to see you." She waited for him to come to the living room. "Let me show you the rest of the house," Stuart said as he pulled Sergeant away who had already started begging for attention.

Stuart gave her a quick tour of the first floor with Sergeant leading the way.

Back in the foyer, he reached for her luggage.

"It's okay, I can carry them," she said scooping up the larger bag.

"I know," he said with a little laugh, as he picked up the other bag "but you've got to let me feel like a host."

The wide, straight stair led up to a sitting room lit by the large arched window at the back of the house. Two corridors stretched in opposite directions away from the sitting room, one to the west side of the house and one down the east wing with rooms opening on both sides. Emily followed him to the large bedroom suite at the east end. It had once been Stuart's bedroom and extended the full width of the house directly over the sunroom. It had windows on three sides and the interior wall was dominated by a brick fireplace.

As Stuart placed the bag on a high queen-sized bed, he said, "This was my room growing up, but it's yours as long as you want. You can see down the river from the window left of the bed."

Pointing to a door beyond the fireplace, he said, "There is a private bath through there. Feel free to use the closet and dresser drawers, and whatever else you need. If you look in the bottom drawer, there's a second set of clean sheets and pillow cases. Clean sheets are on the bed, but whenever you feel you're ready to change them, use the ones in the drawer and wash the others in the laundry room downstairs—and feel free to use the laundry for your own personal needs. What I'm trying to say is, please make yourself at home."

She walked to each of the four windows, then sat on the bed. Twirling a small ring around her finger, she started to say something, but stopped, hiding an embarrassed glance at him.

"I'm just so glad there's someone staying here," said Stuart. "Why don't you take your time to unpack or whatever. I'll be back at my spot downstairs."

He walked to the door and paused, "It's a big old house and makes big old house noises. If you'd like, I can leave Sergeant here to stay with you at night."

"That may be a good idea."

"Just let him out for a few minutes before you go to bed. He'll come right back. Trust me, he'll love having you here and love the responsibility of looking after you." Sergeant looked at her for a moment as if to confirm Stuart's words.

As Stuart started to leave she said, "Stuart, I'm just curious about something."

"Sure. What is it?"

She started twirling her ring again. "You told me you spent summers here with Sarah and Tad. Where did you and Sarah sleep?"

"Right here in this bed. If...if that's a problem, I have other rooms, but this has the best views."

"It's not a problem—not really. As I said I was just curious."

As soon as he and Sergeant left, Emily lay back on the pillows and looked around the room. The small, subtle pattern in the wallpaper had a slight lavender tone and was just dark enough to contrast with the pure white wood trim around the room. A punch of blue on the mantel above the fireplace drew her to a large clump of violets in a small, glass vase.

She stood to look out the window again and opened it as wide as it would go. An avalanche of chilled air rolled down the side of the mountain into her room. With her eyes closed, she let the breeze flow across her face. The sleeves of her blouse rippled. For a few minutes she let the cool air soak into her skin.

After changing into blue jeans, a sweatshirt, and white sneakers, Emily folded her clothes and placed them in the top drawer of the bureau. After a moment of hesitation, she opened the bottom drawer containing the clean sheets. They were the same violet blue as the flowers on the mantel. Out of curiosity she looked into the other two drawers which were mostly empty except for a few miscellaneous items, some blank paper, fountain pens, an old book of poetry, and a picture frame placed face down. She turned the picture over without removing it from the drawer. It was of Sarah in her wedding dress. One corner of the wood frame was crushed and the glass was broken in a spider web pattern starting from that corner as if it had been smashed against something hard. Emily immediately placed it back in the drawer face down. Looking around the room she realized there were no other pictures anywhere. Small holes in the wall over the fire place and between the windows revealed places where paintings once hung.

Emily returned to the sunroom. Stuart was again absorbed in his work. She sat on the couch by the fireplace, unlaced her sneakers, and placed them on the floor along with her canvas bag. Sergeant seized the opportunity to climb beside her and put his head across her lap. She wished she had brought Stuart a gift and wondered what it should have been. Alone with a man she barely knew, in a remote, almost forgotten nook of North Carolina, watching him paint images stored in his mind—she didn't dare speak.

Sergeant continued to get his head stroked, eyes sealed in extreme dog bliss while she pondered a question she wanted to ask Stuart.

It had only been a week since the County Manager told her that the commissioners had decided to expand her company's contract to include designing a new jail. This would be in addition to the original contract to prepare plans for the renovation of the courthouse. The public meeting to announce the expanded project was scheduled for the following morning—Friday. Emily had no experience in jail design. She was originally picked by her partners as Project Architect for the Redbriar job because it was expected to be only courthouse renovation and a good project for her—the most junior of the four architects in the firm. She knew how difficult jail projects were and she already had a firsthand impression of what it was like working with Sheriff Hodges.

Emily's mind raced forward to the following morning when she would be sitting in a public hearing in front of the commissioners with the sheriff somewhere behind her staring down his large, overbearing nose. In addition to this, with the exception of Sergeant Evans, she would be working entirely with male deputies. There were few women architects in North Carolina at that time and none had ever been the lead designer for a county jail.

After about twenty minutes, Stuart finally put down his brushes. Emily broke the silence by saying his name. Surprised by her voice, he spun around on the stool.

"Oh, I'm sorry. I've been ignoring you," he said before moving his stool closer to the couch.

"I think Sergeant's in love," he said looking at his dog still stretched across her lap.

"He's a sweetheart."

"He is, but in his dreams he thinks he's a wolf."

Stuart pushed back a little on his stool to look at her nestled in the spot where Tad, as a young girl, loved to sit and watch her dad paint until late at night. He remembered how, each night, she fell into such deep sleep, he could carry her from the couch to her bed without waking her.

"Stuart, I have a couple of things to ask you," she finally gathered enough courage to say.

"Ask away."

"I want to know if you will to do something for me." She reached into a canvas bag and pulled out a pair of scissors.

"Okay, you've got my attention."

"I thought of this just last night and if you don't want to

do it, it's okay, but I have my first public meeting about my project tomorrow and I need for you… I really would appreciate it if you would sit with me at the hearing.

He looked down then back at her before saying, "I don't think that would be a good idea."

"I understand. I shouldn't have asked."

"But, you've *got* to tell me what you were going to do with the scissors."

"I was afraid you wouldn't go because it has been so long since…," she paused realizing she was, again, starting to say something really stupid.

"You're trying to say it's been so long since I had a haircut?"

"Only if you wanted to. I thought it might make you more comfortable with the idea of going to a big meeting at the courthouse."

He looked at her, then at the scissors, and then turned his head trying to keep a smile from growing into a laugh.

"You probably think this is silly," he said, "I've been up here over sixteen months and I'm sure by now I look like a real mountain man, but this is the way I need to stay—at least for a while. I sort of blend in with so many of the other guys around here with long hair and bushy beards. Even you, when you first saw me at the restaurant, didn't recognize me."

Emily put her scissors back in the bag and tried to hold back the red tide filling her cheeks. She said, "If you'll go, I don't expect you to say anything, just steer me clear of land mines. I don't know anything about the people here. Just give me a little secret kick or something." Her lips stretched into a crooked smile which made him laugh.

After throwing his head back and giving up a long exhale through half-closed lips, he said, "Okay. I'll just pretend to be the mountain man you picked up on the way to town."

"That's all I need."

Jack Hemphill

CHAPTER ELEVEN

When Emily and Stuart arrived at the courthouse, Chuck Cunningham, the County Manager, was already stewing on the front steps. The well dressed, middle aged man, long thin hair combed over bald spots that couldn't quite be hidden, started talking the moment he saw them. He was a chipmunk of a man, constantly propelled by short bursts of energy.

He put his arm on Emily's back and walked to the courthouse steps without a word to Stuart, who he obviously didn't recognize.

Before entering, Emily scanned the façade of the old brick building that gawked back at her with solemn authority. Cunningham held the massive wooden door open still ignoring Stuart. The numerous renovations and repairs over the years couldn't cover the inescapable scent left by seven decades of history.

A wide central corridor led them past the north portico doors where the defendant had been murdered only a few weeks earlier. She noticed the doors were still taped closed. The county had temporarily sealed the north entrance because they had not been able to scrub off the blood stains soaked into the granite steps.

Whenever a crowd was expected, the commissioners met in the Superior Courtroom on the second floor. Cunningham dragged open one of the ten foot high, two- inch thick doors and they all three walked in.

At her request, two seats had been reserved on the front row for Emily. All five commissioners, the county attorney, and the Board Secretary entered together and found their designated positions at a long table in the front of the room. Stuart noticed a uniformed deputy sitting in the back, but there was no sign of Sheriff Hodges.

Casually dressed men and women sat shoulder to shoulder. The old air conditioning system was useless and all windows on both sides of the room were open inviting a slow but constant breeze to float over the crowd perfuming the air with a mixture of tobacco and breakfast bacon.

Women sat without talking while men spoke softly through the corners of their mouths.

Redbriar never had a murder on its courthouse steps before and schemes of how to prevent it from ever happening again gathered and circulated throughout the little town like flocks of birds in autumn.

Stuart saw people he hadn't seen for years. Some he recognized merely by family traits sculpted in their faces. The Crunks had massive foreheads and Neanderthal jaws; the Wellborns had more skin flapping under their neck than gobbling turkeys; and the Watkins were always large, round-faced people punctuated by long pointed noses. Three of the Jenkins sisters were there. Only daughters were born in the Jenkins family for several decades and all of them were hopelessly gorgeous. All three sat on the back row so that their seventeen-year-old cousin could discretely nurse her two month-old daughter.

Scattered around the room were several herds of Weavertown men with oak bark skin covering their hands and the back of their necks.

As he and Emily took their seats, Stuart glanced around

to see if anyone recognized him. No one looked at him for more than a moment.

After a pledge to the flag and a brief prayer, the county manager opened the meeting by saying, "We are here to explore changing the scope of the current courthouse project and updating the building program. This usually takes place in closed session, but because of the recent events, we have decided to allow the public to attend so everybody can appreciate what steps are being taken. We are fortunate that our architect, Emily Budd is here with us today."

Emily tightened her lips and stared at the floor. The county manager continued, "The renovation of the courthouse and addition of a new vehicular sally port will stay part of the program as before, however, we realize the need for additional security in our judicial process so we are proposing to include building a new jail and law enforcement center adjacent to the courthouse."

The crowd began to fidget.

"This county may grow, so the new building program includes enough space to increase the potential inmate population by about twice its current level."

The fidgeting became a flutter. Some people had already guessed they were going to propose a bigger jail; others were surprised and horrified at the thought. A few were still so disgusted by the blood on the side steps that they were glad something was being done to make the town safer. If the people had anything in common, it was the fact that they all wanted to keep Redbriar a small, southern, mountain town.

"Some of you are probably wondering why we are proposing such a big change. We are projecting our needs twenty years into the future, but the money to build the additional cells will not be wasted. The state prisons are overcrowded and will stay that way for a long time. The state is currently considering paying counties to house state inmates. This money will go a long way toward paying for the new jail."

Nervously trying to read the crowd, the commissioners shifted their eyes from the papers in their hands to the faces around the room.

The county manager said, "It seems to me there are only two logical places for the new buildings. One site is to the west between the courthouse and the river, and the other is to the north. Now, I understand that many of you are already aware of those two choices and I'm sure already have some strong opinions."

The crowd's flutter increased to a low rumble.

"We all know the sites, but let me give a quick overview of whys and why-nots for each. The west site has the advantage of being behind the courthouse and mostly hidden from downtown. Plenty of land is available for everything." He walked forward, put his hands in his pocket, and lowered his voice. "The project will require a lot of digging and grading and most of the trees would have to be cut down. Ellie's Knoll would have to be lowered. Now, the commissioners realize that big hill back there has a lot of sentimental value to all of us, but I'm afraid, however, building on that site would pretty much level it."

Stuart pulled a piece of paper from his pocket, tore off part of it, and jotted a note. Secretly, he slid it into Emily's hand. The note read, *Ellie's Knoll, sentimental only to people who live in Redbriar. The Weavertown people couldn't care less.*

A dozen people yelled out a jumble of words at once.

Cunningham quieted the room by shifting attention to the second option. "The only other obvious site for the jail is right over here to the north. That site would run from the existing parking lot along River Street all the way to the edge of town. I know that means we would have to move the General Bucknell Monument."

An angry, garbled, continuous clatter like a freight train

rattled parts of the room.

Stuart passed her another note, *Bucknell, a Civil War hero. Moving his grave would start another feud.*

Cunningham spoke louder, "That site's big and flat enough, but we'd lose existing parking and from downtown, the jail would stick out like a frog in buttermilk."

"Where you gonna put the General?" someone from the audience grunted.

Three men stood and waved their hands wanting to speak. Cunningham cut them off by raising his voice again and continuing, "If everyone will please keep their seats and be patient, we will discuss all sides of this."

He looked around at the commissioners for signs of support. Getting no response, he turned to the audience again. A man wearing a blue shirt yelled out again, "Where you gonna put the General?"

"Yes, we are well aware that the general is buried under the monument." said Cunningham. "If the jail goes there, we will have him dug up and re-buried with a big new monument on another site."

"That's my great uncle!" insisted the man in blue. "That's been his gravesite for over a hundred years. Why doesn't that matter to the county? I don't want no Redbriar backhoe diggin' up his grave."

"I know, I know," said the county manager, "but, please understand these two sites are the only options available. We realize everyone's concern about destroying the knoll and we know there are lots of people who have special feelings about the General. I think half of Weavertown claims to be related to him in some way, but…"

With that, the auditorium exploded into a half deafening roar. Cunningham raised both his hands, palms forward, calling for silence, but it did no good. He looked back again at the commissioners for some help, but they continued to cower behind their papers.

Right on time, Sheriff Hodges marched into the courtroom and down the center aisle. Slowly, one-by-one the crowd took their seats.

"I see the sheriff is here now," said Cunningham.

"Sheriff, do you want to say anything?"

Cunningham sat down without waiting for an answer.

Sheriff Hodges, after a few words with his deputy, strutted to the center of the courtroom. Instead of facing the commissioners and addressing them he turned and faced the audience standing directly in front of Stuart and Emily like he owned the room. His stubby, brown hair curled slightly over the tips of his ears in just the same way his thick eyebrows protruded over the top of his dark green eyes and his mustache spilled over the corners of his lips. His wide, battle-worn, angular face bore scars from every part of his life.

With a half-concealed leer, which was his typical demeanor when put on the spot, he said, "Mr. Chairman, I apologize for being a little late. Urgent business had me tied up for a while this morning. I understand from my deputy that some options were suggested for the jail location. Would you please have the county manager give me a summary of the options."

Hodges stood still as he looked around the room to acknowledge his allies.

Chairman Caldwell nodded to Chuck Cunningham who lowered his head for a moment to think how to summarize the options.

"The two choices are to either go to the north of the courthouse and take the existing parking lot and the monument, or go to the west behind the courthouse and remove the old hill we all know as Ellie's Knoll."

With that, the sheriff snapped around with a look that could drive railroad spikes. Realizing he alone knew the bloody secret buried in the middle of that hill, and remembering the need to keep his composure, he coughed, strutted back to a spot directly in front of Emily and Stuart, then barked, "The jail has to be placed where it is most secure."

Emily noticed the sheriff's ears were starting to glow red as he continued to thunder. "It's most secure where it's most visible. Is there anyone here who doesn't believe that it would be more visible and therefore more secure on the north parking lot site along River Street, and not behind the courthouse? Isn't security the number one issue here? Didn't a man just a few weeks ago get his brains blown out not seventy-five feet from where I'm standing? Doesn't some of the blood on those steps belong to one of my deputies?" Once again he gazed around the room until he finally saw Emily in front of him and for the first time, recognized Stuart. "Shit," the sheriff blurted out loud.

The crowd was silent for an awkward moment, then mumbled among themselves, swaying back and forth. The sheriff shook at least a half dozen hands on the way back to his seat, whispered, joked, and punched a few arms in typical good-old-boy fashion feeling out how many were still on his team.

"Hey, Roland how about that no-hitter. That boy of yours got an arm...How's that knee, Bill?"

An old man extended his white, boney fingers across the aisle. Sheriff Hodges held them in both of his hands without squeezing and said, "Glad to see you back Mr. McGill,' then he kissed Mrs. McGill on the only spot on her cheek not covered by her frizzy white hair. After regaining his victorious smirk, he sat down.

With that, the chairman rose, looked at Emily, and said, "Would the architect like to make a few comments at this time?"

Emily felt a jolt go through her body. She instinctively reached into her pocketbook and pulled out a notebook and pen, as if she actually had notes to present. She stood, walked a few steps toward the commissioners' table, turned, and faced the crowd. The first face she saw was Stuart's, who was giving her a reassuring smile. She looked around the room. Everybody waited in silence. The sheriff gripped the chair in front of him with both hands while fixing his stare on her.

"I haven't...I mean my company hasn't had the chance to see any site surveys yet, so I really don't have a recommendation at this time." Her voice trembled a little at the end of her sentence.

"It looks to me that the two sites each have their own advantages and disadvantages. I'm certain the site with the knoll would be more expensive because of the excavation costs alone, but the county may feel it's worth the cost to place the jail in a location where it's not constantly visible from Main Street...especially since they are considering building it big enough for eighty-five or more prisoners."

She glanced over at Stuart who gave her a nod that only she could see. Looking back at the county manager and giving a little gesture with her hand she said, "Okay?"

The sheriff had already risen half way out of his seat before she sat down.

With both hands, the sheriff continued to grasp the chair in front of him as he said, "Wherever you decide to put it, it's the architect's job to make it look good. Right?" He smacked his thick lips then continued. "I'm sure our pretty little lady architect can muster enough talent to make it look beautiful from the town, and I'm sure she's smart enough to figure how to design it so that monument to General Wesley Bucknell can stay right where it is. What else do you need to know?"

He glared for a few seconds at each commissioner. Emily

fixed her eyes on the county seal mounted on the wall behind the commissioners to avoid looking at the sheriff.

Caldwell stood and said, "Miss Budd, would you agree with the sheriff?"

The breeze through the windows had stopped. Ladies started fanning themselves with whatever they found in their pocketbooks. The Jenkins' baby started to whimper.

Again Emily stood with no idea of what to say. She searched every corner of her mind. Nothing came. Someone in the middle of the room coughed. Feeling empty, and naked, and stupid she looked around the room for something intelligent to offer. Knowing her face was beginning glow brighter than the two red exit signs over the rear doors, she took a deep breath. The first words that came out were, "Maybe the sheriff's right."

He was still standing and gave a confident glance at his deputy, as if he had already crushed her. The deputy's shoulders shook in silent mocking laughter. Sheriff Hodges looked back at her and straightened up to display his full six foot-five ego. She cast her eyes at Stuart briefly and started over.

"The sheriff may be right...about one thing. The architect is talented enough to design the jail appropriately for either site."

She walked toward the commissioners scrambling through her mind for another thought. "I can also tell you she is talented enough to design it so that it will be secure in either place."

Sheriff Hodges' posture wilted slightly as he slid both thumbs under his belt.

"I think ..." she paused, "I think I should tell you something else," She looked back at the crowd, "No matter how well we design it, it's not going to look like a courthouse, or a fire station, or a grocery store, or an office building. A jail large enough to house nearly a hundred inmates is going to look like a jail, but my company will make it as compatible as it can possibly be with your town."

She looked at the group around the sheriff who had slithered as far away from him as they could. "One last thing," she spoke softly to hide the tremble coming back into her voice, "If the general's monument is anywhere near the jail, with all the fencing we're going to put around it, no one will ever see that monument again except the inmates."

She turned and sat on the bench sliding close enough to Stuart for their shoulders to touch.

Cunningham rose to his feet and said, "It appears that we have discussed the issue and need to take it into private session for a vote. So, we will recess for one hour."

With that, the five commissioners, County Manager, and Secretary to the Board stood to leave.

Sheriff Hodges flew out of the courtroom yanking the two large doors so hard they banged into the wall as loud as rifle shots. The Jenkins' baby burst into a full scream which set the crowd off like a pack of fire crackers.

Stuart stood and gestured to leave. As he followed her up the aisle, the crowd closed in around her grunting out questions. She looked back for Stuart. He pushed his way through the mob and locked elbows with her then plowed a path through the courtroom and out the door. A woman's voice cracked through the clamor saying, "That's Stuart Burns!" A momentary silence was replaced by a new roar with air-borne fists and pointing fingers.

A dozen clusters of people with tight white lips and red faces churned outside the courtroom and along the main corridor.

Emily didn't look at Stuart until they reached the stair. She was still clutching her notebook with both hands.

They left the building through the south portico and paused between two columns. Emily shook her head like she was trying to clear her mind before saying, "Now I'm supposed to go over to see the old jail."

"Are you going to be okay?"

"I don't want to go by myself, but no choice. I have to meet Sergeant Evans for a tour. I've never been in a jail before for any reason." She was hoping he would get the hint.

"Emily, you know I can't go with you."

The jail was only two and a half blocks away. She wished it were further. They walked past the building where the sharpshooters perched only a few weeks earlier then pushed through a weed-covered vacant lot.

In front of the old dungeon, he said, "This is as far as I can go."

Emily smiled, "Can you wait an hour?"

He returned the smile, "I'll be on the front steps of the courthouse."

Jack Hemphill

CHAPTER TWELVE

The anger and suffering that filled the old jail extended beyond its walls and hung over it like a dusty haze. As she opened the front door, Emily was struck with the smell of old wood, aged concrete, and vinyl tile that had been recently scrubbed with a strong cleaning solution.

"I've been expecting you," said Captain Morgan, the chief jailer.

"I'm Emily Budd. I'm supposed to meet Sergeant Evans."

"Yep, Chuck Cunningham told me you would be here, but Sergeant Evans is out today."

"If you know who I am, you know I need a crash course in county jails," she said.

"Learning about county jails and learning about *this* jail are probably two different things," he replied through a large wad of gum.

"What's different here?"

After glancing out the window for a moment, the captain said, "Our sheriff pretty much makes his own rules."

"What are his rules," Emily asked knowing she would probably regret it.

"Well," he said slowly, sitting on the edge of his desk with his head cocked slightly backward. "These men and women are already in a sardine can that's too hot in the summer and too cold in the winter, with no privacy and nothing to do but try to survive and not piss off the stinking fish lying in the bed beside them. But, if they don't do what he wants, or don't quiet down at night, or if they fight or yell at the staff, all the water in the building will be turned off for the weekend including sinks, toilets, and showers, or the heat will be turned off on the coldest nights, or the air circulation shut down until the stench seeps all the way into the Booking Office."

"Why don't they revolt or something?"

"They just want to get the hell out of here, and...I know you're going to ask if the sheriff is ever threatened. The answer is 'yes.' He's without doubt the most feared man in the county, but he gets a threat on his life every week. And you know what? He treasures each threat like a war medal." Captain Morgan looked out the window again, then continued. "I work for the guy, but I don't understand... that is, nobody understands him. Everybody knows to do just what they are told to do and if they don't...well, they learn quickly just to do what they are told to do."

"Obviously I need to learn about how to design a jail. Would you give me a tour?"

"Absolutely, I can show you the male cell blocks, but Sergeant Evans will have to give you the tour of the female area when she gets back."

"You're not allowed in there?"

"Yes, but only if she's with me or if it's an emergency, Otherwise, I'm not even allowed to open the door without a female guard."

Captain Morgan walked to a secure door between the Booking Office and the Detention Area, swung the door until it knocked against the wall and said, "The cells are in the center with a corridor all the way around the perimeter. There are six cell blocks and each cell block holds four inmates plus the two isolation cells on the end. That should be twenty-six beds but we got twenty-nine inmates in the male wing right now, which means we got three sleeping on the floor. The female wing is through that door over there. We'll do the whole male side, but keep at least an arm's length away from the bar front." He then gestured with his hand for Emily follow.

"Okay, gentlemen listen up," he yelled. "There's a woman on the floor. Put your pants on, get off the toilet, and behave for a few minutes."

Morgan walked to the end of the corridor and around the corner out of sight, repeating his orders two more times to the cell blocks on the other side leaving Emily alone. She crept cautiously expecting the guys to be bothered by a woman looking at them like caged animals in a zoo, but most of them went about their business of doing nothing.

Many of the men were asleep. About one-third buried their heads in paperback books. Some stared back. Only a few spoke. Time had stopped in a self-conscious silence. No churning tempers, no cat calls, no screams of anger or anguish. One man, bare from the waist up, was doing push-ups on the floor. Just behind him an older man hovered over a half-finished game of solitaire, his eyes fixed on the blue tattoo covering his right triceps. With his left thumbnail, he constantly stroked the letters of what appeared to be a name inscribed on his arm.

She noticed drawings had been scribbled on the walls. A small, dark man with long, straight hair was carefully crafting a scene on the dayroom wall using colored crayons. She had been told by the County Manager that the guards encouraged inmates to draw on the walls as a type of therapy and to keep them occupied. Crayons were given out whenever requested. Every few years the walls had to be scrubbed and painted over. New drawings would start appearing the moment the paint dried.

Windows were spaced on the outside corridor walls at ten foot intervals, allowing sunlight into the cell blocks.

She paused for a moment to look out the window at the far end of the corridor. The river rushed past the jail with nothing but forest and mountains beyond.

A stare coming from one of the isolation cells burned the back of her neck.

"How ya doin?" the inmate said as she turned around.

She hesitated, then replied, "Well... I'm just doing *fine*. How are *you* doing?"

"Well... I'm just doing *time*," the inmate said with a little bounce in his voice. "You're Miss Budd aren't ya?"

Emily squinted her eyes, "Do I know you?"

"I'm Chigger," he answered. "Chigger Morgan—Captain Morgan's cousin."

His muddy brown hair was cut short on top and long on the sides with a single braided rat-tail that hung down his back. The skin on his face was gray, leathery and tightly stretched over the bones.

"Are you from Redbriar Mr. Chigger?"

"I grew up here and been here my whole life, and I've been in and out of this old jail more times than you can imagine. Right here's the best room in this hotel. I can see the mountains, the sunset, and since this is isolation back here, nobody messes with me."

"Do you know why I'm here?" Emily asked.

"Yep, you're gonna build me a new hotel. Don't forget my view."

"How did you know that and how did you know my name?"

"Whatever my cousin knows, and Sergeant Evans knows don't take long before everybody around here knows. Also we got twenty-nine families outside feeding information to us all the time. Even in isolation I can hear what's goin' on in the other cells, and we got nothing better to do but talk 'bout and think 'bout what's goin' on outside."

He explained to Emily that he only had a couple of weeks left in his sentence and the next time he saw her would be on the outside.

"So you're really the Captain's cousin," she said, moving a little closer.

"Yep."

"That must make being here a little easier."

"Hell no! Other than getting my own private suite."

"Why not?"

"Cause the sheriff makes sure I always get the maximum amount of time here."

"But why?"

"Anybody that has anything to do with drugs is flagged. Once a week he picks a work crew of inmates to clean this side of the river. Only druggies get picked. You see these scars on my arm? That's from the briars and thorns along the river."

"Why does he single out...." a little embarrassed, she waved her hand toward the other cell blocks then continued, "guys like you?"

"You mean druggies?" he said.

"Yes, I guess."

"Cause we're the bottom of the toilet," he said so softly she wasn't sure she heard him. He attempted a smile through gray teeth then eased to the rear of his cell.

"Nice to meet you, Mr. Chigger," Emily said, as she walked a few steps and took off her suit jacket. She tucked it under her left arm and opened her writing pad. As she leaned her shoulder against the bars of an empty cell to scribble a note, she felt a slight nudge against her back. She turned just in time to see Chigger reaching through the bars far enough to stroke his fingers across the blue silk lining of her jacket. She took a few steps backward, switched her coat to her right arm, and looked at him as he pulled back his hand and laid face down on a pillow.

"Goodbye Miss Budd," he mumbled.

Captain Morgan was waiting for her in the Booking Office.

"Are you finished?" he asked.

She said that she had seen enough and would come back another time to meet the Sergeant.

As Emily left the building, she had an odd feeling. Something she couldn't identify at first. The only picture of prisoners she ever had in her mind were of remorseless, sweat-soaked faces, grilled by the sun, tethered together with chains as they picked up garbage along the highway. What she expected to see at the jail was nothing like what she found there.

She walked across the vacant lot, looked back at the old building, then looked beyond it, over the mountains. She realized that the place where she was standing was the farthest she had ever been from her mother, from Charleston, from wrought iron rails, and leaded glass doorways.

The helpless wretch buried in his pillow, embarrassed for touching the silk lining of her jacket, stuck in her mind.

She walked through the weeds and smashed them to the ground, then, with her jacket flung over her shoulder, she marched down the street toward the courthouse. The bright sun left dark shadows under the south portico. She saw Stuart in the shade, leaning against a column.

"Any word from the commissioners?" she said as they both sat down on the top step.

"Cunningham walked by a while ago." Stuart replied, "He

was talking to somebody about getting a survey completed of Ellie's Knoll."

"So they sided with the guys from Weavertown?"

"That's what it looks like. I'm just glad I don't have to be around the sheriff right now."

They sat for a few minutes without talking. The courthouse cast a diagonal shadow that covered them and wiggled its way down the front steps. The crowd had gone home. It was the middle of the day and only three cars were driving through town. On the other side of the river, a woodpecker hammered at the side of a dead tree.

From the top step, they looked all the way down Main Street. A few men and women walked by and old men sat in chairs outside the barber shop. Emily wondered what it would be like to live here. She loved the way houses were clustered close around the village center.

Stuart said, "They never told you in school about projects like this, did they?"

"No, in school they don't teach you about real people in a real world…and angry sheriffs, and all that stuff." With her legs crossed at the ankles, she shoved both hands into the deep pockets of her jacket, raised her shoulders for a moment and then let them fall. Without saying anything further, she closed her eyes for a minute.

"Are you okay?" he asked.

Just then a grayish-brown dog caught their attention as he sniffed his way along River Street, turned down Main Street, and sat with the old men in front of the barber shop. After receiving his reward of a pat on the back and a long scratch behind the ears, he disappeared into the open door at the fire station. Emily looked at Stuart, and gave him a smile as her only answer.

CHAPTER THIRTEEN

"Try these," said Sheriff Hodges as he walked into the Booking Office.

Captain Morgan was sitting at his desk finishing reports. "What are they?"

"The best chocolate chip cookies in the world. Made them myself this morning." Hodges placed a dish of a dozen five inches diameter cookies on the table in front of the captain.

"Brought you a mug of coffee too. Can't eat chocolate chip cookies without coffee."

"Jesus!" Captain Morgan said as he took a bite. "How'd you make them?"

"Three secrets. I'll tell you two of them, but if you tell anybody else I'll throw you in the cell block naked."

"Then don't tell me."

"Secret number one—use twice the amount of butter as the recipe calls for. Number two—twice the chips. The third will stay my secret. Greatest cookies in the world. Where's Ceda? She should be on duty now."

"She's back with the women. Just be a minute. When you gonna tell me about your meeting with the state guys this morning?"

The sheriff raised his index finger while he finished chewing an entire cookie stuffed into his mouth, and washed it down. "Yeah, we're going to have some interesting months ahead."

"In what way?"

"We're going to have some state officials and Feds screwing around here. They're investigating something that's already got its tentacles stretching from North Carolina to Colombia."

"South Carolina?"

"No the other one, below Mexico."

"Gotta be drugs."

"Yep. The Fed guy said South American traffic has exploded."

"So what's that got to do with us?"

The women's cell block door slammed as Ceda returned.

"Ceda, come on over here," the sheriff said.

"What's going on?"

"Got to tell you something."

Ceda placed her clipboard on the counter and stood by Captain Morgan. "We're out of coffee," Hodges said as he held up his cup, "regular for both of us."

Ceda collected both cups and walked toward the break room. Before opening the door she turned just enough to glance back at the two men who were obviously waiting for her to disappear before they resumed whatever they were talking about. Once inside the break room she put some water in the coffee maker, then she walked back to the door and opened it just enough to let the conversation ease through the crack.

She heard the sheriff say, "The druggers know now that there's a limitless supply of cheap labor in South America, so endless and so cheap that they can manufacture and ship drugs at twice the rate U.S. junk-heads can consume it. They also know that right now it's easy to find places to bust through the thousand-mile Mexican border. Nixon's 'War on Drugs' we've heard do much about will be kicking in soon so that long border will start closing down. It'll be completely sealed off—maybe in ten years or so."

Captain Morgan picked up his fourth cookie. "I can't stop eating these damn things, tell me the final secret."

"I thought you'd never ask. It's a touch of almond extract in the batter."

"Okay, now tell me where we fit into this drug thing?"

"You aren't listening. They can manufacture the cheap shit and get it into the U.S. at twice the rate American-idiots can suck it up. Understand?"

"Uh, yeah."

" So what do you think they do with all the extra stuff they gonna bring in?"

"Hide it?"

"Yep. Stockpile the garbage. Stockpile it in places where it can't be found. Morgan, listen to this, if you drew a circle that connected Miami, New Orleans, Chicago, and New York, can you guess where the center of that circle would be?" "Somewhere around here?"

"Closer than that—right on top of Jefferson County. They suspect some of it has already been stashed around here. Best place in the country to hide things? Hell, people that lived here all their lives sometimes get lost in these hills."

The water started to boil in the coffee-maker and Ceda eased the door shut, ran back and poured two cups of instant coffee with two tea spoons of sugar in each cup. Holding both cups in one hand, she once again pulled the door just enough to follow the conversation.

"The SBI guy told me in the next twelve years the network of interstate highways will be woven into such a web that you can drive from here, right here, and be in any one of those big-ass cities in a few hours."

"I still don't know how we fit in."

"Remember everything that I just told you is secret, but the truth is they don't know beans for sure. They're just putting the little pieces together and that's the way it looks right now. But if somebody from South America or anywhere else is trying to pull this off, he's going to need some local help, a good ol' Jefferson County thug who can kick around these hills without anybody thinking anything about it."

"So we're supposed to grab this guy?"

"We're supposed to do nothing yet. Nothing but watch for anything going on strange or suspicious. Then report it. Then do what they tell us."

"Sheriff, we don't really know what's going on five miles out of town. How we gonna watch the whole damn county? Hire more deputies?"

"No! This whole thing's got to stay a bigger secret than my chocolate chip cookie recipe."

Ceda took that as her cue to bring in the coffee. The two men stopped and watched her put the mugs on the desk.

"What are you guys talking about?"

"Try one of these." The sheriff handed her the plate and watched while she took a bite of the cookie. "What do you think?" He asked.

"Good. Chocolate chip is my favorite… especially when it has that little touch of almond extract."

Sheriff Hodges always backed his car two lengths into his steep driveway next to his house. Before he climbed his steps to the side door, Pinky appeared and nuzzled against his legs. Hodges' long-legged orange friend was the only one of his cats allowed to stay outside all day.

He stomped his boots beside the door, stepped into the kitchen behind Pinky and then flung his hat across the room to a single chair beside the small kitchen table.

After hanging his blazer on a door knob, he placed a large frying pan on the stove, added grease and dumped in a can of scrapple. It immediately began to crackle.

As the fragrance from the pan drifted into the rest of the house, cats of all colors and sizes appeared from their favorite hiding places around the house. Hodges had to take one cat off the stove and another one off the table where he had placed small bowls filled with dried cat nuggets. As soon as the scrapple was cooked, he heaped a portion over the dry food in each bowl, then placed the bowls in a circle on the kitchen floor. The scrambling cats created a storm of fur, which immediately turned to silence as each chomped at his dinner. Sheriff Hodges sat and watched for the next few minutes. When they finished, two cats jumped into his lap begging attention. The two cats, Buford and Cougar, were the most affectionate of his eight pets. Cougar had a litter of four kittens just three months earlier and the strongest and unquestioned leader of the kittens, Sampson, was crawling up his pant leg. The sheriff picked up Sampson by the scruff of his neck and placed him on the table beside his mother. This was the time of day he loved best. His eight friends (plus four kittens) had been napping all day and now with full stomachs, they all wanted to play. Beside the kitchen table, he kept a drawer full of toys that instantly converted his little kitchen into a roller derby. Rubber mice that squeaked when bitten, balls that jingled as they rolled across the floor, and four cloth balls with a pinch of catnip inside each. Even Buford and Cougar jumped into the ring. Sampson, however was content to keep his spot under the sheriff's stroking hand.

For a half hour to forty-five minutes at the end of each day this was the sheriff's therapy. It was a little journey from the insanity of a sheriff's world to the pure imaginary world of his cats. It was just enough to let him forget, until morning, the collection of suffering he had locked away.

CHAPTER FOURTEEN

STUART

By the end of the summer, Sergeant learned the sound of Emily's jeep as it turned into the driveway. She found me in the carriage house where I was packing food and equipment into canvas bags.

"I'm glad you decided to come. It's a perfect time," I said.

"I can't believe I'm doing this," Emily said as I handed her a sleeping bag, blanket, and a fully packed bag.

"I've never camped anywhere before, much less on a rock."

It had taken me months to convince her to do it. I was afraid she would change her mind at the last minute.

"You'll love it, but don't worry about the rock, I put a folded air mattress in your bag," I said.

We walked together down the rocky ravine to my favorite place on the big flat rock by the river. Sergeant ran ahead of us and jumped into the stream. Within minutes the simple camp was set up and a fire was started in a natural depression in the stone ledge. I laid a blanket directly on the rock and my bedroll on top of it. Emily blew up the air mattress and smoothed out her sleeping bag. Less than an hour of sunlight was left, which was just enough time to reheat a pot of stew I had cooked in the carriage house. I also placed a pot of cider and a long roll of bread wrapped in tin foil by the fire.

Emily took a little taste before filling her plate. She got seconds. We ate it all. With good food and a breeze following the gurgling river, it's almost impossible not to relax, open a little bit, let go. We both needed it.

Sergeant, who had been given his share of food, curled near the upwind side of the fire. Once the black night surrounded us and the fire settled down, Emily wrapped a blanket around her.

"I used to lie in that same spot," I said.

"Did I get your place?"

"No, it's okay I'm in Bakkuk's place."

I still didn't know what she thought of my odd friend. It was easy for me to picture Bakkuk there on the rock beside me. He always rose after midnight, stood by the water, and watched moonlight dance in the stream while I lay on my back, looking into the black sky like it was a giant canvas splattered with a billion silver spots.

"I guess the first time we camped here I was seven or eight," I said.

"Were you afraid...the first time?"

No, not with Bakkuk here. Everything seemed easy with him. We always cooked simple things like hotdogs on a stick and a pot of baked beans or something like that. Before we went to sleep we listened for animals."

"What kind of animals?"

"Just about everything."

"Great," she said sarcastically. She waved to Sergeant with her fingers and he moved a little closer to her.

Emily sat up and rested her back on the rock behind her, pulled her blanket tighter over her shoulders, and listened to the night sounds that never stopped. High-pitched cricket songs fought with guttural sounds somewhere in the distance.

"What's that?" she asked.

"That's a male bullfrog."

"How do you know it's a male?"

"Just listen. What does it sound like?"

"Sounds like a frog."

"He's trying to tell all his girlfriend's he's got a 'jug of wine, jug of wine, jug of wine.'"

"You're right! That's what it sounds like."

"I know this is going to sound really odd, but frogs were once my favorite animal."

"Uh, yeah—pretty weird. You've got every kind of wild animal in America running around these hills and your favorite is a frog?"

"I know. Hard to believe, but when I was a young boy, Bakkuk brought giant frogs from downstream for us to play with. We staged frog jumping contests and things like that. I never told him this, but I used to think frogs were turtles that had escaped from their shells."

"That's um…" She tried to hide her laughter. "That's actually kind of sweet."

"I can remember thinking, back then, that turtles seemed so slow and bogged down by that the little suit-of-armor they were born with, that it was more like a built-in prison. Young turtles needed to hide in their shells. You know, for protection. I could see that, but, I figured sooner or later, when they grew up and could take care of themselves, they escaped from their shells and became frogs—free to hop around and swim and do frog things."

"I suppose so. It's not exactly the kind of thing I ever thought about."

"That was a little boy's imagination, but part of it stuck with me. I always wondered how it felt."

"To have a shell?"

"No, to drop something that was part of you, that you were born with, and then one day just swim away with a freedom that you couldn't possibly have imagined."

Sergeant sat up and looked at me for a moment, checking to see if everything was still okay, then settled back against Emily's leg.

"Didn't you tell me Bakkuk trapped animals?" she asked.

"Bakkuk was always trapping. Even before he was a teenager, he was making money catching pests—ten dollars for skunks and raccoons and fifteen for foxes that had a taste for chickens. His favorite spot for releasing raccoons and skunks was on the northwest side of the county, close to Weavertown, but he had several places for releasing foxes. Sometimes he went as far away as the other side of the French Broad River to let them go. Most of the time he caught red or silver foxes, but every now and then he caught a cross-fox."

"What's that?"

"They're rare, but you know what? He always released cross-foxes on Mt. Tsula either in the woods around the base or on top of the mountain, and he never charged the farmer for the catch."

"Why?"

"To be honest, I'm not sure I can tell you why Bakkuk did any of the things he did, but I have my theories. When the French were trying to settle this part of the mountains, trappers let cross-foxes go. They're wild looking critters. Their name came from the dark stripe that runs down their back and across their front shoulders. When the pelts were hung, the markings formed a perfect cross and so no one wanted them."

Why?"

"They were afraid of them."

"Because of the cross?"

"Yep."

"Okay then, Bakkuk didn't trap them for their fur, but why didn't he release them on the other side of the French Broad like the others?"

"I have a couple of theories about that too. I think he also was a little bit superstitious about them, but more than that, I think he somehow thought they were special."

"How ?"

"In all the times I went with him to check his traps, I only saw a few cross-foxes, and I can tell you they don't look like silver or red foxes at all. The black stripe runs up their spine, crowns the top of their head and fills their face with a mask that makes their yellow eyes shine like a pair of fog lights in the dark. They're just wilder looking critters."

"But why did he think they were special? Was it because nobody wanted them?"

"Yes, I think that was part of it. Anyway, several times a month I helped him carry animals across the county and let them go. Every now and then Ceda went with us to take raccoons over to Weavertown—to the dump."

"Who's Ceda?"

"Ceda Evans."

"Sergeant Evans?"

"Yes.

"Met her a few weeks ago."

"She's almost my age. We pretty much grew up together following Bakkuk around."

"She was a tom-boy?"

"Oh yeah. She could skip a rock across the stream better than just about anybody…except me. Big hands and feet for a girl, now that I think about it, big shoulders too."

"She ever marry or anything?"

"Yeah. Long time ago. Didn't work out. He turned out to be an alcoholic."

"Abusive?"

"He got violent when he was drunk, but every time he did, Ceda beat him up. The last time she broke his nose. He ran away, drew all his money out of the bank and never came back. That's when she started working for the sheriff."

"So when she was young, she went trapping with you guys?"

"No, she didn't like the trapping part all that much; she like letting them go. Bakkuk believed that raccoons liked the smell of the Weavertown dump, so we took them there thinking they would like it so much they would never return to Redbriar."

"How'd you carry them?"

We strapped wire cages to our backs—that is, Bakkuk and I did. Ceda walked with us but without a cage. The way to the dump was through the woods and over small creeks, except for the Deep Pine River. It joins the Redbriar just south of Weavertown. Crossing that river would have been really tough except for the big sewer main spanning over it."

"Don't tell me you made a bridge out of the sewer main?"

"Yeah. The big pipe was flanked on each side with two steel beams creating what seemed to us the perfect pedestrian bridge. It was one of the best parts of the trip to Weavertown. It was hard work with the cages on our backs, inching our way over the three-foot wide bridge with a twenty-five foot fall to the river below. Bakkuk always led the way, with me in the middle, and Ceda following."

Emily filled her cup with cider and nestled back into her blanket.

I continued, "I've got to tell you about a trip to the dump

late one morning during a long dry spell. The river was running very low. The usual roar and gurgling of the water was reduced to a slight background whisper. By the time we reached the halfway point across the river, we heard voices under the pipe from the Weavertown side. We shuffled our feet slowly so the cages wouldn't rattle. At first, the only sounds were garbled words, and a young girl's high clear voice. When we got near the far bank, Bakkuk dropped to his knees then stretched his belly over the top of the pipe. We copied him a few feet behind."

Emily scooted her air mattress a little closer.

"A small gap between the steel girder and the pipe allowed us to spy directly below without being noticed. Every word spoken by the three people on the bank below reverberated against the pipe and concrete abutment. By then we heard deeper voices like a young man and an adolescent boy. As we peeped through the gap, we recognized Chigger Morgan and his friend, Dab Nettles."

"Chigger Morgan?"

"Yes, have you met him?"

"Oh yeah, I had a chat with him in jail."

"I'm not surprised. Anyway, I didn't know the girl then but guessed she was about thirteen. A blanket had been spread over a flat area of the bank. They were smoking something and insisted that the girl try it, too. After a few minutes the voices became more exaggerated and distorted. Ignoring her squealing protests, Dab ripped open her blouse then held her arms behind her while he pulled her to the ground. Chigger watched motionless. I saw Bakkuk's finger nails digging into loose paint on the girder. He was breathing through his teeth. I couldn't imagine what he was going to do. He reached into the wire cage on my back, lifted the raccoon, maneuvered it to the edge of the girder, and dropped the animal fifteen feet directly onto Dab's back. With screeching and flailing arms and legs, both Dab and the raccoon rolled over and over down the embankment until they landed in the thorns at the water's edge. Righting himself, still screaming, Dab bolted downriver.

"It was too much for Ceda, who started squealing like a baby pig. With one hand, I pulled her on top of me, while I wrapped my other hand over her mouth.

"Chigger stood still in a half-stunned—half-drugged stupor, as the second raccoon landed on his shoulders digging its claws into his back and its teeth into his neck. Chigger let out a shrill scream and took off running in the opposite direction— raccoon still attached."

"What about the girl?"

"The young girl climbed up the bank and ran down a dirt road that paralleled the river to Weavertown. On the way back, we found Chigger sprawled on the ground, soaking wet, exhausted, head against a tree. By that night both boys were arrested and both were sent to juvenile court. As first-time offenders, they were given supervised probation."

"Did you ever see the girl again?"

"I didn't see her again until two years later when she entered Jefferson High school with me. She didn't know me then. I waited a couple of years before I got to know her. We were very different. She was very studious and I was…me."

"But, did you ever really get to know her?"

"It was Sarah."

"Oh, my God. Your Sarah?"

"Yep, my Sarah."

"Did you ever tell her about seeing her on the river bank?"

"No."

"She never knew where the raccoons came from?"

"Nope."

"What was she like then?"

"She was outgoing—a natural-born talker. Smart as hell. The only person in her family to get an education."

"Did she get along with your parents?"

"Of course not."

"Did you get along with her family?"

"They never liked me and, of course, I never saw them again after the trial."

"You haven't spoken to any of them at all?"

"No, but I saw their faces staring at me in court and knew they wished I were dead instead of Sarah."

We both listened for a while to the fire crackling.

"Tell me more about your family," she said.

"Well, my family came from good Scots-Irish clans. Calvinists. Good people, but seldom showed their emotions. Didn't believe in giving into passions and all that sort of thing."

"That must have been hard for you, I mean, as an artist—right?"

I nodded as I asked, "Were you close to your family?"

"I was an only child, like you. There were just three of us, but we had strong feelings—held nothing back, affectionate, chatty. It took forever just to get through our meals—we even talked simultaneously sometimes."

"That was never a problem at the Stone House."

After looking at the spray of sparkling lights above her, Emily glanced at me. A steady breeze kept the embers glowing giving enough light to see a faint outline of her face.

"Did Sarah like coming here?"

"She came here from time to time, but never stayed through the night. She never understood sleeping on a rock with a perfectly good bed not two hundred yards away."

"Stu...you know I came to the trial."

"Yes, I saw you."

"You saw me in the audience on the first day, but to be honest, I couldn't watch. I didn't come back. When my friends talked about it, I couldn't listen. It was just too hard for me to hear what they were saying, especially the medical reports. I can't imagine what it was like for you."

"It's always going to be painful."

"I saw the verdict in the headlines, but never read the articles."

"Emily, you know it was nothing but an accident, no matter what the DA wanted everybody to believe."

Emily slid the blanket off the back of her head and leaned forward.

"Would you tell me about it?"

I rolled toward her propping myself up on one elbow.

"It was an accident. The summer was almost over and Tad stayed here with my mother while we went back to Charlotte. I had an exhibition opening at the gallery, the next day. I ate an early dinner at home by myself, then went to the gallery where they were hanging my show. I needed to be there. When I finally got home, late, I couldn't find Sarah. Her dinner dishes were still on the table and nothing had been cleaned up in the kitchen. About eleven-thirty, Charlotte Memorial Hospital called and told me they had Sarah and I should come right away. When I got there, she was dead. When she realized she was in trouble, she called 911 and by the time they arrive, she was face down on the kitchen table gasping for breath. It took days for the hospital to figure out she died from complications caused by eating blueberries containing arsenic."

"I heard about the poison, but what made the DA think that pointed to you?

"The press was being fed a lot of junk by the DA who thought he smelled a high- profile case. He built his whole attack around his suspicions about me and he never looked anywhere else."

"What suspicions?"

"It was all—or mostly—circumstantial, but that boils down to one thing—they couldn't quite prove it and I couldn't really disprove it either. So they left me dangling."

"But, they found you guilty and sentenced you. That's not exactly dangling."

"Yep, but not for the first degree murder the DA wanted. The jury exercised their right to find me guilty of a lesser charge— reckless homicide. From the DA's evidence, they were certain I was somehow involved, but couldn't prove pre-meditation."

"But, what evidence did they have?"

"I guess for someone who didn't know me, it probably looked like a lot. The truth is I had some of those same blueberries that night before I left for the gallery, but nothing happened to me. They tried to create scenarios as to how and when the poison got into the fruit. My lawyers presented medical records that showed Sarah had been taken to a hospital once before with symptoms of arsenic poison. It happened years earlier right after we were married, before we moved to Charlotte. I drove her to the Jefferson Hospital. Turns out there's a small percentage of people in the world who are easily affected by extremely low levels of arsenic. It's just like some people are affected by low levels of peanuts in food. The tiniest amount of arsenic sent her into convulsions. The first time it happened, the hospital in Redbriar concluded that the arsenic probably came from pesticides spread around our farm that accumulated in the vegetables."

"So how did it end up in her food in Charlotte?"

"It's not as hard as it sounds. We brought the blueberries home from the farm—from our own bushes. We still use pesticides."

"But, she pulled through that first time."

"Yes. Sick as hell for a little while, but as far as I know that was the only other time it happened. Anyway, my attorneys presented all that in my defense."

"So what's the evidence against you if she had a history of this problem?"

"They used her medical history against me. It wasn't hard for them to show I knew she had this condition, and the same compound in pesticides that contain arsenic is also found in certain pigments of artist's paint. It's been used since the mid-eighteenth century especially in France."

"Pesticides in paint?"

"Actually, yes. The pigment is called *Paris Green*. It was first used to kill rats in Paris, but many artists loved to mix it their paint because of its intense blue-green color."

"What kind of artist would mix rat poison with their paint?"

"Famous artists. It was Cezanne's favorite pigment; he used it in most of his paintings. Some experts believe that the fumes caused his death. Many people believe it also caused Monet to go blind and Van Gogh to become insane."

"So why did you mess with it?"

"Lots of artists *messed* with it. Like I said, because of its powerful, beautiful color."

"So they tried to claim you put *paint* in her food?"

"Yes, that's exactly what they said. It would only take a tiny amount"

"But how? Wouldn't it taste bad or something?"

"Yes, if you're using oil paint. Oil has an odor, but a teaspoon of water mixed with a small amount of Paris green found in certain watercolors is odorless and tasteless and still contains a tiny bit of arsenic."

"They still make paint with that stuff?"

"They did until a few years ago. Today other chemicals have replaced it. Anyway, that's what they found in her and made a case that I laced the blueberries with my watercolor."

"But, where was the *real evidence* against you?"

"There wasn't any."

Emily sat up, leaned on her right hand, turned toward me and said, "Any idiot can see that. I don't understand why they thought this was such a strong case."

"Well, I agree of course, but there were a few more things they put in the mix. They produced as evidence, letters I had written a couple of years earlier to LeBlanc and other artist's paint companies in France and other parts of Europe asking which of their paints contained Paris Green. Two answered with letters giving me the exact colors they sold that contained it. Tubes with each of those colors were found in my studio. The detectives also found small amounts of green paint on the kitchen counter."

"Anything else?"

"Yes." I stood and added a few logs to the fire.

"She had already packed her bags," I said as I sat back down on my blanket. "She was going to move out the next day and stay with her sister in Weavertown. Tad was still at the Stone House with my mother and apparently Sarah had planned to pick up Tad as soon as she got back to Jefferson County and move in with her sister."

"Stuart, she was leaving you?"

"Separating."

"I had no idea."

"Nobody did. Not even me until her sister testified, but the truth is, Sarah gave me plenty of warning—I just chose to ignore it. I thought she understood what an important time that was for my career."

"Did Tad know about it?"

"No, I don't think so."

"So the DA thought that was the motive?"

"Yes, that's what they suggested as my motive; with her sister testifying against me they presented a damn convincing argument that I had perfect opportunity and a believable motive, but it was still all circumstantial. The jury apparently concluded that I didn't mean to kill her—only punish her for threatening to leave—so they went for reckless homicide."

"And you can't prove you didn't know she was leaving?"

"No. I'll never be able to prove that. Why?"

"Well, how did the paint get on the kitchen counter?"

"Do you think her death was my fault?"

After staring into the embers far too long, she said, "I don't know."

"Sometimes I cleaned my brushes in that same sink where she prepared meals. Okay, maybe that was stupid. Maybe I left a few smudges of paint there and maybe that was enough to kill her. I'm never going to know and I'm never going to be able to convince anybody that I was unaware of the danger."

Emily stopped talking at that point.

As the campfire darkened and the steady breeze grew cooler, Emily settled deep into her sleeping bag and Sergeant tucked himself underneath my right arm.

I still couldn't believe she agreed to sleep on the rock. I wondered if I told her too much about me. The embers faded. I couldn't see her any more. I wanted to stoke the fire just enough to watch her sleep, but I didn't dare. Until that night, I had never talked to anybody, except my attorney, about it. As usual, I was awake all night.

A muffled silence settled at dawn. Clouds stood still in front of a slowly brightening horizon. Crickets went to sleep and bullfrogs had long since given up or had found their mates.

Coffee penetrated the air. The unmistakable sharp fragrance pried open one of Emily's eyes just in time to see me with a towel in my hand pulling a pot from the embers.

"How do you want your coffee?" I asked as she sat up.

"Well, I usually take cream and sugar."

"You think I don't have them?" I pulled out two small metal containers with screw caps and two small silver spoons. "Okay it's real sugar but powdered cream."

"Perfect, but, please tell me you're not a perky morning person."

"I'm afraid that's one rumor about me that's true."

"What time is it?"

"A little before six."

"Believe it or not I only have a couple of hours before I've got to be at the jail."

"What's that all about?"

"Sergeant Evans is helping me measure it. The county wants me to do a plan to show how to convert the old building into another use after the new jail is finished. If I'm not back by noon, come get me."

"Don't worry; you're in good hands with Ceda."

By seven-thirty, Emily was on her way to the jail. I let Sergeant run around the farm for exercise while I caught up on some painting. After a couple of hours I stepped onto the deck to get some air and call Sergeant. I looked toward the river then into the open field behind the carriage house. No sign of him.

From the front side of the deck, I saw someone getting into an old, gray Studebaker parked on the far side of the road in front of my property. The driver backed into my driveway, then shot off toward town. Still no sign of Sergeant. I walked around the back of the Stone House toward the duck pond when I heard a slight yelp. I saw Sergeant lying on his back under a bush thirty yards away. Thinking at first he was just napping in the shade, I jogged toward him. I called his name and he answered with a louder yelp which caused me to break into full sprint. As I got closer, I saw he was in deep pain, throwing his head from side to side, and writhing on his back. As soon as I pulled his head and shoulders across my lap he calmed down, and my voice immediately reassured him I was there and everything was going to be okay. The more I talked, the more he seemed to recover.

It took two weeks to get the report from the lab that tested the contents taken from Sergeant's stomach. The report was clear. The problem came from partially cooked hamburger laced with rat poison—a common type of rat poison used by half the farmers in the county. The main ingredient was arsenic.

A little grassy clearing rested between the duck pond and the flat rock. My family used it as a cemetery for most of the last century. Granddad had the highest spot. My mom was placed beside my dad. Cleo was buried closest to the river. A little patch of land off to one side was used for pets. We buried Sergeant there.

CHAPTER FIFTEEN

Armed with a clipboard, pen, and measuring tape, Emily returned to the jail. She hoped to get all the important dimensions of the existing building in a couple of hours. The old jail came into view like a toothless dog that had been in too many fights. She parked her car in front, walked into the Booking Office, and waved to the large female officer at the desk.

"So you think you're ready to face this crowd again?" said Sergeant Evans.

"I'm ready to get it over with."

"How 'bout some coffee before you get started?"

"Sure, why not." The sergeant walked into the break room and returned with coffee and a box of doughnuts.

"I'll pass on the doughnuts," said Emily raising her right hand as if she were being sworn in. "I'd love to have one, but I really don't need them."

"Well hell, nobody *needs* doughnuts—you don't eat 'em 'cause you *need* 'em. You eat 'em 'cause they're great, they make you feel good, they give you a doughnut high." Emily helped herself to one light brown doughnut.

"Captain Morgan let me go through the jail a while ago, so I know a little bit about what to expect." Emily said, "But, I'd still like to get this over with as quickly as possible."

115

"I'm sure the guys and gals will be glad to see you again."

Emily shook her head slightly, "When I was here before, I didn't have a chance to go through the female side. I only saw the male wing. It wasn't nearly as bad as I had feared, but I can't pretend that some of the guys weren't a little weird."

"What? You don't like our fine guests?" Sergeant Evans said sarcastically.

"Well as an example, I met a guy in isolation."

"That would be Chigger."

"I guess you get used to anything here," Emily said.

"It's all routine if you do it long enough."

"I suppose."

Sergeant Evans sucked jelly out of the side of a doughnut then said, "But, there is one thing that I'll never get used to. It's when my friends or their families are locked up."

"How do you deal with that?"

The sergeant rolled her eyes a little, "It's tough. I don't even pretend to act like it doesn't get to me." She blasted out a short laugh then continued without taking a breath, "To tell you the truth, since I started working for the sheriff, half the people locked up in here were people I've known. I make sure they get what they need." She looked down while her eyebrows tightened. "Actually most of the guys do okay. It's the women I worry about."

"What do you mean?"

"Some of the women in here are no more prepared to be an inmate than you are."

"Me? I wouldn't make it through a day in here."

"Believe it or not, you may be tougher than some of the women we have right now," said Sergeant Evans.

"I find that a little hard to believe," Emily said a little embarrassed. "But not all of the men looked all that tough—like the guy with the Brussels Sprout collection. What was that about?"

Sergeant Evans chuckled. "A lot of the guys like to save vegetable from the meals, carefully dry them out, and then smoke them during their weekly hour in the outside exercise yard."

"Smoke them? How?"

"They roll them in pages torn from their Bibles. People are always donating Bibles. Some like broccoli with the Bibles, others spinach. These birds have become very creative. Did you notice we had to weld tight the little steel plate behind the shower handles? We found they were removing the security screws and steel plates so they could stick plastic cups, filled with orange juice and peels, against the hot water pipes. After it cooks for a month they pass around cups of fermented liquid from their own little wineries. Jail life is a thriving art form. In the exercise yard, we let them smoke whatever they want as long as it's not dope.

"I know they look docile and remorseful, and they are most of the time, but when drugs get in here, anyone of them, or all of them, go crazy in a flash. The misdemeanants, the vagrants, the wife beaters, and thugs don't stay more than about ninety days; however, more than half are here because of serious crimes and are waiting for their trials. Some wait two years before they even have their day in court."

"That's awful."

"Yes , but it's their attorneys that delay the trials, not the state. I've got a guy in here now facing his third murder trial. Never been convicted. You can't imagine what they and their friends on the outside will go through to get drugs to their buds back in the jail. Sometimes the inmates, especially the women, smuggle drugs into the jail the very day they're arrested."

"How in the world do they do that?" Emily asked.

"Body cavities."

"Oh, dear God!" Emily slid her unfinished doughnut onto a napkin.

"I think I've heard enough."

After emptying her coffee cup and licking the last trickle of chocolate from her thumb, Evans said, "Okay. Now, I'm ready to go in."

Sergeant Evans wore a brown uniform with a long-sleeve starched shirt, well creased slacks, and official black shoes exactly like the male officers. Emily followed closely behind through the secure doors into the male cell blocks. Once again, Emily was struck by the peculiar stuffy, sweaty, stagnant odor. As Sergeant Evans walked ahead of her, she called out to be sure the men were dressed. As before, most had found a way to be detached from the scene around them by reading, sleeping, drawing on the walls, or staring at the ceiling and creating their own imaginary paradise.

With Sergeant Evans watching, Emily measured the halls, dayrooms, and cells as quickly as she could, but she took time to look at all the drawings etched in pencil and crayon on every available surface. The scribblings were somber insights into their thoughts, honest cries of desperation. Sketches of angels, grim reapers, poems they created, quotations from the Bible, Euripides, Shakespeare, Bob Marley, Bob Dylan, prayers. Several Bibles were lying on the floor.

Both isolation cells at the end of the male wing were occupied. One man was asleep—or more likely passed out, obviously arrested the night before. The other cell was still the home of Chigger Morgan who, as soon as he saw her, started talking.

"Miss Budd, I'm glad you came back." He stood with his face wedged once again between the bars waiting for her to walk by.

"Hello Mr. Chigger, I thought you'd be out," she said as she continued down the corridor.

"I was! I must've missed you. Don't forget my view of the river and mountains in the new jail." He watched her walk away.

No direct door existed from the male side to the female cell block. It took two locked doors on either side of a vestibule to go from the male wing into the women's area.

Like the male side, all surfaces were gray, hard, and cold, and bore the patina of frustration. But, the female side contained a different scent like sweet starch. The still air clung to the inside of Emily's nose causing her to sneeze. From the corridor, she saw through the gray steel bars into both dayrooms—ten feet wide and fifteen feet long. Across the back of each were two cells with two double bunks. The cell doors were open to the dayroom, but the women lay motionless in their bunks. Two toilets and one shower were on display in the dayrooms in plain view with no privacy from either the cells or the main corridor. The two inmates in the first cell appeared to be asleep; the other two in the next cell were quiet, but awake. One woman was reading a book, and one was lying on her back in bed staring at the ceiling. To Emily it felt more like a morgue than a jail. She tried to imagine what crimes the women had committed.

Emily wanted to talk to them, but didn't dare ask any personal questions. "Excuse me ladies. I have to measure your room," she said as she walked into the second cell.

"We gonna get new drapes and carpet?" a large woman asked with a sneer.

"No, just have to draw this old place up and then figure out what the county can do with it when we build the new jail."

"Why do they want to pay you to do that? I can tell them what they can do with it for free." As Emily ignored the first inmate's question, she noticed the drawing done in blue crayon on the wall over the second inmate's bed.

The picture was a striking image of a blue horse swooping from the sky pulling a chariot. The drawing was sketched out in perfect proportions and the prisoner had mastered the difficult task of foreshortening which gave the impression that the animal had flown directly from the clouds, through the wall, into the cell.

"Did you do this?" Emily asked. The young woman who was still staring silently at the ceiling cast her eyes to the wall for a moment. "Yes, but I can't finish it."

"Why not?"

"My crayon stubs gave out. All I have left is blue."

"I have to tell you it's beautiful just like it is." The young woman sat up, smiled, and thanked her.

A jolt surged through Emily's gut, like she saw the dead. The young woman, with her short blond hair, small chin, slight overbite, and large blue eyes looked exactly like Sarah. Emily glanced again at the drawing on the wall, then back at the young woman and knew, at that moment, beyond any doubt that the young woman was Tad. Trying to hide her surprise, Emily asked in a slow, quiet voice, "Are you from Redbriar?"

"No… I mean I guess I am… now."

"Who taught you to draw like this?"

"My dad."

"Is he anybody I might know?"

"No." Becoming a little suspicious Tad asked, "Who are you?"

"I'm Emily."

"I heard you say you're designing a new jail."

"Yes that's right, and I have to suggest to the county what they could do with this one, but I really don't know what it could be. I don't see anything to save except these wonderful drawings on the walls. Can I take a picture of yours?" Still suspicious, without replying, Tad hopped off the bed to get out of the picture and Emily snapped several shots. Emily felt like crying. Her heart raced as she left the cell and dayroom and looked back one more time. Tad had returned to her bed and lay motionless again watching the gray concrete that surrounded her.

Emily didn't speak until she and Sergeant Evens walked back into the Booking Office, "I know who that girl is."

Sergeant Evans said, "I know you do."

" I knew her mother."

"And you know her father."

"Yes, but why hasn't he been told that she's here"

"Why do you think?"

"I would guess because she doesn't want him to know."

"You're right, but only half way there."

"What do you mean?"

"She's old enough now to make that decision, but frankly I don't want Stuart to know she's here."

"Why?"

"Emily, you know him. He makes his own rules. That's what his family always did. He don't give a shit what the sheriff or the courts say about anything. I know what he would do if he knew she was here. He would come and wouldn't leave until he got her out. You've met our sheriff—what do you think he would do?"

"The sheriff would probably throw him one of his cells."

"He'd throw him in a cell and if Stuart protested, which he would, the Sheriff would beat him and charge him with resisting arrest—and that would be just the first five minutes."

"I know you and Stuart grew up together and you're doing this to protect him, but isn't there anything he could do for her if he knew?"

"She won't be in here long, if he stays away." Sergeant Evans walked behind the counter and sat down. "Stu's a little older than me, but we're almost like family except way back then, when we were kids, I had a crush on him."

"Did he know it?"

"Hell no. I mean, to him we were always buddies... well,

maybe a little more than buddies. We're like kin folk."

"Then why can't you tell him about Tad?"

"I wanta tell him, but I know him better than anybody. I know what he would do. I'm not gonna tell him about her for his own good.

"So you really are like kin folk."

"More like brother and sister, but I think the only girl he ever really loved was Sarah."

"Did you know her well?"

"No, she didn't hang around with us, with me, but I know she was probably the smartest girl to ever graduate from Jefferson High. Ended up with a degree from Carolina in psychology... Lot of good that did her up here."

"Did you know, before she died, she had plans to leave him?"

"Yep, that's what I heard."

"Why would she do that?"

"Because she was an *idiot!*" Sergeant Evans leaned against the counter beside Emily. "Emily, you can't tell him about Tad, understand? For some reason, the sheriff has left him alone since he's been back, but Stuart can't come down here, understand?"

Emily dropped her eyes without answering.

The ride back to the Stone House was too short. Emily crept along trying to decide what she should do. She knew he would eventually find out and be furious.

"How was the Jefferson County Pokey?" Stuart asked as she stepped onto the deck.

"Sad."

"The building or the people?"

"They're both the same. I had a nice long talk with Ceda."

"Good, how's she doing?"

"She was very helpful. You two were really close

growing up."

"Me and Ceda? I can't remember her not being around. If you're close enough to someone to go skinny-dipping with them half your life, then you're pretty close."

"I guess so. Anyway I got close to the inmates this time."

"Do you want to take a shower?"

"No, really I'm serious. They all screwed up somehow, but I couldn't help thinking that every one of them has a family or somebody somewhere worried about them."

She stopped talking for a moment and looked toward the river. A steady wind cascading down the mountain whipped Emily's thick hair like leaves on a tree. She noticed the pictures he was poring over were of Tad. Emily said, "I know you worry about her, but you don't talk about her very much."

"Of course I worry. But, I believe she'll come home someday soon. Can't tell you why, just a feeling." He lifted the leather folder full of pictures and said, "Look at these." She opened it and pulled out five or six dozen shots. Because of the wind, Stuart had clamped them together in bunches. All were of Tad taken the last summer they spent together in Redbriar. "I still want to finish her portrait."

Emily leafed carefully through the stack, placed them back into the folder's inside pocket, and then with the care of a midwife handing a newborn to its mother gave them back to Stuart. "That's a wonderful idea, Stu," she said realizing she couldn't do it—she couldn't tell him that his daughter at that moment was only a few miles away lying on her back staring at the ceiling of a seven by ten foot concrete cell.

Jack Hemphill

CHAPTER SIXTEEN

TAD

I was suspicious of Emily right away. I was suspicious of everybody, but Emily especially. She marched into my cell and took too much interest in me and my wall drawings. Even Novie, my cell mate, thought at first there was something peculiar about her.

All I wanted was to be left alone. Mostly I didn't want anybody to tell Dad where I was. Some of my cousins were in there, on the male side, and I thought, at first, all I had to do was wait out my time and we would all go back to the cabin, but I had a feeling that once again everything in my life was getting ready to change.

It's funny, being locked up didn't bother me that much. I felt safe. Didn't have to do anything but wait out my time. No one on the outside knew where I was and I thought they would never find me there.

Emily wasn't what you call a pretty woman, but she had the kind of face artists loved. Strong cheekbones and heavy eyelids. The first thing I noticed was the color of her hair. I thought about how much my dad would like to paint her. Of course, I had no idea then what would eventually develop between them or the effect she would someday have on him and me.

125

Jack Hemphill

CHAPTER SEVENTEEN

STUART

Even in late July, Redbriar is cold by the river at 4 A.M. A light was on in Possum's workshop. I peeped in the window. He was sanding a piece of carefully carved blond wood. Didn't notice me for a minute until I tapped on the glass. He screamed like he had seen a ghost and dropped the wood on the floor.

"Shit Stuart! what the hell you doin' in the dark ?" He turned his back to me to light another cigarette. I let myself in through the front door and by the time I walked into the shop he was busy sanding again. I pulled up a chair and watched.

"It's beautiful but what is it?" I finally said.

"Don't know."

"What are you going to do with it?"

"If I knew that, I'd know what it was."

"I guess so."

"What you doin' here?" he asked.

"Walking."

"In the middle of the night?"

"Yep."

"How come?"

"Lots of reasons . But, maybe you can help me with one

of them."

"Me?"

"Yep. You're good with dreams. At least you say you are."

"Wha'dya dream?"

"It's the same dream over again each night ever since ..."

"Since Sarah died?"

"How did you know?"

"I'm good with dreams. So what happens in them?"

"Almost nothing really. I'm walking around the county, and I see Sarah standing in that big window at the back of the Stone House watching me. Just watching me no matter where I go or how far I walk. Nothing else. It's driving me crazy. What do think it means?"

"It's simple. She wants you to join her."

"That doesn't make sense. Before she died, she was getting ready to leave me."

"Now, she wants you back. Simple as that, 'cept for one thing."

"What?"

"You wouldn't be havin' those dreams if you didn't want her back also."

"I can't stop thinking about her that's true, but I've got to make the dreams stop."

"Why?"

"Because I almost never let myself sleep anymore. I feel like if I don't stop the dreams, I'm never going to be able to sleep or rest again."

"Contact her."

"You know I don't do that sort of stuff."

"Then enjoy your dreams and leave me alone."

"Come on Possum, if you were me, what would *you* do?"

"Okay, what I'm goin' to tell you came from my great

uncle's tribe, but keep it to yourself, understand?"

"I guess so."

"He taught me things before he died and I've contacted him hundreds of times since then. I taught some of them to Habakkuk twenty-five years ago so he could contact his dead dad. The most important thing is you gotta have a big fire."

"Bakkuk and I used to make fires on the rock ledge at the quarry."

"That's the perfect place. You need to send something up that belonged to her."

"Send something up?"

"Yes, burn somethin' that belonged to her. She's watchin' you. She'll contact you."

"How is she supposed to contact me?"

"*How* is up to her." He shrugged his shoulders.

"I still don't get it."

"You'll see a sign. Can't tell you what, but you'll know it when it happens."

"Give me an example."

"Watch for things that fly. Flyin' things are close to the spirit world."

"Birds?"

"Anything that can fly, but in your situation, I would watch for ravens."

"Not my favorite bird, so why ravens?"

"Because you need answers. That's the one thing you and Sarah have in common. Sarah's death was too sudden and neither one of you understand it."

"But what the hell do ravens have to do with *me*?"

"Ravens got somethin' for everybody. They bring healing and they also bring death."

I got up and put the chair back by the wall. "I don't think I want to play this game."

He continued talking ignoring what I just said, "They say if ravens call you and then fly away, they're asking you to follow them."

"What do you mean 'follow them'?"

"Follow them into the spirit world."

"You mean die."

"Same thing."

"And that's supposed to stop my dreams?"

"Contacting her will stop your dreams, but there's more. Watch for a sign. I don't know what she has to say or what the sign's gonna be. Like I said it's up to her."

"And if I don't get a sign?"

"If you contact her and she don't give you a sign, she has decided to go away forever."

"And the dreams?"

"If you contact her, they'll stop. Don't know what happens after that."

Working three hours per night, it took me two weeks to haul a cord of wood, strapped to my back, one load at a time, from my truck up to the ledge at the side of the quarry. Finally sometime after midnight, I strapped a long but narrow cardboard box to my back and climbed the mountain. With paper, twigs, dry branches, and well-dried split logs stacked crisscross, I created a blaze that towered twelve feet. It was at that moment I cut open the cardboard box and removed Sarah's clothes. That was all of her clothing that I still had—four blouses, two sweaters, a pair of shorts, and one blue dress. I loved her in that dress. I once painted a portrait of her wearing it. Clutching the dress, I threw all the other garments into the fire and watched them disappear.

I had to get away from the heat, so I sat on a rock forty feet away. The fire consumed itself and crumbled into a furnace of flame and glowing white ashes. There was no breeze to sway the long black arms streaming from the fire straight into the sky. No bats, no birds, no butterflies, no insects, nothing flying, just black smoke rising into an infinite dark blue.

I pulled the dress to my face and inhaled its fragrance. She was still there. I called her name before tossing the garment up into the hottest part of the flame. My face burned.

The dress was silk and ignited in a sudden burst and was carried upward by an invisible column of heat before it became lodged in the branches of an old dead pine sticking out of the mountain above the quarry. The dead tree was a white skeleton against the dark sky and ignited like a fuse on a fire cracker. It burned to the top where I saw the unmistakable round form of a large raven's nest. Two birds circled above the nest until the flames engulfed one of them who screeched and spiraled to the ground while the other raven continued to circle until it flew away into darkness.

Exhausted, I drove home and parked my truck in the barn by the carriage house. I pulled off all my clothes and threw them into the burn pit below the garden. I laid my boots by the back door of the carriage house, showered, dressed, joined Emily for breakfast without a word about what I did.

After that, there were no more dreams because sleep was impossible.

Jack Hemphill

CHAPTER EIGHTEEN

STUART

What is it about the sizzle of eggs hitting a hot pan—especially one that has just been used to cook bacon? It says "wake up." It says, "Something good is going to happen today." It says, "Life is worth living." Sergeant used to love the sound.

We bury our friends but they never leave us. I still felt Sergeant's soft tongue kissing the side of my hand.

For several months, early each morning after breakfast, I stood for a few minutes on the hill above the river beside Sergeant's grave. Sometimes I talked to him. Sometimes I just stood there and remembered. I had never seen Sarah's grave. She was buried not five miles from there. Until then I never gathered the courage to see it. Her family buried her and, of course, I wasn't invited.

It was a Thursday morning. No one goes to graveyards on Thursday mornings. I decided to slip into the old church yard, pay my respects, and leave before I was noticed.

A good two hundred yards from the Weavertown Baptist Church is a dirt road where I parked my car. From there I walked across an open field to the church. The white clapboard building glowed in the morning sun. Except for the brick chimney, rough foundation, and dips in the roof, it would be hard to tell the building was over a hundred years old. Near the rear, a wrought iron fence guarded the graves of Civil War soldiers. Traditionally families were buried as close to each other as possible. Sarah took me there several times to put flowers on her fathers' grave and I guessed she was buried somewhere close to him. A stone wall separated the open field from the church property, and I walked in the field along most of the wall's length before climbing over into the graveyard.

Not forty feet from her father's grave was a new headstone with the name *Sarah Remington*—her maiden name. I knew they would do that. I don't think the family ever really accepted the marriage or thought it would last. They were right. I hated that. Week- old flowers drooped over a mason jar.

Being careful not to step on any part of her grave, I sat off to the side in a patch of clover. I wanted to say several things to her, but I couldn't remember any of them. I guess an hour passed. In silence, I picked clover and tossed them petal by petal on her grave. None of the feelings I thought I would have came to me, and it was becoming clear that trying to wait for them wouldn't do me any good.

I was about to stand when I heard a sound from the front side of the church. It was a deep, muted noise like the slam of a car door. I quickly slipped between the tombstones, crawled over the stone wall, and waited. With a slight crouch, I was completely hidden behind the shoulder high wall. The sounds of footsteps on the gravel road were definitely that of a man. He plodded steadily forward until he was directly beside me on the other side of the wall, then he turned into the graveyard. After a minute, the low muttering of a man's voice floated over the wall. I couldn't understand a word. Slowly I raised my head higher. At first I couldn't see him. Again I rose higher. A man was kneeling beside Sarah's grave replacing the flowers. I still couldn't see his face until I moved another ten or fifteen feet further down and peered over the wall again. He was partially hidden by her tombstone, but as soon as he sat up I knew who it was—Dab Nettles. Older and skinnier than the last time I saw him, but it was he. My hand clutched a stone on top of the wall so hard that it broke loose and crashed to the ground. Nettles turned his head toward me just as I dropped to one knee out of sight. I thought to myself, *What the hell am I doing hiding from a twerp like Nettles?* I stood upright and walked half way across the field toward my car when I heard another door slam in the church yard. It was a gray Studebaker identical to the one I saw at my house the morning Sergeant was poisoned. Even from that distance, I recognized the man who hopped out of the car. It was Judd Remington, one of Sarah's older cousins. I bolted toward him in full stride kicking up a cloud of red dust behind me.

When I got to the gravel road, I marched toward the two men in the graveyard. I don't even remember hopping over the wall. As soon as they saw me they stiffened as motionless as the tombstones around them. Judd called out my name like it was a curse. I answered, "Judd, where the hell's my dog?"

He replied, "Why don't you ask Sarah?"

At that point there was no doubt in my mind what he had done. I felt like killing him on the spot. He bolted and tried to run around me. With my right hand I grabbed a handful of jacket and skin under his left arm pulling him off balance enough to slam him against a stone monument. I wrapped the fingers of my left hand around his long skinny neck and pressed my thumb deeply into his Adams apple. He managed to squeal out a cry to Nettles, "Call the Sheriff!"

Nettles ran behind me down the road. Shoving Judd backwards, I ran after Nettles, but he had too much of a head start so I turned back just in time to see Judd dart behind the church. Realizing I had lost both of them, I walked back to the front of the church where Judd was waiting for me in his car with the front window rolled a quarter of the way down.

In a breathless squeal he spit out the words, "Where's my goddamned cousin—you piece of chicken shit! You're not going to get away with it." His rear wheels showered the yard and church porch with dust and gravel as he caught up with Nettles whose car had already reached the paved road.

Old memories can be more nagging than pain. As I drove home, all the things I had refused to think about for the last few years screamed at me—all of them fighting for attention. Nettles was a skinny little lizard with bug eyes and large red lips forever slobbering after Sarah. He was uneducated and barely made a living. His family had a business of buying pottery made by people around the county and taking them to Asheville and Charlotte to sell. Before Sarah died, I knew he visited her in Charlotte, twice. Thought they were just old buddies, but after she died, I found his letters.

My keys bounced off the bread table and landed in the fireplace. Ashes and powdered smoke shot from the embers. Sitting on the raised hearth, I fished the keys out with a bread knife and then slid my back against the brick wall. Again, I felt Sergeant's soft tongue licking my hand with kisses of comfort. With my toe, I traced the worn lines in the brick floor where Cleo's rocking chair once sat and rocked endless hours while she sang and watched the fire.

A late September sun was shining through the window onto Cleo's square wooden table. Cleo always sat on the left nearest the stove and I always sat on the right. When Bakkuk was with us, he sat in the middle chair, the best place to look out the window while he ate.

"Stop gazin' and eat," Cleo always said in a way that only she could. She would then say, "I'm not goin' to have no scrawny boys in my house." The food was always piled high on our plates and if we finished eating it too quickly, she immediately piled it on again. She seemed to think the more food she stuffed in us, the more love she had given, and she had lots of love to give–real love–not just affection, but the kind that made us glad just to be who we were.

Even to that day, I still felt safe inside the walls of that little house. I remember when I was a kid, how much I loved to spend the night there wrapped in blankets and pillows lying on the floor of the loft while Cleo sang us to sleep. Her voice resonated in deep, haunting sounds like bass notes on a cello. It was both sweet and powerful at the same time.

Those memories were my best therapy. I wallowed in them, but even they couldn't stop my mind from returning to Judd and Dab Nettles, and what they had done to Sergeant. The sheriff was the only law enforcement in the county, and I couldn't imagine him lifting a finger to help me. I thought of Emily who was arriving in a few hours. Should I tell her? Over the last several months, she slowly became comfortable about being there with me. I needed her to keep coming and I needed her to stay.

On Thursday afternoons, she usually arrived around five. By then, I always had the carriage house filled with aromas from one of Cleo's recipes, but Emily was running a little late that day and I lost all track of time. The sun was sliding behind the mountains when she finally sprang through the door. She immediately sensed my mood and sat beside me at the table. It took me a minute to crawl out from under my thoughts. She waited. Finally, I told her about finding out that it was Judd Remington who had killed Sergeant. Then I told her about what they said and why I didn't think they were through with me. Emily reached out and squeezed my hand. I don't think she knew what to say. She just looked at me and squeezed and didn't let go until darkness filled the house. She turned on a small lamp at the kitchen table. She trusted me. I don't know why. She didn't ask any questions—just listened, but I couldn't tell her everything. Not then. Not everything I knew about Sarah and certainly not about my suspicions. I couldn't tell her about how I felt when I had my hand around Judd's throat—the same way I felt when I tore up Sarah's letters and crushed them until my fists shook.

Two weeks went by before we discussed it again. Emily waited for me to bring it up. She knew it was best to wait. There had been no sign of any of the Remington boys or of Nettles. "Do you think you scared them away?" she asked.

"I'd like to believe that, but…"

"You think they'll call the sheriff?"

"No, not now. Not unless I scare them again."

If Emily was nervous at all, she never showed it. She came every two weeks from Thursday through Sunday whether she had any meetings with the County or not.

In a lot of ways, Emily missed Sergeant as much as I did. He loved staying with her at the Stone House and he made her feel safe. I noticed after Sergeant was gone, she lingered longer with me at night in Cleo's house before returning to her room across the drive. Even late at night, we never seemed to run out of things to talk about. Sometimes we read to each other.

At first Emily didn't want me to draw pictures of her, but by the end of fall, she let me do quick pencil sketches, then more detailed studies, then charcoal followed by pastel studies. In the dark winter months, she relaxed even more and was willing to pose for me under different types of lighting and in different positions. She never stopped blushing and I worked hard to capture the color–the beautiful coral pink that lay across her cheek competing with the fire in her hair.

Emily had a natural love for art and enjoyed talking with me about paintings. I explained the importance of making everything in the picture work together–the model's pose, the composition, and the colors.

"If I use a model in a painting," I explained, "then I have to paint her so she appears to have something on her mind, and if I do it right, she becomes a window into her own character and sets the mood of the painting."

What do you mean, "If I do it right?" she asked.

Knowing that I didn't always explain things well, I pulled up a chair and placed a drawing of her on it.

She studied it. "What do you see in me?" she asked.

I pushed the chair closer to her. "Tell me what *you* see," I said.

She leaned closer to the drawing. I watched her face as she pondered it before glancing back at me. Right then, still bending over the drawing with her eyes fixed on me, she mirrored the pose captured on the sketch. I loved that look. I had seen it dozens of times—especially when she was embarrassed or not sure what to say, with her head tilted downward, and away from me, and then out of the shadows, her light blue eyes shining back at me with a flash of new found confidence.

Emily gave me a slow and easy smile. She understood the drawing and a glimpse of what I saw in her. I never stopped finding things about her I wanted to paint.

By December, I persuaded her to start sketching. At first we sketched together. After a while, we took turns posing. She had a natural talent and listened carefully to my critiques, but she had her own style. I loved it. It helped me see further into her mind.

I wondered what she was thinking of me—a quirky artist, a widower living alone on top of a mountain, a man with few friends, a man who, according to Sarah, was just about as exciting as a pile of granite.

Every week she took off another layer of the armor

carefully wrapped around her and showed me another piece I didn't know existed.

By the end of winter, we stopped talking about Dab Nettles and the Remington boys. But, neither of us forgot about them, and as we later discovered, they never forgot about us.

CHAPTER NINETEEN

As usual, Emily cut through the studio after her Saturday walk. Stu was gone. She thought it odd that he wasn't there, but then, maybe he had gone back to the carriage house.

She didn't notice the door was already open as she untucked her blouse and walked into her room. Something crunched under the heel of her sneaker. It was a sliver of glass the size of her finger. She remembered the picture of Sarah with a broken frame in the middle drawer of her dresser. As soon as she opened the drawer, she knew Stuart had taken it. She wondered why he didn't just ask for it. Why he waited until she was out of the room?

She hurried to the carriage house and called up the stairs. No reply. It wasn't like him to disappear with no warning. The sound of the old winding stair made her feel like a burglar as she climbed to the loft. Sunlight shone brightly through the skylight onto the blue blanket covering his bed. There were no other windows in the room. It was sparse and neat and the only other furniture was a bedside table with a reading lamp, a large bureau, a small bookcase, a wardrobe matching the one in her room, two floor lamps—one on each side of the room—one bentwood chair with a blue cushion, and one additional chair placed in the center of the room on an oriental rug. The ceiling followed the roof slope to a peak that ran the length of the room.

Emily turned on both floor lamps then sat in the chair in the middle of the room. The long walls on either side of her were filled with photographs of Sarah. The chair was placed exactly between the two displays. On the floor was the broken picture frame from Emily's drawer. The picture was gone. She looked for it on the wall but it wasn't there.

A ticking clock beside the bed was the only sound she heard for the next half hour. She studied every photo on both walls trying to get some kind of grip on what he was doing. He had never shown her the pictures of Sarah and never talked about the shrine in his room to her memory.

She turned off the lights, walked downstairs and eased into Cleo's big wooden rocker and put her feet on a small footstool. The silence surrounding her combined with the brisk walk earlier that morning caused her to fall asleep so deeply that she didn't hear Stuart come in, take off his boots, and deposit his muddy clothes in the laundry room. He tiptoe up to the loft, changed and returned to Emily. She awoke when his fingers stroked hair away from her face.

"Looking for me?" he said.

"I didn't know where you went."

"Took a ride in the truck."

"Where?"

"Just a ride." Once again, he pulled a strand of hair from her face. She noticed his gold watch was missing. He wore chinos and a light blue long-sleeved shirt and was barefoot. His shoes and socks were still beside the front door. A dirty D-handled shovel was carefully placed beside the muddy boots.

"Emily, come upstairs, we'll be more comfortable there." She followed him up the winding stair. He had already turned the lights back on even though the shaft of sunlight had moved to the rug in the middle of the room. The walls were bare, all photos were gone. Stuart pulled both chairs into the center of the rug beside the patch of sunlight and motioned for her to sit on the bentwood with arms and blue cushions. He pulled the broken picture frame from the top drawer of his bureau, and sat on the other chair, which had a straight back and no arms.

"I know it's odd I didn't tell you where I went today."

"It is, but I'm not going to ask unless you want to tell me."

"I do want to tell you, but I'm not sure I can."

"All I know is you were gone for a few hours and came back with a small shovel and mud on your boots. To tell you the truth, I'm not sure I want to hear about it."

"I was at Sarah's grave."

Emily leaned forward and looked straight at him. "What did you say?" she asked.

"I drove to the cemetery. Nobody was there."

"You dug her up?"

Stuart clasped his hands, looked at his feet and groaned. "I don't know if I can do this, but I feel like I owe you something, some kind of explanation about lots of things."

"I don't want you to think you owe me anything, but I'm not good at hiding my concerns and sometimes I don't know where my boundaries are supposed to be. Always been that way, so you be the judge about what to tell me, but, dear God, please tell me you weren't digging in her grave!"

"I have to go back a ways...It may take a while."

"Stu, there's nobody here but you and me, and I'm not going anywhere for the next few days, so take your time."

"There's something I told you last year that's not quite true. It's about Sarah." When he leaned forward his face was directly in the sunlight. He looked at his feet and squinted, then leaned back and looked at her as if he found a place to start. "The night Sarah died, I was with her."

143

"You told me you were at a gallery opening with Pierce."

"Well, I was, but I came home; she was gone. Got the call from Charlotte Memorial and went straight there. I told you before that she was already dead when I arrived, but I was with her when she died."

"What's the matter with that?"

"Nothing, but there's a part I just didn't want to tell you before. She knew she was going. Weak, but determined to hang on until I was there."

"That's actually kind of sweet."

Stuart pushed forward in his chair. The sunlight deepened the wrinkles in his brow and around his eyes. "No. It's *not* sweet," he said firmly, "she held my finger exactly the way Tad did when she was a newborn baby. After taking three last shallow breathes, and in a faint voice, she exhaled her last words. 'Look at me,' she said. I hadn't really looked at her face until then. The moment our eyes connected, I saw the light going out inside her." Stuart swallowed and paused to catch his breath. "Do you understand what she did?"

"No."

"Emily, her last wish was for me to watch her die. That's what it was all about. She knew how I remembered images, especially faces and now that picture is *branded* in my mind, just as she wanted it." He stood and walked to the bed and back. "At first, I saw it in my dreams once a month or so. After a while, she woke me I the middle of the night at least once a week. Now...I don't sleep at night, any night, more than about two hours without seeing her and hearing her say 'Look at me,' but , in my dream, beyond the words, she's saying, 'I know what you did.' That's the memory she wanted me to keep."

"Stu, you know what I'm going to say."

"You're going to ask me why I didn't tell you before."

"Yes, exactly. I never thought she was that cruel."

"I know, but there's a little more. I loved her and my mind pulls me to her even when I'm awake. When Possum was sixteen, he accidentally cut off his pinky finger with a table saw. He told me many times he never missed the finger, but it constantly itched and he couldn't scratch it because it was gone. The finger as well as the itch was stuck in his mind. All he could do was endure it. That's the way Sarah haunts me and all I did today at her grave, was try to stop the itch."

"Stuart, what did you do?"

"I filled a wooden container the size of a jewelry box with everything she ever gave me, including my watch. I also placed inside the box my ring and our wedding picture." Stuart picked up the broken frame. "You probably saw this in your dresser."

Emily nodded.

"Her family forbad me to attend the funeral and I never felt like I buried her…until tonight."

"You buried the box in her grave?"

"Yes."

"How deep?"

"Very deep."

"How do you feel?"

"Exhausted."

"Do you think you'll be able to sleep now?"

"I'll find out as soon as the sun goes down."

CHAPTER TWENTY

Emily arrived fifteen minutes early for her meeting with the Jail Committee. Delores Minton, the County Manager's secretary, was bending over the bottom drawer of a file cabinet when Emily walked into the reception area. Emily placed her boards and briefcase against one of the visitor chairs, but remained standing trying not to wrinkle her brand-new pantsuit. She had borrowed her mother's coral earrings because they matched one of the primary paint colors she would be presenting that morning.

"I *swany*, I didn't hear you come in," Delores said as she closed the file drawer and walked across the room toward her. "You probably don't remember me, but I'm Delores. I saw you in the courtroom a few months ago. Come on in to the conference room and let's find us some coffee before the guys drink it all up."

Delores was a full-figured woman with pixie-length hair the color of strawberry Kool-Aid . She had one of those smiles that filled her face and it never completely went away. She took her coffee black, but made sure that Emily had plenty of cream and sugar.

"How many do you expect at the meeting?" Emily asked.

"Oh, we always have two commissioners besides the sheriff and county manager, but don't worry sweetie, I'm not going to let 'em bite you. Go ahead and put your stuff on the table. I'd love to

147

look at the colors."

For the next quarter hour the women discussed the choices and possibilities from carpet and fabric samples and color chips. They laughed at some daring ideas they knew nobody else had the courage to suggest. Delores always made everybody around her feel more comfortable and Emily forgot all about her nervousness. Emily had been up since five that morning practicing her presentation. Since this was the approval meeting for the Design Development Phase, the managing partner of her firm had offered to come with her, but she insisted on doing it by herself and wanted it to be perfect.

Chuck Cunningham, the county manager, arrived and filled his cup. Then Commissioners Skeeter Marsh and Nelson Harris came in together already discussing county business. Sheriff Hodges was the last to arrive.

He nodded to the commissioners then to Emily. One of the primary items in Emily's contract was a design for the complete reengineering of the antiquated air conditioning system at the courthouse. The August sun was already hotter that morning than the system could handle. Even though the county manager's conference room had high ceilings and northern facing windows, the men were fanning themselves with Emily's handouts. Earlier that summer, other preliminary meetings had been held in the Sheriff's conference room at the jail. This was the first meeting in the County Manager's conference room.

Emily started by saying, "Our mechanical engineer was here earlier this week and is in the process of designing a completely new HVAC system, so hopefully you won't have to live through this heat after this season."

The crude sketches shown at those meetings had slowly evolved over the summer into presentation boards, blue prints, and color boards. Emily carefully explained the ways the jail design coordinated with the old courthouse. With her drawings, she discussed the brick details, window spacing, proportions, and proposed overall appearance of the new structures. With photographs, she illustrated ways the new design would blend with the architectural character of Redbriar. Emily guided them through color-coded floor plans carefully put together to indicate different types of spaces, such as secure and non-secure spaces, office areas and booking, inmate areas with the medium, and maximum security cells.

The presentation was going exactly as practiced, but something was wrong—something felt unsettled like rustling leaves before a summer storm. No questions were being asked by the committee. When she finished presenting the plans, an excruciatingly long and awkward pause seemed to make the temperature in the room rise another ten degrees. Each committee member looked at his stack of papers or shifted his eyes toward the Sheriff who was seated in the center chair at the conference table exactly opposite Emily. Finally Sheriff Hodges crossed his arms over his barrel chest and said, "Miss Budd," he paused, "what is it like to be responsible for watching, all the time, dozens of individuals who are either predators, victims, or suicidal?" He paused again and waited for Emily to answer his obviously rhetorical question.

She smelled the trap being laid out. "I know it's got to be hard," she answered reluctantly, knowing that she was about to be blasted with whatever the Sheriff was holding in his mind.

Sheriff Hodges never had the ability to hide his gloating sneer and that morning it was oozing out of every cranny in his face. After leaning forward and placing his left index finger on the table, the sheriff said, "Whether these fine men and women are awake or asleep, we watch 'em. All day and all night. Inevitably, sooner or later, at any hour, no matter how quiet they have been, somebody's gonna to kill someone else, or somebody decides to end his own life, or an escape will be attempted, or they try…God knows what. Look at your drawings. From this design, how the hell do we see these jerks when you lock them away at night, out of sight, in solid concrete block cells? At least, in what we have now, we can walk around and see them through the bars any time day or night. I thought you understood this." He leaned back in his chair, once again crossed his arms, and cocked back his head with his eyes still fixed on her.

Emily, who had been standing, removed her suit jacket, carefully folded it over the back of an empty chair, and sat down across from the Sheriff. She looked at her drawings and said, "Of course, all I know about prisoners is what I'm told, and I'm told counties are moving away from the kind of jail that you have now—the old-style jail is too spread out. Obviously in the old-style jail, the guards can't see anything in the dayrooms until they make their rounds and people are getting hurt when the staff isn't looking."

"But," the Sheriff interrupted, "when we *do* make our rounds, we still see through the bars into the cells any time and that's what I want here. If you're going to do this jail, you're going to have to let me see those birds—all of them—all the time, whenever I want to. I don't want the little sons of bitches out of my sight."

Skeeter Marsh leaned forward and asked, "You say, Miss Budd, your design is what other counties are building now in their jails?"

"Yes," answered Emily, "I've researched this and the officials down in Raleigh strongly recommend that counties get away from the bar front designs and, of course, they have to approve these plans before we can build it." Without realizing it, she sat back and folded her arms over her chest creating a mirror image of the Sheriff. "I'm not sure I know how to produce a design that provides you with a state-of-the-art jail that you need *and* at the same time keep the style you have now."

"Well, Miss Budd," he paused again. "it seems to me you told us not long ago, in the courthouse, how you were smart enough to make it secure no matter what, and I still believe, as I said, that it's my job is to tell you what I want and yours is to figure out how to do it."

"What Miss Budd has drawn is similar to what they have in Asheville," said Marsh, "Maybe, Sheriff, you should drive over there and take a look before we make a decision."

Sheriff Hodges shifted his stare from Emily to Skeeter Marsh and said, "If that Sheriff down in Asheville ever moves up here to run this jail, *then* you can do whatever you want, but for now Miss Budd is going to make me a new set of drawings and she's going to do it in two weeks and it's going to be designed so I can see every damned soul in there all the time. *All the time*! I don't care if they're asleep, awake, in the shower, or on the pot, I'm going to watch 'em—got it?"

With a half-muted, almost apologetic voice, she said "But, Sheriff, be sure you understand that in this design the guards in the control room, elevated above the main floor, can see into the dayrooms all the time."

"Miss Budd," said the Sheriff, "suppose I put you and Miss Minton in one of these cells overnight and nobody knows but Miss Minton that she's gonna to kill you. What good is it to you if that guard over there in the control room is watching the *dayrooms* all the time? What good would a *hundred* guards do if *nobody* can see into the cells?"

"I didn't think about it that way, but I would ..."

"Then think about being a prisoner in there and what that architect, the one that's *clever enough to make it secure no matter what,* should have done to save your life."

Cunningham decided it was time to move on to the color presentation. "Miss Budd also has sample boards showing suggested color schemes for both this building and the jail." Emily hoped the sheriff would leave when she started the color presentation, but he sat still as a stump watching her arrange the boards.

She explained the new color scheme for the courthouse first. The committee discussed how much better the new colors would look and they made only minor suggestions to the selections. In addition to the colors, fabric for office window treatments, and flooring material, Emily also discussed the changes to the building, stairs, doorways, and bathrooms to meet state standards. The group took another coffee break as Emily gathered up the courthouse boards and began arranging the color presentation for the new jail. With a fresh mug of coffee, the Sheriff studied each color. Starting with the Sheriff's offices, she discussed paint samples for walls, color for the porcelain tile floor in the lobby and carpet for the office areas. Next she presented colors for booking and inmate processing with displays of paint chips using neutral warm tones. To keep her mind on what she was saying, she spoke mostly to the two commissioners.

Just as she so carefully rehearsed that morning, Emily described various studies from highly respected institutions such as the *National Correctional Association* and the *American Institute of Architects* which listed colors believed to have a calming effect, especially on inmates locked up for long periods of time. Still looking at the commissioners, she said, "The research has shown that the most successful colors for confinement areas are the ones that in some way remind prisoners of pleasant things in their past, things they naturally associate with the softer places in their memories." She placed the color board flat on the table in front of the Sheriff. She didn't notice how his jaw was beginning to throb as he ground his teeth. "We, my office and I, have looked at hundreds of colors, and the one that we suggest for the confinement areas is made by Devoe Paint. It's right here on the color board and is called 'Coral Buff.'"

Without any warning, the sheriff jumped to his feet, reached into his back pocket and slammed his black wallet onto the table. It bounced off Emily's notebook and knocked the pen out of her hand, "See that color!" he said pointing to his wallet. "That's the only color I ever want these men to see. No one's heart needs to bleed over them. They're criminals. They don't need to feel close to their mommies. They need to feel like criminals who got caught. They need to feel close to the receiving end of my size twelve boot." He stopped speaking but continued to loom silently above her like a vulture over a half-dead rabbit.

Emily looked up and felt herself rising out of her chair as fast as the red hair rose on the back of her neck. She looked straight into his eyes. The room was so silent she heard herself breathing.

"Coral Buff!" he said mockingly. "Coral...Buff ? Black and the color of their own blood is all they'll see as long as they're in my house."

He perched on both sets of knuckles, planting them in the center of the blueprints crinkling the paper into jagged waves between his fingers.

"Now Sheriff," said Skeeter Marsh. "We have been given suggestions by our architect that are believed by experts as ways to calm these guys down, which means reduce the violence in there and make your life easier. I think you should at least think about it."

Commissioner Harris said, "Skeeter, damn it, listen to the Sheriff! He's the only expert on *his* jail in this room. He knows what he needs. We don't need any national association telling us about how to deal with inmates in our county."

"I've looked at the jail reports," said Marsh. "We've had

twelve fights in twelve weeks—twelve fights in twelve weeks, Harris. Does that sound right to you? I also found out from the state that we have the highest rate of inmate-on-inmate violence in North Carolina."

The Sheriff dropped his eyes to control his boiling anger; his knuckles continued to curl under his catcher's mitt hands as he said, "Miss. Budd's going to be back here in two weeks with a new jail design. She will also bring a color board that has *gray* as its brightest color... Are we clear?"

"Yes," Emily said looking down at the color board in front of her. Cunningham had shrunk at least four inches into his chair. Delores was busy recording every word. The sheriff left followed by Commissioner Harris. Delores got up and helped Emily gather the boards.

Commissioner Marsh walked by and patted Emily lightly on her shoulder then left.

"Honey," said Delores, "believe it or not, the meeting went well." She then collected all the coffee cups and took them out of the room.

Alone, Emily unclasped her mother's coral earrings and carefully placed them back in a little white box in her briefcase.

Emily and her office didn't make the two week deadline and asked for an extension. They didn't make the second deadline either and asked for another delay in the schedule. From their research, they concluded no jail had ever been built the way Sheriff Hodges was demanding. The four partners in the architectural office spent weeks struggling to create a plan that met all the Sheriff's needs and still stayed within the North Carolina regulations for jails.

Emily was finally able to deliver and present a unique design to the Sheriff and Jail Committee. During the short presentation Hodges was completely silent. That was his form of approval. She also presented new interior color boards for the jail displaying nothing more than black bars and gray walls. Skeeter Marsh was absent. Without explanation, he resigned from the Board of Commissioners two weeks before that day and never attended another commissioner's meeting and never again attempted to hold an office in Jefferson County. Nobody knew why.

Emily drove back to the Stone House After the meeting. The odd layout she presented that morning was nothing like her original design. She spent the last few days and all the night before trying not to like it, but there is a built-in magnet in the minds of architects that pulls them irresistibly to unique and untried places. The very fact that the design was destined to be controversial in Redbriar and beyond made her partners love it.

CHAPTER TWENTY-ONE

A brass door knocker startled Emily out of a dream in which she was floating on a soft blue sea. It awakened her to the hard surface of her drafting table where she had fallen asleep on top of her blueprints surrounded by a pile of balled-up tracing paper.

As she opened the front door, the six-foot blond, wearing a black fur coat, short burgundy skirt, and matching cashmere sweater said, "Oh, I'm looking for Stuart."

"You must be Pierce," Emily said.

"Yes."

"Hi, I'm Emily. Stuart told me you would be coming by this morning. He drove down to Asheville for supplies but should be back any minute. Come on in." She stepped aside while Pierce walked through the foyer toward the living room. Emily quickly tucked her gray flannel shirt into her blue jeans.

"Why don't you make yourself at home in the living room until he returns."

"I'd rather go to his studio."

"Sure, that's fine. He wants you to see some paintings. They're in the den, but I'll bring them to you." Pierce continued walking to the studio. Emily picked up the canvases in the den then followed the trail of perfume to the sunroom studio. "These are all his latest—except for the one on the easel, of course."

"Excellent," said Pierce as she dropped her coat on the couch and wiped her hand across Stuart's stool before sitting down. Emily placed the canvases beside her. Pierce flipped quickly through the stack. "These will be going to New York."

"That sounds great." Emily sat on the couch while Pierce slowly placed the canvases in a line against the wall.

"Are you and Stuart related?" said Pierce returning to the stool.

"No, we're just good friends."

"Really. Do you live here?"

"Yes…no, I mean just on the weekends."

"Oh. How long have you known him?"

"Just a few years, but I didn't really get to know him very well until…you know, after the trial and everything."

"Yes, of course," Pierce said followed by an awkward pause.

"I come here on business," said Emily.

"Really, what business are you in?"

"I'm an architect."

"Oh."

"I'm working on some projects for the county."

"So, how long will your projects last?"

"I'll be coming up here a couple more years, but…I'm glad. I really like it here."

"Did you ever meet his daughter?"

"No."

"Too bad. Lovely child. Stu showed me some of her artwork. She could be quite an artist someday too. You know, being Stuart's daughter and everything, her work could someday be very marketable."

"Good."

'So, Tad hasn't come home yet?"

"No. I don't think that will happen for a while."

"I see." Pierce gave her a knowing smile and said, "I've been working with Stuart for at least ten years now. He's been a good client. Not the typical starving artist, you know. He can afford to do what he wants without worrying if his work is selling."

"Yes, he never talks about it or anything that has to do with money, but that's really none of my business." Emily said.

Pierce crossed her legs, placed her elbow on her knee, and her chin on the palm of her hand, then said, "My dear, if you are in a relationship with him, don't you think you should know what he's worth?"

"No. Not really. I know he has this beautiful house, and land, and other stuff from his family, but why did you say 'relationship'?"

"No reason." Pierce pulled a cigarette from her coat pocket, lit it.

"Pierce," said Emily, " I don't think it really matters how much he's worth. He's a nice guy and we're friends. That's all—that's it."

Pierce watched Emily try to hide her red wooly socks by sliding her feet under the baggy cuffs of her jeans. "I believe you." Pierce said.

Emily knew her cheeks were beginning to glow. After turning her face toward the fireplace for a moment, she said, "He's going to be here in just a minute, so unless you need something else, I'll get back to work at my drawing board upstairs."

"It was nice meeting you, dear," Pierce said as she blew smoke straight up. Before Emily could leave, the door to the deck opened. Stuart lugged in two large bags and a half dozen newly stretched canvases. "Sorry I'm late." As soon as he put his supplies on the floor, Pierce extended both hands toward him. He walked to her and wrapped his hands around hers. "How've you been?"

"Never better."

"Great to see you." He then walked to Emily, placed his hand on her left shoulder and gently kissed her cheek. As she leaned slightly forward trying not to act surprised, Emily caught a glimpse of Pierce looking back at her, expressionless, exhaling smoke through her nostrils. Stuart had never kissed Emily on the cheek or anywhere else. She had no idea why he did it then.

"What do you think of these?" Stuart said as he turned to Pierce and pointed to the paintings lined against the wall.

"Just what I'm looking for. But, I need three or four more."

"I've got more underway."

"I know you do. I've never known you to have less than three or more going at a time."

"Well, there's one on the easel and three in the carriage house."

"Why in the carriage house?"

"That's where I stay now."

"Really?"

"Yeah. You want to see them?" He gestured for her to lead the way as he picked up her leather briefcase and fur coat. Before they got to the deck, Pierce locked elbows with him.

As he closed the door behind them, one of Stuart's packages turned over with a loud *clunk*. Emily immediately started picking up the spilled items—pencils that had rolled from their boxes, several tubes of paint in both water color and oil, and a few tubes of acrylic. A small brown box skidded a few feet behind the edge of a canvas. As she pulled it out with her finger she read the words, "32 caliber." With her thumbnail, she gently opened the lid to confirm it was a box of bullets. She then started removing the remainder of the contents of the bag and placed each item on the floor. Sketch paper, pencils, paint tubes, markers, a small can of varnish, another brown box, and a heavy cloth bag sealed with a tie string. Sitting on the floor with her back against the wall she untied the string and looked into the cloth bag at the small shiny pistol.

After returning all items including the gun and pouch into the paper bag, she sat a few minutes picturing Stuart with a hunting rifle and a shotgun, but couldn't imagine him with a pistol. Returning to her room, half way up the stairs, she remembered the view of the carriage house from the den window. Shadowy images rippled through the old carriage house glass as she peered through slightly opened blinds in the den. Emily walked outside and hesitated only a moment before shuffling across the stone pavers. The front door was open. Stuart was sitting at the bread table signing papers. Pierce was behind him looking over his shoulder with one hand on his back. Paintings were placed in a row across the hearth. As soon as he had finished, he looked up and saw her. "Emily, come in." He walked to the door and opened it all the way against the wall. "Come on in I'll make lunch for everybody?"

Later that evening, from the front window in her room, Emily saw Pierce's taillights disappearing in the dark. Stuart had promised Pierce five more paintings and Emily knew he would return to his studio. He was leaning against the brick fireplace with his hands in his pockets looking at the unfinished painting on the easel twenty feet away. That was his favorite spot when he was thinking about his paintings. She wondered if he would mention the kiss.

"Sorry to interrupt," she said.

"No, I wanted to see you." Emily sat on the couch and he pulled a chair close to her. "It was a good day. I'm so glad you were here."

"Well, Pierce is an interesting woman."

"Oh, I know she can be a little hard to take, but you have

to understand—she grew up in Boston."

"She's lovely."

"She's been good for me. Good business sense and a real go-getter."

"Oh, I'm sure she is."

"We've got a trip coming up."

Emily started twirling her amethyst ring around her finger. "How long will you be gone?"

"From Thursday until the following Monday. Pierce has set up a series of meetings in New York. She wants to introduce me to some people she knows."

"Next Thursday?"

"Yes."

"I need to be here. I have an early meeting on that Friday."

"I know. I hate to leave you alone all weekend.'

"I'll survive."

"One of these days, I'm going to get another dog."

"You should."

"Anyway, to tell you the truth, with some of the things happening around here, I wish I didn't have to leave you alone."

"Do you want me to stay somewhere else?"

"Of course not, but I bought something for you to have here while I'm gone. It's a pistol. A small one to put in the nightstand beside your bed. I know it's not the kind of thing you like to think about, but you may feel better at night and I'll feel better too, knowing you have it."

"I wouldn't know how to use it."

"I'll teach you."

"Why do you have to go away?"

"We're making real progress in New York."

The Saturday morning after Stuart left on his trip to New

York, Emily stayed in bed until the sun roasted its way through the thick mountain mist. The night before, she found a large lantern in the pantry and placed it by her door to start her morning adventure as early as possible. After putting on her jeans and sweatshirt, she walked half way down the corridor from her bedroom and cracked open the attic door. Before lighting the lantern she peeked up the winding stairway into the dark.

It was six-thirty in the morning. The dead silence and dusty treads made it feel like no one had entered that sanctuary for a half century. Pale morning light through the dormers made the shrouded furniture, scattered around the dark pine attic, look like a midnight graveyard.

The high pitched roof created an enormous attic room, and just as she hoped, it was filled with antiques, old trunks, and many unidentifiable things covered with blankets and sheets. In the middle, she found a large cedar closet containing old clothes.

In front of one of the dormers, she uncovered a dressing table with a high oval mirror. Gray, muted light, floating past the dressing table, made her image in the mirror look like a scene from and old black and white movie. Each time she found a treasure in the closet she tried it on, posed in front of the mirror, and acted out whatever came to her mind. Each piece—ruffled blouses, long black dresses with big black ribbons, hats of all colors and sizes— took her somewhere else in time and fantasy.

Wearing a deep purple dress that almost fit and a long black fur coat, she said to her reflection in a low mocking voice, "Hello dear. I'm here to see Stuart." She turned slightly and pulled the dress above her knee. "Why is it I believe you, Emily? Especially when you say you haven't slept with him." She took a long puff on an imaginary cigarette still watching in the mirror, "Oh, you're an architect? Then you really don't have any idea how much he's worth—do you?" Turning away from the dormer, she strolled into the shadow then returned swinging her arms and hips, paused at the mirror, snapped her head toward the image and said in a sultry voice, "Really dear, since you aren't using him right now I think I'll take him …" she stopped and whispered the last words in her own voice, "with me to New York."

She put her own clothes back on and closed the attic door behind her.

Breakfast was fresh coffee, bacon, toast, one egg scrambled, and a small bowl of grits with a little cheddar cheese followed by a second cup to be savored leisurely as she walked through the house discovering more details of the antiques, paintings, and other hidden surprises in each room.

Stuart had never taken her into his storeroom under the stairs, and, like the attic, she never had a chance to explore it. The six foot wide and twenty foot long room had a ceiling that started at ten feet high at the door and sloped downward until it met the floor at the other end. A wide flat cabinet filled the shallow end of the room. Paintings on canvases were stacked in rows along both side walls. To the right was a high wooden cabinet with many small drawers containing tubes of paint and other supplies.

The paints were separated into drawers by color. The third drawer she opened contained greens and blue-greens. Carefully she slid the drawer out of the cabinet and took it to the closest window in the den. She laid each tube in a row on the window sill and carefully read the descriptions. One tube plainly displayed in English, "Contains Paris Green". One was all in French, but she recognized the words "Coleur-Verte de Paris," which she understood to be the same poison. A third had the word, "Stockholm". All the tubes were old and all had been opened, but a small dab of color clung to the back of the cap of the French tube. It was still sticky like it had been recently used. She threw the paint back into the drawer and returned the drawer to the cabinet.

A gun rack hung on the left wall holding a double-barreled shotgun on the top rung, a smaller rifle on the middle, and several fishing rods on the lower bracket. Below the rack was a small storage bin for ammunition and lures.

After placing her cup on the top of the small cabinet, she studied carefully each of the paintings against the wall. They were stacked in date order revealing a gradually developing style over the years. Next she turned to the large wooden cabinet at the end of the room containing paintings and sketches mostly on heavy art paper. They were also arranged in date order from the bottom drawer to the top. Along with more finished pieces in watercolor and pastels was a collection of rough sketches and first studies. The top three drawers contained work done in the last ten years. She found lots of sketches and paintings of Tad as a young girl, and sketches along with a few finished works of Cleo working over her bread table.

In one of the lower drawers, she found a series of rough sketches of a young man who Emily concluded must have been Bakkuk, but there was only one finished watercolor of him. It was a powerful, striking figure of a man marching across an open field. Bakkuk's strength was shown in his face with its dark skin and sharp angular features silhouetted against the hazy white sky. His long hair was streaming behind him as if blown by a constant head wind. She wondered why his clothing as well as his hair were painted deep blood red.

The only things in the top drawer were a couple of quick studies and one finished painting of Sarah—a watercolor the same size as the one of Bakkuk. Every single thing about it was exactly the way Emily remembered Sarah. It brought her back to life. Emily studied the delicate details, the color, and the careful composition. She wondered what Stuart thought about as he caressed every curve of her body and face with his eyes before he copied them with his brush and paint onto the paper. Sarah was wearing a long blue dress, sprawled across a couch, and she was reading a book with the back of her left shoulder nestled under a window. Her face was lit only by light reflected off the pages of her book.

Emily remembered Sarah's enormous intellect and how her words gushed out like a never ending waterfall, but filled with deep and fascinating thoughts.

Sarah appeared to be totally focused on whatever it was she was reading. The detailing of her eyes and the color of her skin, her delicate, graceful fingers, and the sunlight embracing each strand of hair, told Emily that this was a portrait where the artist loved his model very much and relished every nuance of her image and memory.

CHAPTER TWENTY-TWO

STUART

"Behind that wall of earth and stone is the water supply for the whole county," I said pointing to the forty-five foot high reservoir dam. Steel pipes penetrated the embankment leaving blue-green streaks flowing across granite stones into drainage ditches below. New boulders covered with fresh clay supported the lower portion of the dike. A series of steel beams resting on piers carried the pipes down the mountain, through the trees, and out of sight to the county water treatment plant.

"Not exactly what I had imagined," Emily said.

"This side of the quarry is what I call the 'underbelly.' They're constantly repairing it to prevent rupture. Where we're standing right now is probably forty feet below the water surface. It's ugly, but just wait until we climb a little higher."

Leaving my car at the base of one of the stone piers, we walked around the earthen wall to a hill of solid granite. I led the way up the steep incline, climbing over boulders, and between rock crevices, finally reaching a point where the whole reservoir, in full view, circled halfway around us like the top of a volcano.

"This is more like it," she said pausing to catch her breath. Emily was never the outdoor type, but I think she was really enjoying herself. She always carried a camera in her bag and had already taken a few shots of the dike and reservoir...and me.

"Now you can see what's left of our first quarry," I said, sweeping my hand in a semi-circle. More than half of the reservoir was surrounded by stone cliffs rising out of the water twenty-five to fifty feet. The open end of curve was closed off by the stone and earthen dike beside us. Above the cliffs surrounding the quarry, mountains rolled upward with rock outcroppings penetrating the surrounding forest of small trees.

"I thought the water would be clear or even blue or something like that—not *red*," said Emily.

"It's usually blue, but when we have a storm like the doozy two days ago, the swollen river gushes red clay into the reservoir. It takes days to clear out." Emily leaned against a large boulder at the edge of the dike. I think she wanted to rest there for a little while. I re-tied my shoes to give her a little time to catch her breath, then I started climbing again. As soon as she saw the steeper incline, Emily took a deep breath, ballooned her cheeks, and let the air out slowly, but never said a word. We reached an overlook just above the side of the dike where a fourteen by twenty-eight foot stone building with a slate roof stood anchored to the rock.

"Wow, what's this?" she asked.

"My family built this at the same time they built our house—same stone, same slate roof. This structure was used back then as the quarry office. It's got a great view of the reservoir. They used it to store records, equipment, and dynamite."

"What's it used for now?"

"It's empty. After we closed the quarry, my family leased the property to the county to make a reservoir."

"Leased it?"

"Yep, I actually still own it all."

"Does anybody use the house?"

"Not now. For a while, we used as a little summer place to cool off. Sarah and Tad loved to spend time here. When we moved to Charlotte, Sarah let her family use it, but I had to put a padlock on the doors and run the Remington's out."

"Why?"

"Because they were slobs. They were wrecking it."

"Can I see inside?"

"Yes, I want to show it to you, but we'll have to do it next time. Believe it or not, we still have some climbing to do." She gave a short pathetic laugh and then followed me up the trail. We continued walking and climbing until we reached an altitude of fifty feet above the water level. That was as high as I intended to go and probably as far as Emily would climb.

"This is my spot," I said sitting on top of a waist-high boulder. Emily sat down cross-legged beside me. "There's a piece of magic here," I said concealing a smile.

"Show me." She bounced a small pebble off the back of my neck as I looked over the water.

"I proposed to Sarah here. Tad loved to have picnics here. Long before that Bakkuk and Ceda and I used to build bonfires here. We'd stay until the fire died, well after dark."

"That must have been fun."

"Bakkuk said he was trying to contact his father."

"Where was he?"

"He didn't know. He didn't know where his mother had gone either, but he thought they were both dead. He didn't really remember much about either of them."

"Poor guy. You said he was raised by his aunt?"

"Yes, and she told him all about his mother, but he learned about his father from Possum. Possum is also half Indian and knew Bakkuk's dad, but I don't think even Possum knows what happened to him. I do think most of what Bakkuk knew about

Indians, he got from Possum. The rest I guess he just made up to be what he wanted it to be."

"So, you said there was magic here. What's the magic?"

I stood up. "Are you ready?"

Emily squinted.

"See how the mountain on this side of the quarry is mostly flat, while the opposite side curves a half circle all the way from the dam on our left to the place where it joins the mountain off to our right. This spot where we're sitting is almost the exact center of that semi-circle. It's a little over a thousand feet from here to any part of that cliff."

"It's beautiful, but that's not magic," she said in a teasing voice.

"Well it's going to seem like magic. Tad always wanted to believe this spot was haunted. If I call out your name standing here, it will reflect off the cliffs, and, because it's curved, all the sound will bounce right back here to this spot, the center of the circle, then bounce off the cliff below and return across the quarry to the curved stone wall, then back again, and so on. So you will hear your name repeated every two seconds at least six times before it fades away."

"Does it have to be my name?"

"Absolutely," I said as I stood and shouted, "Emily." Even though I had warned her, she almost fell off the rock when the echo returned over and over with such clarity and strength it was hard for her to believe it was not someone calling to her from the other side of the quarry. "You want to try it?"

"Sure," she said jumping to her feet, but she tripped on a stone and suddenly fell forward toward the edge. Realizing there was nothing between her and the red water fifty feet below, she let out a shriek. I reached out and instinctively wrapped my arms around her as the scream repeated its echo over and over. We moved to a grassy place away from the edge and listened to the panicked voice bounce back and forth until it shrank into silence.

We both burst into laughter. She lay on her back with her hands over her face. I stretched out beside her. After a minute, she rolled onto her side and propped her head on one hand, quietly gazing across the water. A hawk circled above us.

"Stuart, I've got to talk to you about something." I turned to her and leaned on one elbow. "I know something about Tad," she said. I sat up.

"When I went through the jail, I ...she was in there."

"What?"

"Stu, I wanted to tell you, but Sergeant Evans made me promise not to."

"*Why?*"

"According to Sergeant Evans, if you knew, you would go down there and probably anger the Sheriff or something and I'm not sure how Tad would take it. I thought it would make things more difficult for both of you."

Without speaking, I stood and walked to the edge of the big rock, looked to the other side of the quarry, then to the sky. I said, "Let's go." The hawk circling above turned sharply toward us then made a bullet shot to the edge of the cliff twenty feet away. With a snap of its talons, it picked up a field mouse trying to scramble into a crevasse. The hawk rose twenty feet in the air before the little animal wiggled free, fell into the grass, and disappeared.

We shuffled down the mountain around the green-streaked dike to my car. I was more surprised than angry but too angry to talk. I knew Emily was upset, but my mind was racing. I think she was afraid I would go straight to the jail, but I drove home. She followed me to the den and sat on one of the leather chairs. I sat down at my desk and opened my checkbook. After closing my eyes for a moment to clear my mind, I wrote a check and handed it to her. It was made out in her name for ten thousand dollars. After looking at the check, she was afraid to look back at me.

"Emily, here's what I want you to do. We have to get her out of there. Put this money in your bank account. I'll call my attorneys in Asheville. They will contact you. Tell them everything. I know Redbriar and I know the Sheriff. Somewhere in the process of arresting her they bent the rules. Somewhere they screwed it up and my lawyers will find it. I will not go down there and my lawyers will work with you behind the scenes, but I want you to go to the courthouse and rattle cages and do just what my lawyers tell you to do. My guess is they will get the sentence reduced with a fine of some kind. Pay it in cash. Pay the court costs and whatever else you have to, including the lawyers.

"What do I tell Tad?"

"Tell her it was your idea. You knew her mother and wanted to do something to help."

Still sitting on the edge of the cushion Emily said, "I don't think she's going to buy it. I'm sure she's too smart for that, and she'll figure out I don't have that kind of money. She's going to know it's coming from you and so will the Sheriff."

"Okay. Tell her the truth, but tell her I just wanted to help her get out of that jail and she doesn't have to see me or talk to me or anything. No strings. Even if the sheriff's gang suspects the money is coming from me, having you pay it in cash, keeping me out of there, will take away some of the curse of my getting her out."

After that, neither of us spoke. She knew what the news of finding Tad in jail would do to me and I knew keeping it from me for so long must have been tough on her, but still, I couldn't imagine why she didn't tell me.

Emily carefully folded the check and held it in both hands in her lap while she watched me walk to the door.

"Stu," she said. I stopped. "I know how you feel, but I

want you to know that I think Ceda was right too."

"About what?"

"About not telling you. I'm afraid it could get worse for Tad if you mess with the Sheriff."

"Emily, I can get her out of there. I could have gotten her out weeks ago if I had known—without messing with Hodges."

"But, don't you think Ceda knows what she's talking about? She knows the system and knows the Sheriff and his people as well as anybody." Emily lifted the check a few inches toward me and continued, "I'm just afraid we'll make it worse."

I spun around and slammed my hand against the wood paneling. A watercolor painting fell off the wall and smashed on the floor shattering the glass,

"Damn it, I need your help! Just help me?" I said.

"Everything I've done was because I'm trying to help you!"

"I can't believe you didn't tell me and I can't believe Ceda would keep this from me."

"She did it because she cares for you. Why is it so hard for you to believe that people care about you?"

I returned to the carriage house without answering. I couldn't, I had no answer.

The truth is I was only fifty percent sure I could get Tad out. Maybe Ceda and Emily were right about not telling me, but it didn't matter. I couldn't let Tad stay in that place a moment longer without trying something.

I never knew why the carriage house always cooled me down, cleared my mind. Tad was *my* problem and I dumped it all on Emily. I'm sure I said all the wrong things, but I didn't want to admit it—not then.

It only took a minute in the carriage house for me to calm down. When I grabbed Emily on the cliff, I felt her arms around me for a split moment. I breathed her fragrance. I should have told her how much I loved that moment. I shouldn't have asked her to get involved with Tad again.

I crossed the drive back to the Stone House. She was gone. By the time I got to the front porch, she was making the first turn down the driveway. She didn't see me wave.

Returning to the den, I half expected to find the check lying on my desk, her way of telling me she wasn't coming back, but she took it with her and she contacted my attorneys, negotiated with the judge, paid the fine, and got Tad as well as the Sheriff's Office to cooperate.

I realized then, that some of the things Emily was able to do, I couldn't do in a million years.

CHAPTER TWENTY-THREE

TAD

I don't think there is a single inch of that entire quarry that Dad and I didn't climb or sketch. He took pride in telling me that the dark stain in the granite ledge high over the water was the result of Bakkuk's bonfires, decades before. He also swore that he and Bakkuk loved to dive from that ledge fifty feet into the water below. I always knew it was a tall tale, but he enjoyed telling about those days so much, I didn't care.

Mom, when she came with us, spent most of her time in the little granite house at the end of the quarry. She usually made sandwiches and Kool-Aid, but spent most of her time at her typewriter. I have no idea what, or who, she was writing. When I was little, she loved to read books to me as we sat on a couch by an open window. Even on the hottest days, it was cool there. She had a low bookshelf just for me and a high one for her own books. When she wasn't looking, I enjoyed leafing through her romance novels. Secretly, I tasted new places, feelings, and emotions that took me far beyond Redbriar. I thought I was getting away with something very wicked. There was a big table in the center of the main room. Sometimes I read at one end of that table while Dad painted at the other end.

Some of my Mother's books were written in French. She told me about her trip to Paris with her friends during college. She learned a little French at UNC and taught me a few words. With images of romantic encounters swimming through my head, I spent afternoons draped across the couch acting out in my mind what I imagined to be her secret past. I always thought my Mother was beautiful and I had no doubt she must have had Parisian men following her with bouquets of flowers all over Paris and all the way back to the airport. I concluded she couldn't or wouldn't talk about it with me because Dad was always around, so I made up stories she might tell me someday– dozens of them—romantic, steamy stories, or at least as steamy as my young imagination allowed.

I always dreamed I would make sandwiches and read to my children in that little house on the cliff, but by the time I was twenty-one, an explosion turned the entire structure, along with those dreams, into piles of rubble at the bottom of the reservoir.

CHAPTER TWENTY-FOUR

Within a week, Stuart's attorneys uncovered three violations of Tad's rights and two clearly documented cases of improper conduct by the officers. She had been convicted of marijuana possession, but the attorneys managed to have her case reopened and she was released under two conditions. First, she had to pay a fine, and second, she had to give an address where she would be living, somewhere in the county. At Stuart's request, Sergeant Evans agreed to let Tad stay at her house for a while. Ceda pretended it was all part of her job, but the truth was, she would have done anything to help Stuart's daughter. Privately Stuart reassured Ceda that he would give her whatever money she needed each month to take care of Tad.

Ever since she was a little girl, Tad knew Ceda, so she had no problem with moving into Ceda's little cabin on the south side of town. The five cousins arrested with Tad were still finishing the last few weeks of their ninety-day sentence.

Emily visited Tad every week. One stormy Saturday, looking through a rain- streaked windshield, she saw Tad sitting on Ceda's front porch. A large drawing pad was draped across her knees. Emily pulled a bag from the back seat then sat beside her on the top step. A soft whisper of rain bounced off the trees surrounding the house and dripped in a constant rhythm from the porch eaves. "Got a present for you," she said. "Last time I was here I noticed you were almost finished with that pad on your lap so I picked up another one in Asheville yesterday." Emily handed her the bag.

"Thanks."

"Can I take a look at your sketches?" Emily said extending her hand. Tad turned the pad around and gave it to her. "These are really good, Tad. Do you ever develop them into paintings?"

"I'm working on several watercolors."

"That's great!"

"Keeps me out of trouble, as they say."

"You're very much like your Dad. You know that?"

"No. Not like him at all."

"Tad, I knew your Mom and Dad before I started coming up here …" Emily stopped as Tad took back her pad and turned away. The sound of pencil lead scratching on paper joined the constant dripping from the roof.

Emily noticed a smaller pad lying beside Tad.

"May I take a look at that too?" she asked pointing to it.

"Sure."

As she turned through the pages, Emily noticed that several of the drawings were of Ceda and her house, but three or four were of a man lounging on the porch steps and against the porch rail. "Who's this?" she asked.

"Just a guy."

Anybody I would know?"

"You know his sister."

"I do?"

"Remember that big girl, my cellmate in jail? That was Novie, his sister. When she found out I was getting out, she asked me to call him. I did, so he's been here a couple of times." Emily took a closer look at the drawing. Even though it was a quick sketch, she saw his tall and painfully thin body, his eyes partially covered by sheep hound hair that scrambled across his face from every angle. He wore sneakers, jeans, and a windbreaker over a t-shirt. His head leaned back against the post, but his stare aimed at her. A cigarette dangled carelessly from the tips of his fingers draped over the rail. Even more telling was the detailed sketch of his face, beaming with arrogance. Emily tried not to let her thoughts show.

"Is Novie still in jail?"

"He said she gets out next week."

"These are great drawings. Hope you let me see more."

"Thanks, I will."

"Anything else you need?"

"Nope, Ceda takes good care of me."

"You're lucky to have her."

"Yep, she's almost like a mom.

"Really." Emily looked over her shoulder toward the front door.

"Well, I'm here to help you too, let me know whatever else I can do for you."

Stuart's station wagon sent out rolling plumes of muddy water from the ruts in Ceda's gravel driveway. He saw her in the kitchen the moment he walked in. "Ceda, its me." His usual greeting.

"Come on back."

"I got your note."

"I wish I could tell you more."

"Tell me what you know."

"When I got home yesterday, there was a man on the steps with her. "

"Who?"

"She called him Daggett."

"Well, who is that?"

"I don't know him, but I know he's no good. His sister was her cell mate."

"Great. What did he look like?"

"In his thirties. Hooked nose with small gray eyes, thick dirty blond hair, denim shirt. When I arrived, he flashed the palm of his hand at me without even looking in my direction and then left in his truck, the kind with the big wheels."

"Did she say anything about him?"

"No, but he left one of those thin cigars on the porch—still lit. You know the kind that smells like wine. Anyway in about an hour he came back and she left with him."

"Did she take her stuff?"

"That's the crazy thing. She took a few things in a bag and left the rest. Most of her clothes, papers, drawings—all are still in her room. She just left and didn't come back."

"How do you know she's not coming back?"

"I don't know, except that she acted funny, and there's something just plain weird about that hairball she went off with."

"Can you find out more about this guy at the Sheriff's office?"

"You're god dammed right I can. The detectives have a file on everybody. Keeping up with the bad guys and some of the good guys is their job. I'll go to work an hour early tomorrow to see what I can find out."

"Thanks. Does she owe you any money or anything I need to pay you?"

"Don't be stupid, Stuart. You know I'm glad to help. Besides, she's all paid up."

"Okay," He beat his knuckles lightly on the counter. "Let me know anything you find out as soon as you can."

He started to leave, then asked, "Why in the world would

she do it?"

"Go off with a guy like that?"

"Yes. She was always a sensible girl. Stayed close to home—except, of course, when she ran away to stay with those Remingtons."

"I don't know. We got along fine. She never gave me any trouble here. Just wanted to draw…mostly quiet."

Ceda returned to the kitchen as soon as Stuart left. She sliced a tomato to make a BLT. As she placed the slices and a fist of lettuce on bread drowned in mayonnaise, she remembered there was no bacon in the house, so instead of bacon she piled a double layer of potato chips over the tomatoes and crunched the two bread slices together until they stuck. Ceda settled into her overstuffed chair in her living room and turned on the TV beside her. While waiting for the black and white set to warm up, she took a bite of her sandwich, sipped her Coke, then picked up a picture frame from the table. It contained a snapshot of her at age nine along with Stuart and Bakkuk. As far as she knew, it was the only photograph ever taken of Bakkuk. He towered over both of them and draped both his long dark arms around their shoulders. Her arms were wrapped around his waist and with her eyes closed, she leaned her head against his side. All three faces smiled.

In a drawer beside her chair she had a stack of unused notepads and a pile of used ball-points. She took a pad and pen and placed them on the table, then pulled a small watch box covered in black velvet from the drawer. Light from the TV flickered into the box and bounced against a piece of Indian pottery the size of a biscuit. As she did every night, she looked at the raven figure carved in the baked clay and thought of Bakkuk who gave it to her on her twelfth birthday. With both the photograph and the relic nestled on her lap, staring back at her, she slowly finished her sandwich and coke. She then picked up the note pad and wrote the name "Daggett," grabbed the keys from the kitchen counter, and with the notebook tucked in her hip pocket, drove back to the jail.

CHAPTER TWENTY-FIVE

TAD

I know somewhere in my life I must have met spookier guys than Daggett, but right now I can't remember who the hell they would be.

What kind of person gets barked at by his own dog every time he comes home?

The first thing I saw through the truck window was the weathered farm house half hidden behind a yard of elms and wild honeysuckle. A gray and black dog with more teeth than face darted out from under the porch and launched an attack at the wheels of Daggett's truck.

"That's my dog, *Scad*," he said, proudly. "Lets everybody know when I'm home."

" Does he bark at everybody ?"

"Not usually." He stopped the truck in front of the steps, hopped out, and then tied Scad to a tree.

From her size and kinky blond hair, I spotted Novie sleeping on a porch swing. It had only been a few weeks since I had seen her, but I actually missed her and was anxious to talk to her. We had more things between us that were different than things in common, but at that time those few things we shared were important.

On another part of the porch, a young man leaned against a half-painted post. Below him were two men lounging on the steps. All three glanced curiously at me but continued chatting among themselves. After saying a few words to the guys, Daggett motioned for me to join them. I got out of his truck, threw a bag made from a pillow case over my shoulder, and walked to the steps.

"Joe, Roy, and Miller, this is Tad." Daggett waved his hand loosely toward the men and then to me. Keeping my right hand in my pocket, I managed to wave with my left hand still clutching my bag. Without saying anything, Daggett climbed the five steps to the porch. I followed. "Novie, wake up," he shouted to his sister on the swing.

She raised her head, stared for a moment, then said, "Tad darling, come on in the house." For the first time, I felt like smiling. "Come on in," Novie waved and said, "I've got a place for you upstairs. Your own room."

"Thanks for letting me come," I said as we walked into the house.

"Oh God, let me tell you. I'm so glad you're here. We got to have more than one woman in this place or it's just crazy around here."

"Just you with four guys live here?"

"Yeah. One of Daggett's buddies had a girlfriend living here for a while but they both moved out a few of weeks ago. You can stay in their room."

The long upstairs corridor was dark except for little shafts of light that managed to slip through a few open doors. "Here you go," said Novie, walking into one of the rooms. "All it's got is a bed and a bureau. We all share the toilet down the hall. Daggett pays the rent, but he likes having his friends live here with him. We all just chip in to buy groceries and things like that, okay? Go ahead and put your stuff away and join us back on the porch when you're ready. Okay sugar? "

"Thank you," I said softly as Novie walked back into the hall. I closed the door and pressed my back against the rough wood. The small bedroom had a single window with a curtain on one side. An old pull shade blocked most of the light. With both fists against my chest I held my breath until I stopped shaking. Before coming there, Daggett took me by my cousin's house to get some clothes and other stuff. Two of the cousins had been released from jail and the rest would be out in another few weeks. I tossed the bag on the bed. It landed with a thud. The bed turned out to be as hard as it sounded. It was covered with two blankets, a set of sheets, and nothing else. Before emptying my bag on the bureau, I draped a blue handkerchief across the top surface, then dumped everything else on it—a change of underclothes, a sweatshirt, a blue knit hat, a second pair of jeans, a windbreaker, and my new sketch pad. From my jeans pockets, I pulled a few personal things and placed them across the left side of the handkerchief—a plastic comb, twenty-five dollars and thirty-four cents, a tattered checkbook for an account my grandmother gave me, and a carved wooden frog. The frog was a toy I had since I was a child. It was about the size of the palm of my hand with blue, red, and green spots. Some of the original blue paint had worn down to the wood.

I lifted the shade to let in some light. One pane was broken. Moist air flooded in. A piece of the river wound its way to the east before disappearing in a valley between two hills. I knew the Stone House was just beyond those hills and I saw part of the top of Mount Tsula sticking its bony fist into the sky. For just a moment, I placed my finger on the window pane as if I were touching the mountain. The only lamp in the room was on the corner of the bureau, but I didn't want to turn it on right away knowing the darkness that filled the room hid the dirt I felt under my feet and fingers.

Novie had reclaimed her place on the porch swing, but left room for me. The moment I stepped back onto the porch she said, patting her hand on the wood seat, "Got your place all warmed up for you, Tad."

"Thanks." I sat down and glanced at the crew scattered across the steps. Daggett was whispering something to the two on the stoop while Roy still rested against a post at the top.

"Your room okay?" said Novie.

"Yes, it's fine, thank you."

"Don't worry, Tad. You'll get used to this place and these four idiots. Don't let them bother you. There're just a bunch of dust bunnies, especially Daggett. I'm probably tougher than all of 'em put together." Novie flashed a smile that lasted about two seconds, then in a low voice she said, "If they get too close, let me know—you know what I mean?"

Scad, who had gotten loose from his tether, eased his way up the stairs, then slithered across the porch toward me with his head held low enough to tell us he wasn't coming to play. I sat still while he sniffed my feet and legs, then my hands. Finally, he gave me a lick and trotted off. Roy, apparently becoming encouraged by Scad, shuffled over to the porch rail near Novie and wrapped his arm around the post. Novie ignored him.

When I finally looked at him, he nodded back. I politely returned a half nod. He stared for another awkward minute as if he were trying to think of something to say.

"I understand you're that stone guy's daughter," he said.

I looked at the ceiling without answering. He didn't seem to notice my irritation or my cool non-response. He continued, "I understand you lived in that big house."

"It's been a while," I replied.

"I grew up in a stone house too, but not like that one."

"I don't live at the Stone House anymore," I said a little louder.

"Don't get me wrong, I was just wondering."

Novie jumped in, "Roy, I was just wondering why you don't have a brain!"

Roy walked in front of us then rested his shoulder against the peeling clapboards close to me. "Like I said, don't get me wrong, I'm happy to have somebody new here, Really. Especially as pretty as you. But," he said after thinking about it, "if I had a rich daddy, I'd probably be living with him as long as I could—but I'm glad you're here." I ignored his babbling. He crossed his legs at the ankles and put both hands in his pockets as Miller strolled over from the stairs and took his turn leaning against the same post beside Novie.

Looking at me, Miller said, "How 'bout I give you a little tour of the farm this afternoon?"

I glanced back at Novie, who replied to Miller. "How 'bout I cut off your little testicles this afternoon?" Roy laughed as Miller turned away with a grimace and put both hands on the porch rail. The moment he did, something caught his attention. "Hey, Roy," Miller said, in a slight whisper, then nodded at Daggett, who was silently slinking toward his truck. After rummaging around the glove compartment, Daggett tip-toed like a stalking cat back to the steps. Roy joined Miller at the rail and both men stretched over it as far as they could to watch Daggett. Joe sat motionless at the top of the steps.

I jumped when the deafening crack of a gunshot rattled the window beside me and echoed off nearby hills. My ears were still ringing as Daggett strutted into the thick grass and picked up, by the tail, the dripping carcass of a rat the size of his shoe. He held the animal high enough for the gang of three on the porch to see. Receiving their yelping approval he tossed it into the bushes beyond the drive. With a triumphant march back to the steps, he shoved the pistol into his pants just under his belt buckle.

"Happens about twice a week," said Novie, "you'll get used to it."

Even though I lived over a year with my cousins, I soon discovered I wasn't prepared for the crude routine at the Jenkins' farm.

Novie's job at the farm was to make one meal a day, dinner, always at 6 PM. She made it for everybody even if they weren't there. If it wasn't eaten, it was put in the refrigerator as leftovers for whoever got to it first. I helped her out and took it upon myself to clean the kitchen and pantry every evening. According to Novie, the guys' job was to clean the rest of the house regularly, which meant it never got done. For breakfast and lunch, they were on their own to grab leftovers, or sandwiches, or just drink beer. Daggett kept the refrigerator jammed full of beer at all times. The pantry behind the kitchen was constantly stocked with liquor and drinks. At the back of the pantry, on a shelf, he kept an old wooden box filled with marijuana leaves and a supply of paper. He kept harder drugs locked in his room.

My bedroom door had a key hole but no key. The wind blowing through the broken window rattled the shade constantly. Since I had only one change of clothing, I slept in the nude. My room was cold. To keep warm I wrapped in the sheets and thick blanket and wore my knit hat. I made a pillow by stuffing the extra blanket into the pillowcase. At night, as I always did, I caressed my little wooden frog under my pillow with my thumb across its smooth back and head until I fell asleep.

Two to three times a month the guys would go off with Daggett for several days. They never said where they were going or what they had done, but when they returned, they were dirty and exhausted and ready to get stoned. It would take them the next three days to recover. Sometimes they drank all night and with the only working toilet at the end of the upstairs hall, I heard footsteps crunching up and down the corridor past my room every half hour throughout the night. Roy, Miller, and Joe were happiest when they had nothing to do, like four year-old boys in an over-sized sandbox.

I did all I could to be part of the crowd at dinner time. Before long the gang got used to me constantly sketching them. When Daggett was gone, Roy and Miller battled for my attention and literally fought to see who would get the seat beside me on the living room couch. When Daggett was home, he never really paid much attention to me, but it was clear to everyone that he considered me his territory and insisted I sit near him; nobody questioned it. Actually, nobody ever questioned Daggett about anything. He was the undisputed leader of the pack and he didn't hesitate to bash someone in the face whenever he thought they needed it. They never said a word—just took it in silence, as if it was normal.

Miller, however, couldn't keep his eyes off me, even when Daggett was around. About once a week, I found a single flower placed on my dresser. It was from Miller. I knew it was from him because the others were just too crude to ever think of anything like that, but still, it bothered me. From the sound of his gait, I knew when Miller walked by at night. Even though I kept the door shut, he always paused for a moment outside before continuing down the hall. I stuffed toilet paper into the key hole, but he still lingered outside every time he made a trip to the bathroom.

I found a radio in the pantry that I put on the floor next to the bed. It kept me company at night. A couple of times a month I drank myself to sleep. Early one morning, someone came into my room during the night and stood there a while, but I really couldn't be sure if it happened at all or if it was just the gin. Anyway, after that, I slept in my clothes.

Sometimes after long summer rains, I still smell the Jenkins' farm. From wet clay and breezes blowing through-rain soaked branches come ghosts that refuse to die. To this day, I'm still spooked out by keyholes. I still cringe when I hear floors squeak in the middle of the night. Living there was a self-inflicted hell, and, at that time, I honestly believed I deserved it.

My only escape was my morning walks downriver to the edge of town and back. Before sunrise, invisible, in the morning mist, I found a different world, a beautiful world. I was never cold, never afraid, and never lost. It was that under-the-covers-with-a-flashlight feeling I loved so much when I was a little girl.

I was nineteen, but I still felt like a young girl, not a child, but just stuck at fourteen even though I had been to jail, gotten drunk, tried some drugs, run away from home, and buried my mother and my grandmother. All my choices then were frightening. At least three times a week Daggett's pistol cracked like a lightning bolt beside the house and another rat or squirrel was tossed into the woods. I began to wonder how much better I would feel if I had a little pistol to put under my pillow or keep in my jacket. Just my secret. No one would know. I even imagined what I would do if one of the guys came into my room again at night. I saw myself firing a warning shot in the air and watching him fly down the hall. Eventually, that wasn't enough. I pictured waiting until he got close to the bed then firing through the dark with a point blank blast in his chest. Before that summer, I never let myself think about things like that and now I'm ashamed how much it comforted me.

Today those days are like dirt devils whirling across a dry field somewhere in my memory.

Everything important comes without permission. In the middle of a rainy June night, after drinking myself to sleep, I was carried from my bed and driven away, never to see the inside of the Jenkins farm house again.

It's true, teenagers are notoriously stupid. Of all the idiotic things I did back then, moving in with Novie and Daggett was the dumbest. I know now the kind of trap I was in. It was foolish, but it wouldn't be the most dangerous thing I would ever do—that was soon to come.

Jack Hemphill

CHAPTER TWENTY-SIX

STUART

I just finished cleaning my brushes. The scent of oil and turpentine cut through the air like pine needles at Christmas. I heard Emily talking to someone in the foyer, then I heard the unmistakable sound of Ceda's official shoes clomping through the house as she came toward me.

Before she walked through my studio door, she started talking. "I can only stay a minute, but Stu, I overheard something today I think you need to know."

"Of course. What is it?" I asked.

"It's about Tad. I've finally confirmed that she's staying at the Jenkins' farm with Daggett and his sister."

"How did you find out?"

"I saw Joe Jenkins this morning; he goes to the farm once a month to collect the rent from Daggett. He picks it up in person, because he doesn't trust Daggett to send it in the mail. I found out about this Daggett guy... well, it's not good. He's done hard time, twice—both drug-related. I wanted you to know this, but Stu...I want you to know something else. There's really nothing you can do about it right now, so *sit tight*. Understand? We're watching this guy so stay out of it."

I closed my eyes, not that I wasn't expecting something like that, it's just that I hadn't allowed myself to think about what I would do when I heard it.

"Of course I understand," I said.

Ceda left as quickly as she came, but not without saying one more time, "Sit tight."

"What *are* you going to do?" asked Emily as soon as the front door closed.

"Bring her home." I pressed my forehead against the cool glass peering into the darkness outside my window.

"What in the world makes you think she'll leave with you?" Emily asked.

"I don't know, but I've got to get her out of there tonight, even if I have to drag her out." I knew that old house well. Joe Jenkins and I used to fish together sometimes, but nobody named Jenkins had lived on the farm for years.

I heard myself cry out "Tad! *What* are you doing?" I rested my head on my left hand and without realizing it I smeared red paint through my hair from my forehead to my crown. Furious, I turned and threw my pallet on the floor. Paint splattered all the way to Emily's feet.

Two canvas bags hung from my easel—one with clean rags and one for oily rags. I took a rag from the clean bag and soaked it with mineral spirits. Squatting on one knee, I scrubbed spots of paint off Emily's shoes. When I finished, she took the rag and carefully folded the clean side out and wiped the paint out of my hair.

I didn't deserve Emily, and she didn't deserve my frustration. Even though I pushed it somewhere far inside; I felt it all the time, but I never was able to push it far enough to hide it from her. God knows I tried, but she knew me. Her thoughts were painted on her face and I knew she was searching for a way to help me.

She stood perfectly silent, still holding the rags soaked in red, until I finally said, "Will you do something for me tonight?"

"Okay. What can I do?"

"I need for you to drive me there, wait with the car, and be ready to drive away as soon as we're out of the house."

"Okay."

Emily trusted me more than she should have and I'm sure she thought it couldn't be as dangerous as it sounded. We had to wait until late that night. Emily cooked dinner but I had no appetite. I had no right to ask her to go with me and once again I was starting to feel a little guilty. "Stay here tonight." I said, "You don't have to do this. It was unfair of me to ask you to go with me."

She wrinkled her face and said. "I want to go, and I don't think you should go by yourself."

"I don't even know what I'm getting you into."

"You're not twisting my arm, I want to help."

It was close to eleven when we pulled onto the furrowed dirt drive. Low clouds had completely covered the moon and when Emily turned off the headlights, we were in total darkness except for the luminous dial on my watch.

"Keep your lights off, make a right turn, and climb the bank," I said.

"I can't see a damn thing!" she protested, but reluctantly eased up the jagged hill. The old Chevy jerked back and forth. The front wheels constantly jammed against stones and mud while the rear wheels grabbed chunks of earth and spewed them into the air behind us. I didn't remember the hill being so high. Finally, cresting the top, we saw the lights of the house penetrating the thick brush in front of us.

At my direction, she eased the car to a spot close to the barn. From there we saw amber light trickling through window blinds at the front of the house and reflecting off the wrap-around porch and low bushes. The second floor was dark except for a glow slipping through a shade over a window near the rear. Emily's fingers squeezed the steering wheel. She turned off the engine and whispered, "Where do you think she is?"

"She's most likely wherever the crowd is."

"How are you going to find out?"

"I'm going to walk in."

"That's your plan?"

"What else do you suggest?"

Emily touched her forehead on the steering wheel for a moment then said, "Let *me* talk to her. She trusts me,"

"I know, but she's probably not going to be alone and you'd have to deal with more than just Tad."

"What do you want me to do?"

"Stay here. As soon as you see me coming out with or without her, open the door, and start the car."

"It doesn't feel right." She clutched the wheel again and gave it a little shake.

"No, it doesn't," I whispered.

"Are you sure you want to do this?"

I squeezed her hand lightly, then got out of the car. I felt her watching. She was as scared as I was. As I walked across the old porch, wood under my feet groaned out a warning. The rusty spring on the screen door screeched as I entered the house. Standing in the dim hallway, I remembered the layout exactly, but the house had become worn and grimy. The air had an odor of smoke and yesterday's fried chicken. The heavy wood stair took up most of the front hall. Muted light and a muffled rhythm came from the living room. I put my hand on the door frame and leaned slowly into the room. A man with his back to me lounged across piles of pillows against a wall. He seemed to be asleep. On a long couch, further into the room, a young man in shorts and black t-shirt blew smoke into the air completely unaware of my presence.

Moving back from the doorway, I inched my way down the dark hall beside the staircase, cracked the kitchen door just enough to see the room was empty, then returned to the front hall. Soft light from the second floor made its way down the staircase. The round wood handrail felt rough and splintered. At the top of the stair, I saw light coming through an open door at the far end of the corridor. I remember there was once a long carpet running down that hall. Now the floor was covered with a sandy grit that dug into the wood under my shoes as I crept toward the door at the end. I leaned my chest against the wall next to the door frame and slowly tilted my head far enough to peep into the room. Soft music was playing. All I saw of the woman inside were her feet draped over the end of the bed. She was wearing two white sneakers, blue laces on one shoe and red laces on the other. Without a doubt that was Tad. After listening for a minute, I peered further into the room. She was asleep with her back and head propped up on a folded blanket. The window shade rattled from wind pushed in by an upcoming storm. She wore her faded blue jeans, a blue sweatshirt, and a teal knit hat. Tad's right hand was resting against her cheek. In her left hand she clutched an empty glass. On the windowsill beside the bed were an empty Coke and a half-empty bottle of gin.

I sat beside her and said her name. She didn't move. I said her name again, a little softer, then patted her arm. When I pulled the glass from her grip, her hand fell against her side. She still didn't move.

"I'm taking you home, sweetheart," I said, as I started to lift her. Something fell from her pocket and landed on the bed. It was the wooden frog I gave her when she was a little girl. She used to sleep with it and she once told me she would someday give it to her children. I didn't know she still had it. After I slid the toy into my back pocket, I picked her up. Grit dug deeper into the floor as I returned to the stairs. Walking down the steps in the shadowy light,

I watched her face. Her long thick hair was held back by her knit hat. It was hard to believe I had her in my arms.

As I reached the bottom of the stairs, a shadow from the living room floated across the floor. I stopped for a moment, but with my very next step, a man swung around the corner and blocked my path. He pushed slurred words out of his mouth, "Where you're goin'?"

"Taking my daughter home," I said, attempting to act nonchalant.

He squinted as if he were trying to recognize me, "She don't want to go with you, old man."

I tried to walk around him, but he stepped in my path again. A flash of light and a quick sharp pain under my chin stopped me. He pushed his blade hard, forcing my head upward. Both my hands were under Tad. There was nothing I could do. I froze. Ever since that night, I've thought of at least ten thousand things I should have said or done. Ten thousand brave, manly, macho, gutsy things that would have blown him aside, but the truth is, I was petrified. There was no way, however, I was going to turn around, put Tad down, or leave there without her.

Looking down into his eyes, I saw his steel gray stare looking right past me. His eyes were watered over, half vacant. It was obvious that whatever drug he had been taking or drinking had fogged his brain. I felt myself step forward. The knife pressed further into my neck, breaking the skin. A warm trickle rolled over my Adam's apple. The cold blade suddenly felt hot. With a quick twist of my body, I slammed Tad's feet into his side, knocking him off balance. He staggered in slow motion, then fell. Tad's left arm hung toward the floor as I walked past him, through the front door. I never looked back.

As soon as Emily saw me, she flipped on the lights and pulled the car to the front steps. I laid Tad across the rear seat, with her head in my lap. As we drove away, I slid my hand into my pocket, pulled the little toy out and slid it back into her front pocket. I then blotted my neck with the top of my sleeve.

It was beginning to rain, but by the time we got to the road, the clouds exploded into a steady flood. Tad moaned a little as I carried her in the rain from the car into the Stone House.

"All the sheets have been taken off the bed in her room," said Emily. You better put her in my room." We were soaked, but I continued to carry her up the stairs the way I had done so many times before. Emily pulled back the covers while I placed Tad in bed. I put her hands and arms by her side before I pulled the covers up to her neck. The flicker of sheet lightening and rain against the panes caused liquid shadows to run down the walls, over the bed, and across Tad's face. I took off her hat and stroked her hair away from her forehead. I watched her in silence for a good half hour.

"She's probably going to be out until morning," Emily said, standing beside us. "Why don't you get some rest? I'll stay here with her."

I stretched out on the couch in the sunroom. Tad was home, but I couldn't get around the fact that she didn't just come home—she was carried home. I really wasn't any closer to her at all, and maybe she was slipping further away from me. Sleep was impossible. Thunder, like wooden barrels rolling across a brick floor, rumbled in the field and passed over the house. Raindrops the size of marbles bounced on the deck just outside the window. I closed my eyes and listened for a minute, then stepped onto the deck and walked all the way to the rail, leaned over while the downpour washed across my head and neck. The flowing water reopened the wound on my neck. The rocks, gully, and trees below all shined and vibrated. Waves of water rolled across the ravine's long stone fingers, but they couldn't hold back the flood. I began to laugh. The warm rain continued to stream across my face and down my neck. The small rivulets gathered strength as they overflowed the rocky crevasses and increased their speed until they became an unstoppable force cascading away from me into the dark swollen Redbriar all the way to the French Broad, which carried it to the Mississippi, and finally to the Gulf of Mexico.

The place where laughter had been slowly turned hollow inside. I began to cry, a feeling I had forgotten. Rolling my head toward the sky and then down below my shoulders, I couldn't distinguish tears from rain on my face. Ever since I was a kid, I never let myself cry except in the rain. The warm stream felt like the gentle dark fingers that stroked my head at night. After returning to the couch, I finally settled into sleep.

The next time I opened my eyes a blanket had been placed over my back, and Emily was sitting beside me spreading adhesive tape over a bandage which she carefully placed under my chin. Dawn was struggling its way through the continuing storm.

"I just came down to see if you're okay."

"Yeah, I actually got some sleep. How's Tad?"

"Still unconscious. She rolled onto her side an hour ago. I put her hat in the drawer beside the bed and pulled the covers back over her. It seemed like she woke up for a moment, but her eyes closed and drifted away again. Other than that, she hasn't moved all night, but I think I'd better go back to her now. Try to get another hour of sleep."

I nearly slipped back into unconsciousness when I was awakened by Emily's voice calling me. Instantly I found myself sprinting through the house, up the stairs, and down the hall to Emily's room. "She's gone!" Emily cried. The bed was empty and the drawer beside the bed was left open. Emily looked into the drawer. She then slid her hand all the way to the back of the drawer. "Tad got her hat," said Emily, "but something else is missing."

"What?"

"The gun you gave me."

The front door was opened slightly. Both of us ran out into the rain. After looking in all directions, Emily jumped into her car and said, "I'll look down the road toward town."

"Okay, go." I ran around the property calling Tad's name. I fell three times as I flew down the sloped gully to the flat rock. Instinctively, I turned upriver and walked along the bank. The rocks and grassy bank were shiny and slick. The water boiled under pounding rain. After walking another hundred yards, I saw something in the water as it flowed over the rocks. Holding onto the limb of a river birch, I stretched most of my body over the stream and extended my arm into the water.

Emily was waiting in the sunroom when I finally returned. I sat beside her and immediately closed my eyes. She saw I was holding something in my grip and I felt her move closer. I opened my fist for her to see the blue wooden frog dripping muddy water through my fingers.

Jack Hemphill

CHAPTER TWENTY-SEVEN

Emily met weekly with the jail staff, hammering out the new jail design. By the end of the summer it was finished. As far as anyone knew, there was no other jail like it anywhere. It was a plan where no inmate would ever be out of direct vision of the guards. Emily and her office were pleased even though everyone knew that the peculiar concept was extruded from the mind of Sheriff Hodges.

The design was organized around a central corridor that ran through the building. The only access into the dayrooms was from each side of that spine. Two floors of cells overlooked the large dayrooms and the cells were separated from the dayrooms only by a continuous wall of bars. The main control room was placed above the entire length of the central corridor creating a room that was ten feet wide and a hundred feet long. Through secure windows along each side of the control room, guards could observe all dayrooms and all cells 24 hours a day without ever leaving their posts. Security was maximum. Privacy was nonexistent.

After the normal thirty-day bidding process, a contractor was awarded the construction contract. By the middle of August, earth moving equipment began gobbling up the site. A construction trailer was installed behind the courthouse, and Emily found herself on site weekly to check the progress and review the design details with the superintendent, Jeff Morris. Only three months were left before winter would begin to affect the construction. She needed to have all the excavation and initial grading done and all concrete slabs and foundations poured before snow and freezing temperatures set in.

"Emily, you have a call from a Mr. Jeff Morris," the voice blurted out of the intercom on her desk. She had just finished packing papers in her briefcase and stuffing rolls of drawings in long tubes to take with her to Redbriar. She would be there in a few hours and she wondered if she should take the call or just go. After pausing for a moment, she pushed the little white button on the phone and heard Jeff's voice.

Out of breath, he told her he had a totally unexpected problem pop up at the site and asked her to come there as soon as she got to Redbriar.

"What's up?"

"I've shut down all my dozers and told them to go home and stay there until I call them back."

"Why do you need me right away? What's the problem?"

"I think we may have an Indian mound on top of the knoll."

"Oh, great. That would be a doozy! What do you want me to do?"

"Well, if I'm right about this, it's going to cost us a shitload to fix it. I want you to confirm my decision to stop work."

After hanging up, Emily realized she would probably be stomping around the construction site until well after dark. She immediately called Stuart to let him know there would be a change in her routine.

"Please be there," she said out loud as she waited for him to answer his phone. The closest phone to his studio was in the study. He picked up on the sixth ring. "Stuart, something has happened at the site."

"What?"

"When they started clearing the top of the hill, they dug up some Indian stuff. Jeff thinks they've got an Indian mound or something up there."

"Indian mound? You mean a grave site?"

"I think that's what he's saying. He wants me to come straight to the construction trailer to confirm it."

"Why can't it wait until tomorrow?"

"Because it's an Indian thing, and you know about all the controversy lately over Indian sites. Morris sent all the grading people home. Anyway it'll be near dark by the time I get there and even later by the time I get to your house, but I wanted you to know I'll be late."

"I'll be here and I'll have dinner ready for you whenever you come."

"Thanks. I have to get on the road. Of course I have no idea what an Indian relic looks like, but I've got to go through the motions."

From Emily's office in Charlotte to Redbriar was just over three hours. Jeff was waiting for her in the construction trailer. "Thanks for coming on short notice, but I know you wanta see this. Help yourself to coffee while I get some things for you to look at." He returned with a burlap bag and placed it gently on the table in front of her. She didn't know what to expect as Jeff scooped out a handful of arrowheads, spear points, and some broken pottery. After giving Emily time to carefully examine the pile, Jeff laid a large bone beside the relics.

"Okay... it's a bone," she said, holding the object with two fingers and studying it carefully. It looked old, had turned partly red from the clay around it, and had a crack on one end.

"There are more bones in the ground," he said, "we dug up

a half dozen or so and left the rest in place."

"Well, the arrowheads are obviously Indian and the dirty red bone certainly looks old. That's about the extent of my expertise." She slid the bone back into Jeff's sack. "This is what I would suggest, tomorrow I'll find out in the morning who to report this to. Keep the bones along with the arrowheads and pottery pieces to show whoever is supposed to look at it. They'll tell us what the heck to do next."

Relieved that the architect was taking some responsibility, Jeff placed the bone back into the burlap bag. "So far, I haven't told anybody about it except you, but I left a message for the Sheriff."

The moment Emily pulled out of the parking lot by the courthouse onto River Street, she saw a flashing light rounding the curve at the edge of town. Seconds later Sheriff Hodges flew past her without slowing down and turned into the construction site leaving tire marks on the street and parking lot. He didn't see Emily.

Nine o'clock the following morning, Emily returned. The trailer was locked and everyone was gone. The only person she found in the courthouse was Delores, the County Manager's secretary.

"Emily, I had a feeling you'd be comin' by," Delores said.

"You know about the things they found on the site?"

"Oh yeah, and I betcha by noon time, everybody in town will know about it. Mr. Cunningham and the Sheriff were here an hour ago."

"What do they want to do?"

"The Sheriff roped it off last night, kept everybody out. Just a little while ago, the Sheriff contacted the state archeologist in Raleigh and asked him if he wanted to take a look. He showed me the collection of stones, pottery and stuff they dug up."

"What about the bones?"

"What bones?"

Emily dropped her keys and placed both hands flat on the counter. Bending forward she said, "Delores, last night I saw a large bone in the construction trailer, a dirty big ol' red bone."

"Nobody said anything about any bones."

With a puzzled voice, Emily asked, "My God, what the hell is he doing?"

"You saw bones?"

"One bone. I know it had to be a leg or something."

Delores came around the counter. "They didn't tell me anything else, but I heard the Sheriff talking to Mr. Cunningham. The Sheriff wants to try to have part of the property from the top of the hill to the river declared some kind of historical site."

"Which means we move the project," said Emily.

"I don't know, but I heard Mr. Cunningham say it would be easier to move the building than to fight with the Indians. He's going to call you later and tell you what to do."

That night during dinner, Emily said to Stuart, "Why did he do it? Why would the Sheriff want to hide the bones?"

"Don't know. I'm sure everybody remembers Lester wanted the jail to be built on the other side of the courthouse. If they actually found a burial site up there, then this discovery would give him the perfect opportunity to get the project moved, but nobody is ever sure what the sheriff has on his mind," Stuart said.

"You remember how long it took me to design the jail on that site? If they move it, I might have to redo most of the floor plan."

"Okay, but it's not your fault. They paid you to design it, they'll pay you to redesign it."

"I know. I guess I just don't like to see the sheriff get his way – again. And, if I have to change the plan, I have to meet with him as many times as it takes to get him satisfied.

"I know and I'm sorry if you have to go through that again."

Emily closed her eyes, leaned her head forward and rubbed the back of her neck.

"You know what? It's my problem," she said. "I shouldn't be dumping this on you, especially now ... I mean with Tad running off again and everything."

"Yeah, I thought I'd hear something about her by now, but ..." He slid out of his seat and picked up the diner plates and then continued, "You know what I do when I'm really down?"

"Yes, you get quiet as a mouse."

"That's true, but before that happens, when I'm really low, I skip dinner altogether and go right to the dessert, double sized."

"You're learning too many of my weaknesses."

"Stay where you are," he said as he carried the half full plates into the kitchen. Emily sat still for a minute then slipped into the hall to get a set of blue prints, returned to the dining room, and spread the drawings out over an empty place at the table trying to imagine another location for the jail. The lights went out. She jumped. Stuart, had flicked the switch off as he walked back into the room carrying a pound cake, a tub of ice cream and two large empty bowels. A lit candle was stuck in the middle of the cake

"Did you make this?"

"I bought the ice cream but I made the pound cake this after noon."

"I've never seen one with a full candle sticking out of it like that," she chuckled.

"I know, it's not exactly romantic," he said.

"No, it's very romantic ... I mean ... if that's what you wanted it to be," Emily said as she looked down at the table.

Stuart was afraid he had embarrassed her, but couldn't think of a way out of it so he just cut two large portions of cake and smothered them with ice cream with blueberries. Neither spoke much while they devoured their sweet meal.

"Feel better?" said Stuart as he shoved aside his empty bowl.

"A little."

"But?"

"But, it's still going to be a nightmare." Emily pushed her chair back slightly, intertwined her fingers behind her head and rubbed her neck.

"I'm afraid you're going to see a lot of me over the next few weeks."

"You think I don't want to see more of you?"

"Oh I didn't mean that—I just don't want to start over on the jail. It's going to be a ton of work; it's going to take a lot of hand holding to get them to understand, and they're going to want it all done right away." She turned her head to one side and rubbed her temple.

Stuart walked around the table, stood behind her chair, and placed his hands flat against her back just above her shoulder blades, then while gently pressing, he moved his fingers slowly in a circular motion. Both hands moved from side to side, across the top of her shoulders, then down the middle of her back.

"Oh God, that's just what I needed," she whispered.

He turned her toward him, pulled her hand away from her face and said, "Come with me." together they walked to the sunroom couch. "Now lie down."

Emily looked confused but sat down and started to recline on her back. "No, lie down on your stomach," he said.

"Oh, of course," she said, with a little laugh. He sat beside her and placed his hands on her blouse in the middle of her back, applied a little more pressure than before, and continued his caress with long, deliberate, circular strokes. He rolled his long fingers across the top of her shoulders, squeezed as he pulled her shoulders back and then with his palms, pushed forward. Starting at the small of her back, he placed his hands on each side of her spine and rotated his thumbs in an upward motion, gradually making his way to her neck. He repeated the routine three more times, with a lighter touch on each round.

She closed her eyes. He watched her smile fade in and out while she exhaled soft sighs. When he finished, she was silent for a moment, not wanting it to stop.

"Feel better?"

"Almost."

He ran through the routine three more times the exact same way. Unhurried, gradually lightening his hand with each pass.

"Feel better?"

She rolled onto her back facing him. "Yes."

"What were you saying about needing to spend more time here?" he asked. "Emily, I …," He was interrupted by the phone ringing in the study. He ran to answer it. Emily sat up to listen.

"She is?" he said. "Yes, thank God. I understand. Yes I promise. Thanks, Ceda." Stuart returned and sat beside her. "That was Ceda. She found Tad."

"Where? Is she all right?"

"Yes, she's back at the Remington's—the cabin."

"And she's okay?"

"Yes, Ceda made me promise not to go there or try to see her."

"Do you think you can stay away?"

"I don't know."

Construction stopped for three weeks. Rumors of the Indian mound sprang up around town and grew like kudzu running in all directions and entwining itself around any remotely plausible story.

The commissioners set up a meeting with Emily to discuss

the project and explore how to shift the site without having to completely redesign it. She explained to the commissioners, "We're going to rearrange the plan and redesign contours to squeeze the new buildings north of the courthouse. Because it will be visible from town, the walls will be designed to match the stone base of the courthouse."

To be sure the commissioners understood the impact of moving the project and how difficult and expensive it would be, she explained the changes and the expected additional costs in great detail, but the commissioners had already made up their minds. They voted unanimously to go ahead with the change, partly because it was the path of least resistance and the best way to keep the project somewhat close to the original schedule, but also because of the excitement flooding the county about the discovery of an historic site.

CHAPTER TWENTY-EIGHT

There were no clouds or breezes in the air as Emily drove back to the Stone House after her meeting with the commissioners. The late August sun hung in the sky in a mercilessly slow path. All Emily thought about was a shower and the constant flow of cool air through the windows of her room. But, that sweet thought vanished the moment she saw Sergeant Evans sitting on the front steps.

"Ceda it's too hot to sit out here," she said, getting out of the car.

"I'm glad you came. I was just finishing up a note to Stuart. Would you give it to him?" She placed it in a white envelope and licked the glue on the flap.

What's it about?" Emily asked.

"Just some information he wants to have."

Emily wondered why Ceda wouldn't tell her what was on the note.

"I'll be glad to give it to him, but I thought he was here," Emily said.

"His car's around back, but I couldn't find him anywhere. Knowing Stuart, he's probably halfway down the river and over the mountain or who knows where."

"I'll be sure he gets it." As soon as Ceda left, Emily placed the envelope in the south-facing window of the pantry, with the glued edge facing the sun. She then proceeded to change her clothes and cool off. It only took about a half hour for the moist glue, cooked in the sunlight, to let go of the envelope's flap. It was open by the time she returned. She eased the two page, handwritten note out of the envelope.

Stuart,

Forgive the hurried note. I'm working 'til midnight tonight, and I didn't think you wanted me coming by your house that late.

The whole staff met with the Sheriff this morning. He is planning another raid, but not like any of the other ones in the past. This one is serious enough that they have sworn us to absolute secrecy about everything that has anything to do with it. They have given it the stupid code name, "Garbage Dump." Every now and then the Sheriff's Office has had small raids on marijuana farms and things like that, but nothing like the scale of this one. There is a local thug who's working for a drug ring. The ring is hauling in and hiding large amounts of stuff here in the county. We don't know where just yet. The Sheriff asked the captain to make a list of twelve of us on the staff to participate.

I finally did it. I volunteered. Surprised myself, but surprised the Sheriff more. Guess what my first thought was after I did it? I thought how proud you would be of me. I felt the same way I did that day when you and I were kids. Remember when we marched behind Bakkuk all the way to the school yard, and scared the shit out of Lester? Anyway, I felt like that again.

Don't think for a moment that the Sheriff has put this thing together by himself. The SBI, along with the Feds, came to him some time ago for local assistance. He didn't know anything about it before then. He's mostly doing what they asked. The truth is, the raid will be done mostly by the state and federal guys. We're providing support.

Stu, there is something else important that I need to tell you. The guy who is the local worker for the drug ring, it's Daggett. I told you he's been involved in drugs, but I didn't know anything about his involvement with this until today. Detective Nelson told me that everything is starting to point to

*him. I thought you would like to know because of Tad's connection with him
and his sister and living over there with them for a while and all that.*

    Ceda

    She slid it back into the envelope, resealed it, then laid it
on the kitchen table in the carriage house for Stuart .

    "Ceda was here?" Stuart asked, as he walked into the Stone
House holding the note.

    Emily replied, "I don't know what it's about, but she was
on the front steps just finishing that note when I got back." Emily
sprinkled sugar over a small bowl of strawberries and cream then
asked, "So, what did she say?"

    "Don't know, didn't read it yet."

    "Why not?"

    "I was thinking about dinner."

    "Dinner?"

    "It's your turn to cook, but if you don't mind I'd like to
have it in the carriage house tonight."

    "Sure if you cook."

    "Yep, give me an hour."

    Emily noticed mud on his shoes and cuffs. "Did you go
upriver?"

    "Yes."

    "How far?"

    "Couple of miles."

    "As far as Tad's cabin?"

    "Yes."

    "You know, Stu, the note may be about Tad."

    "Maybe," he said.

    "Why else would Ceda leave you a note?"

    "I don't know."

    He watched her take a bite of her strawberries then asked,
"Em, how do you think she would feel if she came back here? I

mean, with another woman in the house."

"Another woman? You mean me?"

"Yes."

"She *knows* me. I'm not a stranger. I'm sure we would be okay. Why?"

"No reason, really. I just don't know how women feel about things like that."

I'm not sure I understand how women feel about anything…" he paused, as he read the note twice. "She says something here about a raid and about needing to talk to me tomorrow." He looked at her. "You were right. It has to do with Tad."

"Are you okay?" she asked.

"Nope. Read the note." Emily sat down and read it, pretending she had never seen it before while Stuart looked out the window.

"Stu?" She said in a soft, low voice.

"No," he said as he shook his head, "I'm not going to try to bring her home.

Dinner that night at the carriage house was short and quiet. Emily knew he needed to be alone and she returned to the Stone House at dusk. She read a book in bed for a couple of hours and went to sleep early.

The old house noises had become so much a part of Emily that none of its creaks and groans disturbed her sleep, but any bump in the night other than the usual ones sat her straight up in bed. Early in the morning, somewhere in the house, but still far away, an undistinguishable rattle opened her eyes. Dawn seeped in the windows. She slipped on a pair of jeans and eased down the stairs. She checked the front door. It was locked, then the rear door. It was unlocked. Walking back down the hall, she noticed the storage room door, under the stair, was not completely shut.

The light switch was on the outside of the room just beside the door frame. She flicked it on and leaned her head inside. Nothing looked out of order. Just as she switched off the light, something caught her eye. She turned the light back on and leaned inside again. Stuart's shotgun was still there, but his rifle was gone. In a flash, she flew across the drive to the carriage house. He was gone. She ran around the house to the garden. A figure of a man walked in the dim light past the end of the pond into the trees. Emily buttoned her pajama top all the way to her neck and ran around the pond, through the woods, and to the river where she saw him on the bank moving upstream.

After a ten minute march, she was only thirty yards behind him at a place where the river narrowed and water cut its own path through solid rock giving out a constant triumphant roar. She hurried faster knowing her footsteps wouldn't be heard over the sound of the river. At the end of a long curve in the stream, low hanging thick trees blocked the morning light. She eased her way through the shaded tree tunnel. At the very end, someone from behind grabbed her around the waist and pulled her back. She twisted toward him and stumbled over a stone and they both fell to the ground.

Whenever someone's head hits a stone, there is always an ugly unmistakable sound. A sickening, dull, hollow knock. They both lay motionless for a moment until she rolled to her knees. From light reflecting off the river, she saw Stu's face. He was flat on his back and his eyes were closed.

"Stu!" she said shaking his chest. He didn't move. Carefully she stroked her fingers through his hair. The left side, just above his ear, was wet and sticky. She crawled over him, lifted him slightly, and rested his head on her lap. Blood trickled down the side of his cheek. Emily unbuttoned the lower three buttons of her pajama top and ripped off a section of cloth, folded it neatly, and pressed it against the wound.

The dawn yielded a cool breeze and a uniform dull grey glow across the sky. He opened his eyes and looked at Emily.

"Stu," she said. "It's me, Emily."

"Oh God. It was you following me?"

"Yes."

"What happened?"

"You grabbed me and hit your head on a rock."

He reached to his head and felt her hand still holding the rag against his wound.

"Wow, I really did hit my head."

"You banged the hell out of it."

He held his hand over hers for a minute then said, "Let's go home."

"Let's see if you can sit up first." She removed the rag as he pushed himself to a sitting position. He winced and lowered his head trying to conceal his pain. Most of the bleeding had stopped.

"What do you think? You want to give it a try?" she asked.

He stood without answering, but immediately bent over and reached for her. She steadied him until he stood erect. He held the cloth against his head with his left hand while she held his right arm and carried his rifle. They walked slowly back to the carriage house.

The first thing he said as he eased into Cleo's old rocking chair was, "I didn't know it was you. I thought you were in bed asleep."

"I thought you were asleep too and I thought you weren't going back upriver anymore."

"I wasn't. I made that decision a long time ago, but Emily, you saw the note from Ceda. You know I couldn't stay in bed after reading something like that. I had to get back to Tad."

"What in the world did you think you were going to do with the rifle?"

"I'm not sure. It just made me feel not so alone."

"Why didn't you come to me?"

"I guess I knew you would talk me out of it."

"I would have *tried*, because going there again was *crazy!* But even more crazy with a *gun!*" she yelled.

"That makes my head hurt."

"*Good!*" she yelled again. " I know you haven't had any sleep, but I want you to stay awake for a while. I'm going to make you breakfast and some hot coffee." She sat with him all morning then made lunch before letting him go up to his bed in the loft.

Emily removed all her hanging clothes from the walnut wardrobe in her bedroom, then with her back against the wall, pushed the tall piece of furniture far enough into the room to slide Stuart's rifle behind it. She managed to inch the cabinet back into place completely concealing the weapon. Finally, she replaced her clothing back into the wardrobe exactly the way they were before.

Jack Hemphill

CHAPTER TWENTY-NINE

"How was your walk?" Stuart asked, as Emily closed the door behind her.

"Felt great. The wind was cold, especially down by the river." She strolled to the fire and warmed her hands.

"Saw the dog pack again," she said. "Must have been fifteen of them plowing past me at full speed without making a sound other than crunching dry leaves—scared me to death. The lead dog was the same one I've seen before.

"Big gray dog, no particular breed, short fur, big jaw, and heavy shoulders?" said Stuart.

"That's him. You've seen him?"

"Yeah, half dozen times. They're all farm dogs, you know. About once a month, the big grey gets them stirred up. Nobody knows why they do it, but he starts it by himself and the pack grows as they run past each farm.

"Watching him run was actually beautiful in a way," she said, "looking straight ahead, never breaking stride, such incredible power. Almost weird."

"Speaking of weird, Chuck Cunningham is on the way out here," he said.

"Why?"

"He said he had a proposition for me."

"Proposition about what?"

"Don't know."

"I think this would be a good time for me to do my grocery shopping," said Emily.

Hot, sweet coffee trickled over Emily's fingers onto the leg of her jeans as she pulled onto the county road. She was trying to drive, sip from her cup, and wave at Chuck Cunningham all at the same time as he turned into the drive.

It was the beginning of a typical weekend, with a morning walk and a ride to the grocery store. Emily loved the fact that Redbriar was a completely different world from what she was used to in Charlotte and Charleston.

Early spring lit the village with pent-up energy. Sudden gusts of clear warm air blew away the stillness of winter. Bright morning sun warmed her face as she walked along Main Street. Faithful dogs followed little boys with torn blue-jeans racing off to unknown adventures and porch-sitters returned to empty chairs carefully placed for greeting everyone who passed by.

The usual collection of old men gathered outside the barber shop. Emily's cheerful "hello" brought an instant smile and nod from each faded soul who had lived long enough to earned his right to a wicker or bentwood seat on the sidewalk. Sweaters bearing every conceivable shade of off-white or beige covered the round and bony shoulders of the gentle cronies, but their individuality was preserved in the style of hat each proudly wore: blue rain hats, Scottish-plaid knit hats, baseball caps, and straw farmer's hats. They had long ago lost any embarrassment about watching her as she walked by.

Children on bikes darted in and out of side streets, oblivious to the adult world surrounding them. Outside the grocery store, another white-haired man dressed in a blue coat, plaid pants, and red tie over a light blue dress shirt passed out cards while leaning on a carved wooden cane. "Hi, I'm Mayor Claude Kinkle," he said, with a slight bow.

"You're Mayor Hinkle?"

"Yep, if you're a citizen of Redbriar, I need your help."

"How can I help you, Mayor?"

"Re-election coming up." He said it with such enthusiasm and clarity that Emily could have mistaken him for a much younger man, but she remembered being told that the mayor had recently passed his ninety-sixth birthday.

"If I survive this office four more years, I'll be the oldest mayor in America," he said, as if he had read her thoughts. "Tell me about you."

"I'm Emily Budd. Nice to meet you" As she shook his hand, she noticed it was both strong and soft. "I live here part of the time, but I'm not registered to vote."

Under his bushy white eyebrows, his eyes lit with a sparkle. "There's still time. Just ask Kitty at the library. She'll get you registered. But, I know now who you are. You're the architect on the new jail."

"Yes, I'm a friend of Stuart Burns. Do you know him?"

"Oh yes, I've known his family forever. Saw him grow up, knew his Mom and Dad, knew his Grandma and Granddad. I understand you're living out there with Stuart. Is that right?" He leaned his head back and peered at her through the bottom of his bifocals.

"Oh ..." Emily was so startled by the question she had to catch her breath before answering. "Well, he's been very generous to let me stay there on my business trips."

"How often do you come?"

"I come on Thursdays through the weekends."

"Then I need to get you registered to vote. Anyway I love that old house. I was once a stone mason. Helped his Granddad build it. Some of my crew were Remington's, Sarah's side of the family."

"You knew them, too?"

"Oh yeah, there were a lot of Remingtons. Back then they were either masons like me or worked in the quarry, until it was shut down."

"Is there anybody in the town you don't know?"

"There was up until few minutes ago, but now that I've met you, sweetheart, I know everybody."

She tilted her head to one side. "Did the Remington's get along at all with Stuart's family back then?" She asked.

"My dear girl, the Remington's are Weavertown people. They never think about getting along with folks like Stuart's family."

"I don't understand."

"Well now, the two families just never saw the need to talk to each other, until Stuart up and married one of them. Anyway, tell him you saw me, okay?"

She waved goodbye and walked to the Redbriar Grocery on the next corner. A young boy ran past her with a baseball mitt dangling from the bat slung over his shoulder. Emily watched him for a moment as he scampered toward a park two blocks away. She saw other kids and parents hurrying to a big open field and into a small stand of bleachers.

She didn't notice the car parked outside the store with a bobcat painted just below the word *Sheriff* on the door.

Emily was one of those shoppers who liked to read all the information on each package before buying. She liked healthy food, except when she was sad, working out a problem, or celebrating. That's when she required a stash of emergency chocolate and snack food.

Redbriar Grocery never needed more than two checkout

lines, and most of the time only one. After taking her place at the back of the line, she looked over her list one last time. There were three other shoppers in front of her. Another grocery clerk scurried to open the second register and the first two people ahead of Emily swerved their baskets to the other counter. That's when she became aware of the tall man in a blue blazer standing in front of her. *I don't believe it*, she thought. The Sheriff glanced back, looked briefly at her, then continued to unload the contents of his cart onto the counter. She stood still at first not wanting to get closer. But realizing her reluctance was too obvious, she closed the gap enough to watch each item he was buying as it hit the counter: two cases of beer, instant coffee, various hot sauces, red pepper flakes, twelve frozen meals of Sloppy Joe's, frozen cheeseburgers, already-cooked fried chicken, hushpuppies, fries, barbeque chips, fully-cooked pork sausage, beef jerky, and a jumbo bag of chocolate chips. She dropped her eyes into her own basket filled with salad, eggs, milk, celery, and so forth, then one more time at the pile of spicy garbage on the counter. The Sheriff obviously had the constitution of a great white shark and could digest nails if he wanted to.

She moved close enough to start placing some of her items on the end of the counter. From there, she saw another pile of the Sheriff's items being bagged by the grocer: paper plates, plastic forks, two hot water bottles, a jumbo jar of aspirin, a copy of *Kozy Kitty Magazine*, two dozen cans of cat food, two large bags of Tidy Cat litter, and a birthday card.

With three paper bags tucked snuggly under his burly arms, he turned and nodded in Emily's direction without making eye contact. She nodded back knowing full well that he wouldn't see it. He left.

She still heard the excitement of the crowd two blocks away as she placed her bags on the back seat of the car. Only a minute later, she was walking into the park, watching families and kids of all ages arriving and running in every direction with all the vibration and energy of a kicked-over ant hill. After finding a seat at the top row of the bleachers she noticed a dozen Dads scattered around the ball field mustering skills they had nearly forgotten, coaching their young Babe Ruths who knew and cared nothing more about baseball than what they saw in their dad's eyes. An older group of teens, mostly boys, circled around a small group of young girls sitting on top of the concrete-block dugout. The teenage boys wiggled, wrestled, tumbled, and yelped competing for attention while the young girls metered it out in just the right proportion to stimulate the boy's hunger for more.

Beyond the ball field, at the parking lot's edge near a creek, Emily noticed a small clump of young men with long, stiff hair and colorless clothing. Whatever they were smoking, they passed around in poorly veiled secrecy while they watched the entrances to the park and milled around each other in slow motion like so many earthworms slithering through wet leaves. Emily glanced at them every five or ten minutes. She found herself imagining a storm cloud drifting over just that part of the park, opening up its flood, and washing them away.

A patient Dad pitched twenty, maybe thirty, balls to his son who had not connected his half-sized bat with a single one. Moms set up lounge chairs and juice tables, while most of the young boys and girls ran with exhaustless enthusiasm.

A sudden screeching of tires followed by an earth-vibrating roar caused Emily's head to snap around in time to see a super-loaded blue Ford flying through the back entrance, spewing dust in a towering plume. Literally airborne at every pot hole and bump in the road, the car sped through the parking area behind the bleachers. The bobcat's head and writing on the door were a blur, but she recognized the large square profile of the Sheriff's head.

The slimy bunch near the creek dropped their smokes and ran toward the woods as soon they heard the roar of the Sheriff's car. With a fish-tail stop, the Sheriff jumped out and launched immediately into a full sprint, ran to the edge of the woods by the creek, disappeared for a few minutes, then in a triumphant march, returned to his car.

After parking behind the dugout, the Sheriff briefly surveyed the crowd. Emily pulled the collar of her windbreaker over her nose. With one eye, she watched him open his trunk and remove what appeared to be a body bag. Five minutes after he disappeared into the little room behind the dugout, he bounded out in blue jeans, long-sleeved jersey, and a baseball cap. Five claps of his meaty hands and two long whistles across his fingers resulted in the entire crowd coming to a stop. Four Dads positioned themselves in what were apparently prearranged posts around the field and each kid on the field ran obediently to their assigned coach. One posted at the base, two in the outfield, one in the bullpen beyond the dugout, and one at home plate for batting practice with the Sheriff.

The Sheriff's big bag contained bats and balls which he dumped beside home plate before taking his place at the pitcher's mound. Emily watched each young batter to see how he would react to the gorilla in front of him. After every pitch, the Sheriff gave a critique to the boy at home base who was trying to connect with the Sheriff's carefully placed pitches. Sometimes he would come forward and correct the position and stance by moving the child's feet with his hand or pushing gently down on the batter's shoulders while nudging the back of his knees and lifting his elbows. His words were spoken so softly that Emily couldn't hear most of what he was saying, but each child improved noticeably during the session. *Where did this come from?* She thought. Where is the monster, the sheriff from the Black Lagoon, Attila-the-Sheriff that I thought I knew?

When all eight batters had finished, five more claps and two more whistles caused each of the kids in the five locations to rotate clockwise to the next respective post for a different type of training. Over an hour, she watched him coach each young player, patiently, quietly, genuinely pleased with each improvement. As soon as all players had gone through all five posts, the Sheriff disappeared again into the dugout, then reappeared in his blue blazer and gray pants, got in his car and streaked away through the front entrance.

The predator's predator, the icon of male aggressive energy was becoming human.

On the way back to the Stone House where the road and river parted, she saw the County Manager returning to town in his blue pickup. She slowed to a near stop, rolled down her window and waved, but he whizzed by without seeing her.

Off to her left, a dog limped up a dirt road no doubt going home after his run. Emily's mind immediately remembered the pack she had seen earlier that morning as it followed the big dog into the river, and hopped over rocks to the opposite bank. The last dog, a small terrier with skinny legs and little feet, couldn't quite make the jumps and ended up being washed into deeper water. His little dog paddle was useless against the current. None of the others noticed or cared to look back as they scaled the next mountain and galloped out of sight. Their only mind was keeping up with the leader. Nothing else existed. The little guy soon became just a white spot near the river's bend washed against large rocks, where he squirmed out of the water and hopped to the far bank. Without a moments rest, joyfully, he dashed up the hill and out of sight using whatever strength he had left to rejoin the pack.

Emily finally concluded that what she had been watching all morning, both in the woods and at the ball park, was a perfect guy's morning out—a kind of lemming run with all paws beating the ground in innocent rhythm behind a well-meaning, but flawed leader on a righteous mission, with a purpose known only to him.

Emily put her groceries in the pantry and refrigerator, then looked for Stuart, but he wasn't in the Stone House or carriage house. She found Possum in the barn spreading a thin line of a pesticide around the inside perimeter. "Where's Stuart?"

"Don't know. Thought I saw him going toward the river a while ago."

Shuffling down the gulley, she saw him by the river throwing something into the water. Secretly she settled in a spot just above the flat rock concealed by a boulder and low bushes. He gathered a handful of stones, threw them one by one into the river, gathered another pile and repeated the ritual all over again.

Emily loved watching him when he didn't know it. He was wearing blue jeans and a long-sleeved jersey. A folded sweatshirt and his shoes and socks were lying on the rock behind him. He was methodical and self-controlled most of the time, but she never saw him when he didn't seem to have something trapped in his mind wanting out, and every now and then it burst free.

After watching him for ten minutes, his pile of rocks was down to the last two. She picked up a rock and tossed it high in the air simultaneously with his throw. He watched his stone splash and before he could pick up the other one, Emily's rock landed with a loud splash beside his. He looked for a moment without taking his eyes off the rippling water, then picked up the last stone. Again she tossed a rock into the air in sync with his. Once again his splash was followed by a larger one near the same spot. He stood motionless, looked in all directions, then slowly turned around. The moment he spotted her he charged up the hill. With twenty long strides, he caught her, picked her up and flopped her over his shoulder. She beat his back with her fists as he carried her to the edge of the flat rock, lifting her in the air until she screamed. Then the laughter he was holding inside started pouring out. He laughed so hard he had to put her down before he fell to his knees. She got up and kicked him, ran to the other side of the rock, then sat down and tried to hold back her own laughter.

"I just wish you could have seen your face."

"Did I look frustrated?"

"No, you looked like a confused country boy."

"Well, I *am* a country boy, and I like to throw rocks when I'm frustrated *and* when I'm confused."

She walked back to him. "What are you frustrated about?"

He sat down at the edge of the rock, picked up another stone, and threw it. "After Cunningham left, I walked to the Remington cabin."

"Why?"

"You know why."

"Did you see her?"

"No, I sat under a tree on this side of the river, well hidden. No one came or went. Watched clothes flapped on the line behind the house. Couldn't tell if they were hers."

"Stu, you promised me and Ceda you wouldn't do it. What would Tad think if she saw you?"

He threw another stone.

"Are you going to try again?" He didn't answer.

"What did Cunningham say when he was here?" she asked.

He shook his head. "Of all the things they could have asked me to do, what do you think they want?"

"Money?"

"That would be too easy. They want to honor Sheriff Hodges by putting a new portrait of him in the courthouse."

"They want you to do it?"

"Yep."

"Well, that shouldn't have taken you long to answer."

"That's the problem. I haven't answered him yet."

"Why not?"

"I don't know. That's what I can't figure out. I don't want to have anything to do with Lester, and can you imagine sitting with him for hours painting his sandpaper face?"

"Then don't do it! What's the big deal?"

"Doing it would be torture, but every time I started to say no, I stopped myself. He gave me plenty of time and no pressure, but I told him I'd get back to him tomorrow."

"Well, guess who I just saw at the grocery store."

They each picked up stones and tossed them into the river.

Jack Hemphill

CHAPTER THIRTY

TAD

Beside the Redbriar River, I watched the new jail rising out of freshly sculpted earth. Gray foundations and concrete slabs gave birth to rows of steel bars defining future walls. The river's bank was my private conduit to every place I needed to go.

It was only a three mile walk downriver to Possum's place. His chainsaw roared while billows of white smoke swirled around him. He didn't see me standing behind him. I said, "Good morning, Possum."

He let out a bark like an old dog, then, slightly embarrassed, laughed. "Kathleen!" He was the only one that called me by my real name. "How long you been there?" He asked.

"Just a few minutes."

"So what the hell brings you back this way?"

"I've got a job I want to ask you to do."

"Well, hell yeah, sure!"

"I haven't even told you what it is yet."

"Okay, what is it?"

"You know I've been staying with my cousins."

"Yep."

"I sleep in their spare bedroom. It's got a place in the corner where the floor is sagging and I was wondering if you would fix it."

"Well, hell yeah, sure!"

"I can pay you. My grandmother gave me a small bank account that I haven't used up yet."

"Oh, don't worry about the cost, we'll figger it out. Can I come take a look at it?"

"Yes, please."

"How about I drive you back over there now?" he said.

"Great."

In spite of the cool breeze, a light layer of sawdust clung to the sweat on his neck. He picked up his coat from the woodpile and tossed it in the back of his truck, rubbed his hair and neck, and shook off the loose chips from his clothing. The inside of his truck had a smell that reminded me of the days when I was little and Possum took me for rides to town and around the farm. It brought back old, sweet memories even though the odor was the result of two decades of smoke settling into every surface in the cab. He still displayed a long silver chain fastened to the mirror dangling a set of dice over the head of a plastic Jesus glued to the dashboard. The plastic was the kind that glowed in the dark at night.

"So, Kathleen, how you been?"

"I'm okay," I said.

"Been a long time since I've seen you."

"I know."

"God, you look more than ever like your mother."

"Yeah, well, I don't think about it that much. I'm kind of in limbo, I mean, I don't know what I'll do next, but my cousins have been real nice to me. That's why I want to fix their floor."

At the end of the dirt road, Possum turned right toward town and followed the long bend around the base of the east side of Mount Tsula.

"Kathleen," he gave me a fatherly glance, "you got any

friends? I mean other than your cousins?"

"There's a girl I met in jail. I actually lived with her and her weird friends for a while, but other than those guys and my cousins, I don't really know anybody. Mostly I stay by myself."

As we passed the mountain, the road bent sharply back to the left. The Stone House stood two hundred yards away. I wouldn't look at it, but stared at the dashboard until the house was well out of sight. I know he noticed.

"Someday, sweetie, you're gonna have to do it." He waited for me to look at him before finishing. "Someday you're going to have to see him."

I tried to speak, but all that came out was air. Finally, I pushed out the words, "Maybe some things can't be done."

A covered bridge separates Redbriar from Weavertown. Constant clapping of tires rolling over wooden planks made talking impossible the moment we entered the dark wooden tunnel. We didn't pick up our conversation again until we had driven two miles into the Weavertown side of the river. Possum knew I was thinking of Mom. "You miss her don't you?" he said. I nodded yes. He nodded back and said, "I do too."

He slowed down to turn into the dirt drive above my cousin's cabin. "I still see her sometimes," he said with a sandy whisper. I didn't know what he was talking about at first. "Stuart and Emily think I'm a little mushy in the head when I tell them about things I see."

"What do you see?" I asked.

"Sarah... at the Stone House. Sometimes I see her reflection in the window glass. Sometimes she's walking across the far end of the garden. I can hear her laughing in the pantry and I swear sometimes I hear her crying in the morning."

"Possum!" I wanted him to stop and at the same time, I wanted to hear more.

"I don't mean to scare you none," he said.

"No, I'm not scared. It's just…hard for me to talk about her," I said. "The last time I was with her she was mad at me, really mad. We never made up. I wanted to tell her I was sorry or something, but never had a chance. I don't want to picture her crying."

"I thought I should just tell you what I see sometimes at the Stone House…just in case…you know."

"What?"

"I mean in case you ever come back to live there." I looked out the window, even though there was nothing to see but the blur of thick bushes as Possum bounced his truck down the road.

All the cousins were away at work. Possum parked his truck in front of the porch. With his fingernails, he carefully flicked ashes from the stub between his lips. It had been ten years since he had been in the cottage. He said that everything was exactly as he remembered. Bare wood floor with an oval hooked rug in the middle. A large couch and rocking chair huddled in front of a coffee table with a TV on top. In front of the fireplace stood an old black woodstove with a small stack of logs beside it. The fire had gone out but the stove was still warm. The kitchen was off the living room to the right and a door to the left led to large hall with four bedrooms and a single bath beyond. As soon as we walked into my room, the temperature was a good twenty degrees cooler. The floor bounced as he walked across it. "Yep, you definitely need to fix this; I'm going to check under the house." As he walked out, he noticed the sketches and paintings scattered around the room on the floor and on my bed. A makeshift easel sat near the window made out of wooden pickets and a cross piece of an old fence.

In less than ten minutes he returned with the verdict, "Rotten sill, right in the corner- no big deal. The sill sits on a big stone foundation. I can cut out the old stuff and replace it in no time."

"Tell me how much I need to pay you."

"Materials, not more than fifty dollars, but the cost for my *time* will be considerably more."

"How much?"

"It will cost you nothing but a favor."

"Okay. What?"

"I want you to write your Dad a note. Just tell him you're okay. That's all."

"Possum," I said, with a tone of finality.

"Just say, 'I'm doing alright,'" Possum said, as he turned his palms upward.

"Why are you doing this to me?"

"I don't know."

"I'll do it when I'm ready. If I don't ever get ready, I'll pay you something for the work."

"Deal." He blew smoke straight up.

After he left, I looked through some of my drawings before making a fresh cup of tea and warming an old biscuit. When I walked out to sit on the steps, something grabbed my attention. Possum had unloaded then entire truck-load of firewood from his truck and stacked near the house.

Sitting on the top step, I buttoned my coat tightly against my neck. It was cold and the hot cup felt good in my hands and the tea warmed the inside of my chest. The sound of wind swaying the bushy laurel around the house was interrupted by a rumble of heavy wheels over gravel in the drive. I thought it would be one of the cousins coming home, but didn't recognize the heavy black truck making its way around the final turn. Still sitting, clutching my cup, the truck stopped directly in front of me. The tinted window slowly lowered. A head with fuzzy blond hair the size of a squirrel's nest leaned out the window and a familiar voice said, "Well, hello sugar. How the hell you been?"

"Novie, look at you! Where'd you get the fancy truck?"

"It's Daggett's. Brand new. Lets me borrow it," she said, as she slid out the door to the ground. "You doing alright?"

"Yep, what you see is pretty much my life right now. "

"Any more of whatever's in that cup?"

"Sure, come on in. I just have to get a little firewood." We each grabbed an armful of wood, and with a small hatchet on the hearth, I sliced off a dozen slivers of wood to re-start the fire. Novie sat on the couch with one foot on the coffee table.

"So, it looks like you're doing okay."

"Yeah, but I can't stay here forever. How's Daggett?"

"Well the good news is he's no more obnoxious than when you saw him last."

"That's the good news?"

"I guess the other good thing is that he's not around as much as he used to be."

"That's good."

"He goes all the way down to Cherokee County once a week and gives me a break for a few days."

"The rest of the gang still there?"

"Yeah, except for Miller."

"What happened to him?"

"Just disappeared, but I always knew he'd go that way. He's about as clever as tree moss. Are you still drawing?"

"Yeah. Drawing and painting. I got more time than I know what to do with."

"Tad, got to ask a favor." Novie leaned forward and looked at her hands for a moment, then at me. "I'm helping Daggett with something right now."

"What ?"

'Well, you know he makes a lot of money."

"Yes."

"But I don't get involved with whatever it is. Okay, I have

an idea what it is, but I don't worry about it. Dealing with that kind of stuff is what he does and I don't ask no questions about it. He just needs for me to take his truck to him sometimes and things like that."

"What's the favor?"

"For about a year, I've been driving Daggett's truck once a week to a place on the other side of Cherokee County near Murphy. I swap the truck for a car and drive it back here. That's about it, but now he wants me to drive the truck from here to there, leave it for an hour with him, then drive the truck *and* a car back here."

"How are you going to do that?"

"That's where you can help."

"You want me to drive?"

"Yes. This is how it would work. Each week, Daggett would drive the truck to Murphy. Later we would both drive the car there to the truck then I drive the car here and you drive the truck back here."

"Why would I drive the truck?"

Because if you do this for us, just until the end of the year, he'll give you the truck."

"You said it's brand new!"

"It's one-year old, but it'll be yours by January if you'll help."

"Why me? He's got a lot of friends that could help."

"Because I asked him to let you do it."

"And he said okay?"

"No, he said he wasn't sure if he could trust you."

"Why?"

"Because your Dad came and pulled you out of the farm house."

"Does he know I wasn't even conscious and the first thing I did when I woke up in the Stone House was run away? I never

239

even saw my Dad then and haven't talked to him in years."

"I'm sure that's true, sugar. I told him I trusted you. He said okay."

"I hope you're getting something out of all this."

"He's paid me well—I'm stashing it away. When I have enough, you and Daggett and Jefferson County will never see me again."

"If I do this, where would I take the truck?"

"You would follow me from Murphy back to Jefferson County to a place where you would leave the truck and then ride with me in the car back here. Daggett will come back with somebody else and early the next week somebody will drive him back to Murphy. That's it. It's a six-hour round trip once a week for us. That's all we have to do."

"And by the end of the year, the truck is mine?"

"It's yours. And you'll be safe, don't worry, but if you're nervous, carry a gun in your bag. *I* do. Or, keep it in the glove compartment."

"I have one, but I've never used it. It's still in the cloth bag that it came in."

"Do whatever you're comfortable with."

Tad stood and walked to the window, looked at the black shiny hunk of steel in the driveway, and asked, "When are you thinking about getting started?"

"What are you doing right now?"

Possum was made of mountain soil mixed with granite and clay. He was comfortable with himself and his life, and if he ever felt pain of any kind, he never showed it. In addition to that, he kept his personal feelings and fears, if he had any, well hidden. But I know he loved my family. I also know he enjoyed having me there. I think when we lived on the farm, Possum found excuses to come around and check on me to see what I was doing. He taught me to drive a tractor and his truck as soon as I was tall enough for my feet to touch the pedals.

That was the only truck I had ever driven before the day Novie pulled up at my cousin's house. I drove her black monster for months. Kept the gun in its pouch under the seat with a box of bullets in my jacket. I'm not sure I really knew how to load it or how to shoot it other than just pull the trigger. I'm sure I'll never see Novie again and I'll never know why she trusted me. Outside of my family, she was the closest thing I knew as a friend. Like her brother, Novie was tall, but unlike him, she was big boned. She carried her considerable bulk well. Her skin was pink and smooth. She loved to wear rings. Had one for each finger including her left thumb. All the rings were silver with various colored stones. She never mentioned having a boy friend or any kind of romance, but I think she always wanted to be loved. There was never a moment, however, when she didn't have her chin stuck out as if daring everybody to take a shot at it. But, she's gone for good now, and I'm happy for her. I have no doubt that she's living somewhere far away, foreign and exotic with more money than she will ever need for the rest of her life.

Like Novie, I too wanted to be loved. I admired her strength and wished I had her ability to take control of life, but more than anything else, I prayed I would never end up like her.

Jack Hemphill

CHAPTER THIRTY-ONE

STUART

Sheriff Hodges pounded his fist twice on the front door.

"Stuart is expecting you," I heard Emily say, as she opened the door. His heavy boots scraped across the floor with a determination to get past the event we both dreaded. A bright fire fluttered in the fireplace. I was sitting on the couch, pretending not to notice him and I didn't look up until Hodges walked halfway across the room. I stood. We glared at each other for an awkward moment until I said his name.

He replied, "Let's get it over with."

"Have a seat." The Sheriff plopped in a chair near the couch and stared across the room as I talked.

I heard Emily tiptoeing through the living room trying to hear what was being said.

"It usually takes three sittings for me to do this kind of portrait," I said "but to save time; I've sketched up a few suggested poses and compositions. If we can agree on that much, we can get on with it faster." I opened to the first sheet in a large sketch pad on the coffee table. "These are just conceptual sketches of ideas, so feel free to comment." Receiving no response, I flipped to the second, then the third, and the fourth with no reaction from the

Sheriff. "As you can see, I'm looking for a fairly formal setting such as an arrangement with you at the front of the courtroom with the county seal and flag behind you. I also suggest using raised wood paneling like you see all over the courthouse as a background."

"I got somethin' else in mind," Hodges grunted. "How about a picture of me in my jail with my back against the black iron bars. I want to be in uniform and I want to be turned slightly to the left to display my forty-five pistol."

"I always picture you the way you're dressed right now, in your navy blazer, blue shirt and tie. That's the way I think everybody would expect you to look. I think it's the kind of pose the commissioners want."

"What the commissioners want is a portrait of me."

The Sheriff bent forward stretching his meatloaf forearms across his knees and folding his hands pretending he was willing to listen. I continued, "I agree on the idea that you should be turned slightly to one side...to the left if that's what you want. I agree that you should be standing, but it's got to have *dignity*."

Hodges shook his head and glanced at the ceiling then said, "What the hell is the matter with you? You know perfectly well I'm no dignified kind of guy. I don't understand what's so hard about getting this concept—it's a portrait of *me*!"

"You know what?" I said. "If this portrait ever gets done, it's going to be a picture of you. You're right. But it's going to have my name on it. Your face and my name locked together permanently on display. It's not all about you, Lester."

I walked to the fireplace, picked up a long iron poker and adjusted the burning logs while waiting for the Sheriff's response.

"Dignified?" Hodges stood. "What the hell is *dignified*?"

"I mean formal. The commissioners want something they can be proud of," I said.

"They're proud of me, Burns. Didn't you know that?" I

244

saw him fighting to conceal a slight flash from his lower teeth—a little glimpse of self-satisfaction he couldn't quite hide.

"They're not proud of you, they're scared of you,"

After another arrogant flicker crossed his face, he said, "What's the difference?"

"*Dignity*."

"Everybody knows who I am. Everybody knows what I'm about. Your portrait can't change that. You're either going to paint me or we're wasting each other's time.

"Look at me, Stuart. What do you see?" He strutted toward me with his hands extended outward. "What kind of face do you think I have? How about my hands or my eyes? What do you see?"

I tightened my fingers around the poker, turned, and shoved it with both hands into the fire, then shook the logs until they glowed red while white sparks stampeded up the chimney. I closed my eyes and exhaled "Of course, it has to be you," I said in a pseudo-patient voice.

"You want to paint me? Paint what you see,"

"Yes, it has to be you," I repeated, "but, Lester, if I do this, I'm going to paint a portrait of what you are, not what you *think* you are."

Hodges rocked his head back, closed his eyes, and sucked in his thoughts until they finally erupted like an overdue volcano, "You think you know me? You don't!"

"I know you well enough have an opinion."

"They didn't hire you to have an opinion; they hired you to paint *me*."

"Alright, let's say I don't know you. How do you want people to remember you?"

"Hey, anybody who ever met me never forgets me, just the way I am. Just like this." He pushed closer again. The flickering light from the fire exaggerated the craters in his face.

I walked across the room, looked through the window at the mountain, then down at the unfinished painting of Tad leaning against the wall.

"What's-a-matter, Burns, you don't want to get close to me?"

"No , I don't," I said.

"Neither does anybody who was ever dragged into my jail. And they don't forget me and they don't want to come back once they get out—understand ?"

"No." I turned toward the window again and watched a gray cloud swallow the top of the mountain. Then with my shoulder against the glass, in a barely controlled voice, I said, "So all they remember about you is their own fear; is that what you're saying?"

"Are you going to paint me or not?"

"Maybe not."

"Sheriff Hodges looked at his shoes and said in a near whisper, "No, it's not just their fear of me. After they've been with me they remember something else."

"What?"

"Themselves."

"What does *that* mean, Lester? How does that relate to your portrait?"

"You know how many people have gone through this jail since I've been Sheriff?"

I didn't answer.

"Thousands!" snapped Hodges. "I've given them all something burned-in so deep they can't forget it or me—ever."

"I'm sure they'd like to forget you, Lester."

He slammed his fist on the coffee table and blurted out, "I'm gonna to tell you what I am, Stuart, and you tell me if you gonna paint it!"

Feeling triumphant I walked to my stool, sat down, crossed my arms, and fired back, "Well then, for God's sake, tell me what the hell you are."

Hodges exploded, "*Their god-damned salvation!*"

That was my first real peep into the padded cell of his windowless mind. He stomped across the room and looked downriver for a full minute. His high-pitched wheezing with every breath slowly softened. He noticed the unfinished painting of Tad against the wall. As he bent forward to get a closer look, I hurried over, pulled the painting away from him, and laid it beside the fireplace, facing the wall. Hodges strolled back to the couch and said quietly, "She's a beautiful kid."

Still standing by the fireplace, I turned away from him, picked up the poker and readjusted the logs once again. Hodges tapped on the back of my drawing pad with the nail of his index finger, and said, "Get rid of the fagg poses and do my portrait."

Emily, still standing in the foyer, couldn't hear the last few minutes of our conversation. The Sheriff clomped back through the rooms and nodded to her as he let himself out.

"How did it go?" she asked.

"He's coming back in two weeks for me to sketch his face, then one more time to do the final color. I'm still not sure about the background. I'll figure that out later."

"Are you going to be able to do it?"

"I don't know."

The second sitting was easier. We had already agreed the pose would require the sheriff to turn slightly to the left. With as little conversation as possible, we were able to finish the drawing of his face and outline of his body, then quickly escape from each other.

CHAPTER THIRTY-TWO

Emily's Saturday morning routine was so consistent that Stuart knew exactly when she would be rounding the south side of Mount Tsula. Each week he enjoyed watching from her bedroom window with a pair of binoculars focused on a little opening in the trees that exposed thirty feet of the old trail. Even at the end of her hike, she had a youthful bounce with an exaggerated, almost joyful, swing to her arms. Once she passed that spot on the mountain it took her exactly five minutes to get home—five minutes for him to put the binoculars away and get back to his place at his easel.

Stuart pretended not to feel the cold wind whipping through the door as Emily shuffled from the deck into the sunroom. She had become used to the fact that, when he was painting, the rest of the world didn't exist until something snapped him back, but she was so glad to see him painting again she waited a little longer than usual. He was struggling with the background of the Sheriff's portrait. His tubes were arranged in color order on his side table. She instinctively looked for the blue-green colors and noticed one of them was the French tube with the words, "Verte de Paris." Finally what she had to say couldn't wait any more. "Stu," she said softly.

"Emily, you're back already," he said acting like he was

surprised I'll bet it's cold out there."

"It is, but there's something else out there I need to tell you about."

"What is it?

"I was walking on the back side of the mountain. Because of the wind, I took the path around the east side instead of my usual hike by the river. I was about maybe fifty yards from the dirt road when I heard the sound of a truck straining its way up the mountain."

"No one should be up there. I've got 'no trespassing' signs all over that trail." Stuart wrapped his wet brushes in a rag and put them on the edge of the easel, a sure sign he wanted to hear what she had to say.

"I saw a blue truck slowly bounce up the trail. It's the first time I've ever seen anybody on that mountain before, much less a truck hauling something heavy."

"Did you see what it was carrying?"

"Not right away, but I hid behind a bush and after the driver passed by, I followed him up the road for, I don't know, a quarter of a mile. I saw two men unloading barrels and other stuff in a little clearing near the road."

"Emily, tell me they didn't see you."

"They didn't, I turned around and came straight here." Stuart walked to the window and looked up at the mountain.

"I've got to go see what they're doing."

"Shouldn't the Sheriff's office or somebody like that go instead?"

"The only person I can call is Ceda and I'm not going to get her involved unless I know what's going on." He picked up his jacket from the couch and together they walked through the house to the foyer. "Hold up a second," he said. Emily waited while he rummaged around in the storage room. When he came out, he was carrying a double- barreled shotgun. "It's not very accurate, but it'll get their attention."

Less than a minute after they pulled out of the driveway and headed around the mountain on the county road, they passed an old blue truck driving toward town. "That's it!" she screamed.

"I know that truck. *And*, I know who was driving it, too."

"Who?"

"One of the Remingtons."

"Which one?"

"I don't know for sure, but probably Joe. They all drive that ugly wreck."

He turned his pickup onto the old logging road. The truck struggled its way up the steep trail. Emily held on to the seat with one hand and put the other hand on the cab's ceiling. Close to three quarters of the way up the mountain she recognized the place where Remington had parked.

"That's it—over there." She pointed off the road to the right. They both got out. He brought his shotgun with him.

"You can see they carried something through the brush." They followed a trail of broken bushes and bent branches for another twenty yards until they reached a little clearing beside a small stream. Several large rocks had been dragged to a spot near the stream, forming a stone circle. A rusted barrel about eighteen inches in diameter had been placed on top of it. Another barrel about thirty inches wide was placed on the ground beside it. From the smaller barrel a four inch pipe ran down at an angle into the wider wooden barrel on the ground.

"What in the world is that?" she asked.

"Typical Jefferson County still."

"Typical?"

"Bakkuk and I used to find these things all the time in the most remote places. Always by a small stream like this."

"They're going to make moonshine?"

"No. The Remington's have plenty of places to hide stills on their own property. They don't have to come to my mountain to do that."

"Then, what are they doing?"

"They want me to have one on *my* property. Even today, every now and then, you hear of someone who got arrested for having a still somewhere on his land. He doesn't even have to be making anything in it. I'll bet that's what they want."

"Who would find it way back here?"

"My guess is whoever in the Sheriff's office takes the anonymous call."

"What call?"

"The one that is going to be made by the Remingtons sometime today."

"Okay, now don't you think it's time to call Ceda?" she asked.

"Yep."

"What do you think she'll do?"

"Let's see what she says. You know I can't just report to the Sheriff's office that I've got a still on my property. The Sheriff would love to consider that a confession."

Fifteen minutes after finishing her shift at the jail, Ceda was walking through Stuart's front door. Stuart and Emily were in the kitchen. "Come on back Ceda," he called out.

Ceda was in uniform and carried a small notebook tucked into her belt. "Okay, I checked with Sergeant Maston and, yes, he did receive an anonymous tip that there was a still near the logging trail on Mt. Tsula."

"I'm being set up. Emily saw the Remington boys up there today. When I drove up the old logging trail, we found a barrel-type still."

"Emily, how do you know it was the Remington boys?" Ceda asked.

"Stu was with me when we saw them leaving in their truck."

"Stu, is that the first time you've seen any of them since that day at the cemetery?" Ceda asked.

"Yes. I haven't seen them or heard anything about them since then. So, what's next?"

"Stuart, I want you to file a trespassing complaint right away. Just say you've seen someone up there. You don't know who. That way I can officially check it out based on your request and not based on the report of a still up there."

"How is that going to help?"

"You make the call. I can arrange it so Sergeant Maston and I will check it out, then all that equipment up there's going to disappear."

"How?"

"Magic. You're just a property owner who is concerned about trespassers on your property."

"Ceda, I really…"

"Shutup," she said, as she thumped his stomach with her notebook. "You can file your complaint over the phone. Give me time to get back to the Sheriff's office." Ceda left, looking like a deputy sheriff who had finally been given a chance to enjoy her job.

Serious weather comes to the North Carolina mountains by way of the Gulf of Mexico. After skipping over Louisiana, Mississippi, and Tennessee, it slides into Appalachia with high, gray clouds that gradually lower and thicken over a period of a day or so.

Stuart stacked nearly a cord of wood in a bin close to the deck. By sundown, the cool air had become heavy and misty and he brought in extra logs for the fire. It was Emily's turn to cook dinner and she had placed two settings on the coffee table in front of the couch.

"My favorite!" he said, as she carried in dinner trays.

"Okay, they're just burgers again, but they're special tonight. They're bacon-cheeseburgers. You're going to love them. I also made potato salad and beans."

"Sounds great."

All thoughts of the Remingtons disappeared along with the sunlight. The only glow in the room was the fire.

Stuart noticed Emily was a little more quiet than usual. As they started their second cup of coffee after dinner, he watched her face, waiting for her to speak.

"Stu, there's something I wanted to talk about with you."

"I know—I can always tell when you are stewing over something."

"How can you tell?"

"The corners of your lips get tight"

"Well you know my project here has another eighteen months to go,"

"Yep, a good long way to go."

"My office has been negotiating with the city of Asheville to do a master development plan for the school system. It's a project that will take some years." She stopped and sipped her coffee. "They want me to open a small office in Asheville to be the client contact, work out the building program with them, and be there during the construction phases."

"Emily, that's great! When will it begin?"

"Well, actually it begins on Monday morning."

"This Monday?"

"Yes."

"How long have you known about this?"

"Well, a while."

"How long is 'a while?"

"A few months."

"*Months*? Why didn't you say something about it?"

"I was sort of waiting for the right time."

"I don't understand. The right time for what?"

"Well I want to…I mean I would like to keep on staying here. It's only about an hour's drive to where my office will be."

Stuart put down his cup, paused, then gave a slight gesture with both fists. "Damn it. I thought we went through this. Why did you think you had to ask?"

"I don't really know, except I'll be living here full time."

"Stay! Stay here. Stay with me. You don't ever have to mention it again."

"Stuart, I'm not blind and I'm not deaf. I know what people in Redbriar and Weavertown are saying about my staying here for so long. We have never talked about it, but I know what they are saying about us. I mean, it doesn't bother me, but it's your town."

"You know me by now— at least I thought you did. You should know I have never given the tiniest damn about what they think about anything. My friends here are going to stick with me. The rest of them never liked me anyway. I honestly believe you've been happy here the last eighteen months and you…just stay—stay with me and don't worry about it." They both sat for a while and listened to the fire. Talking with each other had always been as easy as sipping coffee, but they never discussed the future.

"Has your mother ever gotten used to your being here?" he asked.

"No and she never tires of asking questions about you."

They settled back on the couch, laughed about what Ceda would do with the Remington boys, the progress of the jail, cheeseburgers, and Emily's new office. The logs shifted in the fire shooting sparks and smoke up the chimney while fiery fingers found new places to curl around the embers. After another hour, or so, Emily realized she had been doing all the talking. She laid her head on his shoulder. He instinctively lifted his arm and pulled her against the side of his chest. She closed her eyes. He watched the fire.

A dull glow of morning light pushed its way into the dense mist that had settled over the county. Emily's return to consciousness was as slow as the dawn. With her right hand, she felt the silk lining of a blanket placed over her during the night. Her left hand gripped a pillow tucked under her head. Outside, the rising sun found a hole in the clouds, causing the early morning mist to glow as if each one of the billion-billion droplets radiated its own light.

Fresh logs were placed on the fire which popped and snapped with new energy. Stuart was again busy at his easel and had turned it so he faced Emily. She stood and wrapped the crimson blanket around her with the silk lining draped over the top of her head. He continued to paint as she walked to his side. The Sheriff's portrait was on the floor leaning against the easel. She looked over the half-blank canvas Stuart just started. It was a composition of her curled in the red blanket, on the couch, by the fire. Without taking his eyes off the canvas, he gave her an easy smile. The image had already become so fixed in his mind that he continued to paint without looking at her. Walking outside to the edge of the deck, she leaned over the rail into the glowing air and raised her arm above her head, hand facing outward. The deck had been designed as a cantilever, extending twelve feet from the structure of the house without any supporting columns below. The mist flowed around her, over her, and under her. She touched infinity.

Stuart, clutching his brush while he added new layers of paint on the canvas, couldn't see Emily behind him standing outside his window. Covered in red, she stood out in stark contrast with the ever-brightening glow of moist air swirling around her.

She pulled the blanket tighter against the chill, walked to the glass, and watched him paint the red figure in his mind.

Joe Remington was slammed face down on the Booking Office counter. Blood trickled from the corner of his mouth and from a small wound beside his right eye. Both eyes were swollen shut and both hands were cuffed behind his back. Ceda clasped his shoulders while Sergeant Mastin removed the cuffs. The moment Remington felt the handcuffs drop off he sprang from the counter, knocked Sergeant Mastin down and ran toward the door. Ceda grabbed the back of his jacket and pushed him over a bench then planted her knee in his back until Sergeant Mastin cuffed his hands to his feet. Together they dragged him kicking and screaming into a holding cell and left him on the floor.

Captain Morgan heard the fight from his office and came running. "That sounded like Joe Remington." he said.

"Yes, what's left of him," said Sergeant Mastin.

"What happened?"

"We received a tipoff that he had a still behind his barn."

"His barn in Weavertown?"

"Yes."

"What kind of fool would have a still on the outskirts of Weavertown?"

"The kind we got locked in our holding cell."

"Why the fight? "

"When we asked him about it, he went bonkers. He claims it's a setup."

"Why would he say that?"

"Because he's a fool. I had to charge him with resisting arrest as well as owning a still.

By three that afternoon, Joe had seen the magistrate, posted bail, and was gone.

Captain Morgan read over Sergeant Evan's arrest report

and asked Sergeant Mastin if he agreed with it.

"That's the third time I've arrested that boy," said the sergeant. "He's rowdy as hell, but that's the first time I've seen him go psycho like that."

"What happened?" asked the captain.

"I don't know. When we confiscated his still, it was just lying beside his barn, not hooked up or nothing. Looked like it had been used, but obviously not there in that location. Just don't know how he could be so stupid as to leave it out in the open."

"You know this whole affair will cost that boy around $10,000. That's a year's pay for a Remington."

CHAPTER THIRTY-THREE

The gathering clouds descended as mist that thickened into light rain and developed into a storm that increased in strength each day for seven days until it was a blinding, driving wall of water. A cold front had stalled from Alabama to Virginia for the third time that year, dumped on the mountains every drop of water it scooped from the Gulf of Mexico. The swollen river was at the point of overflowing its banks, but on the morning of the eighth day, only a light, but constant, sprinkle remained.

The debris from the storm littered the whole river valley. Sheriff Hodges marched a squad of inmates single file up the east bank, starting behind the jail and working their way to the courthouse. Each prisoner carried a supply of burlap bags. As each bag was filled, the prisoner dropped it in place to be picked up on the return march. A deputy guarded the rear of the squad with a rifle and the Sheriff led the procession. The inmates didn't seem to mind the work even in the cold wet air since this was their only time to get outside the barbed wire walls surrounding the jail. They wore their usual gray cotton inmate uniform with a gray jacket bearing the word *INMATE* across the back.

The bank at the bottom of Ellie's Knoll was too steep to walk, so the Sheriff paraded the crew around the east side of the hill behind the courthouse and behind the new jail construction site. Before being arrested, some of the inmates had worked for the contractor on the jail. Passing by the growing skeleton, they craned their necks trying to see old buddies still at work. A break in the clouds warmed the air and slowed their pace for a few minutes. They reached the turnaround point and the Sheriff gave the men a ten minute break. In a line facing the river, they all sat on their burlap bags and puffed away on whatever they had to smoke. It was the first time some of them had been away from the jail in weeks and as they relaxed and listened to the sound of the river, they thought of going home and getting back to their lives.

The earth began to rumble. Not quite thunder, not quite a quake, nor the sound of a train. It sounded more like a hollow mountain being cracked open. The men jumped to their feet and looked in all directions trying to rationalize what they were hearing, which was totally beyond anything they ever imagined. There was no way for them to know about the massive rupture of the reservoir dike a half-mile upriver. No way for them to comprehend the volume and sheer power of the avalanche of water headed toward them at that moment. The top half of the dyke had exploded like an over-inflated balloon.

It took less than a minute for the fury to reach the edge of town. Even the most hardened felon cried out at the sight and deafening sound of destruction to everything in its way. Trees along the river were snapped instantly. Fragments of buildings, shrubs, siding, roofing, rocks, mud—everything it encountered on its way downstream disappeared and then reappeared at the top of its thundering crest. Its constantly changing form gobbled up mounds of earth and extended its nebulous-shaped arms out over the land. It then retracted those arms, pulling everything with it back into the river. Clay stained the water such a deep red that the oncoming tide looked like boiling, flowing lava.

The full force of the flood struck the south end of Ellie's

Knoll which projected into the river far enough to divert the wave around its west side and away from town.

Although the deputy at the rear of the pack and nine inmates were able to scramble to higher ground near the knoll, the Sheriff was swept under and disappeared immediately. Seconds later he popped to the surface and washed downstream. All they saw of him were his thrashing arms as he grabbed the trunk of a tree in the middle of the flood. As soon as the crest passed, the nine inmates and deputy rushed to the water's edge attempting to find something to pull Hodges back to solid ground, but everything had been washed away. From a piece of land that extended partially into the river, they locked arms, forming a chain, and waded single file with the men at the rear holding to weeds and briars as anchors. The first inmate at the front of the chain, named Bucky, finally reached a tree in the water close to the Sheriff, pulled himself into its branches, leaped to the adjacent tree, and, from one of the lower limbs pulled the Sheriff out of the water into the tree. The Sheriff jumped to the adjacent tree and then, with a long powerful leap, jumped to a small strip of land.

The crew watched Sheriff Hodges put his hands on his knees while he tried to catch his breath. The surge rumbled past the town and around the knoll. It continued to gush downstream through the southern part of the county. As soon as its sound finally died, another explosion, created by the bursting of the dike's lower half, shook the town. This was immediately followed by a second wall of water crashing down the river valley with more violence and speed than the first. The men were calling Bucky to jump to land like the Sheriff had done. But Bucky, who was at least eight inches shorter than Hodges and not anywhere near his physical condition, hesitated. A moment later the new torrent was everywhere. It picked up the two trees and washed them in a swirling motion thirty-five feet away. Bucky held to a limb with his right arm. As the rolling tree pulled him under, he raised his left hand and arm over his head. The tree must have become lodged into something at that spot. All that could be seen of Bucky was his hand sticking above the surface. The inmates were calling out...in horror...in profanity...in prayer...in desperation, "Oh shiiiit, Goddamn, oh Jesus, oh sweet Jesus!" The Sheriff ran along the land until he caught up with a log moving with the flood. He leaped into the water and grabbed the log with both arms until he reached Bucky, whose his hand was still sticking out of the water. Hodges disappeared under the surface for a few moments until two heads emerged and he was able to pull Bucky over part of the log. As the two men were swept closer to the center of the stream, they picked up speed. The log spun further away as the other ten on the bank ran after them as fast as they could.

In no time, the two men were carried to the small mountain at the edge of town. As the constantly flowing water crashed into the steep side of the hill, it caused everything in its course to start spinning. The Sheriff, Bucky, and the log twisted instantly out of sight. The flat farm land beyond the knoll became a churning sea. Even though the surge had moved downstream, the roaring, cracking, snapping, and popping sound was still echoing up the valley as the water continued to wash away everything in its path.

The full poison from the county sewage plant and several small furniture finishing plants located a couple of miles beyond Mount Tsula were immediately flushed out by the surge.

It took twelve hours before rescuers were able to find the Sheriff and Bucky, who were still clinging to half-submerged branches. Massive amounts of debris had created a logjam stopping the larger objects from being washed all the way into the French Broad River. The logjam, however, created a perfect filter to capture and retain much of the pollution, chemicals, and regurgitated sludge. When the two men were pulled from the debris, they had not only absorbed water in their lungs but they had also ingested into their system a number of toxic chemicals and raw sewage. Both men had lapsed into septic shock and were taken immediately to the Jefferson hospital.

Jack Hemphill

CHAPTER THIRTY-FOUR

STUART

On the way to town I was stopped at the bridge by a deputy. No traffic was allowed past that point, so I returned home. I called Ceda and she told me about the Sheriff. After filling me in on the damage along the river, she said she would know more later and would call me.

The next day I phoned Liz Fletcher, head nurse of intensive care. I knew her from high school. "They've been categorized as 'critical,'" she said.

"Is there a prognosis?" I asked.

"The man they call Bucky, whose real name is Simpson Bucknell, has started responding to the antibiotics."

"Did you say Bucky's name is Bucknell? Is he part of the Weavertown Bucknells?"

"Yep, we've had half of Weavertown down here this morning." She paused, then said in a more sarcastic voice, "He's getting more attention than the Sheriff, but as you probably know, we've got a bigger problem right now with the news people than we do with our patients. Media people from Charlotte, Asheville, and even Greenville have camped in the parking lot. They're all over the Sheriff's staff and people at the courthouse. I can't even go home. They keep ringing my door bell."

"What about the Sheriff?"

"The Sheriff is growing worse. His organs are shutting down one by one. The doctor told me confidentially that he's not expected to last another three days."

I let it go, knowing from the prognosis that nature would eventually take its course, but the following morning around eight, Liz called. "The Sheriff regained consciousness last night."

"Any change in his condition?"

"No, not really. They still say maybe three days. He doesn't respond to treatment. But he asked to talk to you."

"To me? Why?"

"I don't know."

"How about his family. Have they been there?"

"No, not yet."

I hurried to find Emily. "He's awake," I said. "For some reason he wants to talk to me."

"Are you going?"

"I have to. He's not expected to live. He's got nothing to gain or lose, no matter what he has to say."

"Do you want me to go with you?" she asked.

"Of course I do, but I don't think this is something you want to see. Maybe he has something he wants to say to me that he can't say to anybody else. I don't know, but I probably should go alone."

"That's fine with me. I'm sorry about what happened to him and all that, but to be honest, seeing him now is the last thing I want to do."

"I understand."

Nurse Fletcher had me wait for a half hour in her office while Lester was being cleaned. "He comes and goes," she said. "Don't expect too much. No one has gotten more than about five minutes out of him yet." She led me to the new wing off the main building. Everything sparkled and gave off an uncomfortably sanitary smell, but the moment I stepped into his room, the feeling changed. Surrounded by strange equipment, tubes running in all directions and entering his body in places I never imagined possible, Lester looked more like a loaded bomb than a man. I pulled a chair beside the bed. He didn't seem to notice me for a while.

I wasted no time trying to rouse him, "Lester," I said softly. "Lester," a little louder.

He moved his eyes toward me, stared for while, then said, "Goddamn it," before he drifted away.

I waited a little while then began again, "Lester…Lester."

Again he opened his eyes and said, "What do you want with me, Stuart?" His voice a little clearer and stronger.

"I'm sorry about what happened, but I was told you wanted to see me."

He glared and turned his face to the ceiling. His eyes watered as he finally said, "It wasn't me." Another minute went by before he spoke again. "I was just a boy, a goddamned boy. They made it easy for me…easy to just keep floating. I never even tried to stop. Didn't want to."

"What are you talking about?" I asked softly. Again he glanced at me then back to the ceiling.

As he continued, his voice became deeper and sounded more like himself. He was still staring upward as if his memories were projected above him.

"We drank more corn that summer than I ever knew existed in Jefferson County, all made from hard grain mash and horse feed and all kinds of other stuff."

"What other stuff?"

"Homemade shit that was strong enough to blow our minds away for half a day." Hodges shook his head slightly and said, "He was asleep under a tree, facing down river. Just sitting there. Quiet. Not doing nothin'."

"Who?"

"Habakkuk …he never even saw or heard me coming."

I bounced to my feet, not believing my ears I leaned over his bed and listened.

"All I remember is how much I hated him," he continued, "Didn't even know why. Still don't know why. With all the junk I had in me that day, it was so easy. I picked up a limb. Walked up behind him, and bashed his head against the tree. I felt…nothing. I felt *nothing*. He just fell, and I felt nothing—like the whole world was numb. Landed behind the tree in a little hollow place that had been dug out by some animal. I knew he was gone as soon as I looked at his face. I've never gotten that stare out of my mind. It looked at me—right through me."

"He had a leather bag on a chord around his neck that fell off and spilled stones on the ground. I kept the bag, but threw the stones into the hole."

I walked to the other side of his bed. "What did you do with him?"

"It was easy to dig in the clay. I made the little tunnel wide enough to stuff his head, shoulders, and hips into the ground. Only his legs stuck out. With the limb I pounded his legs into the hole until his knees were crunched tight against his stomach. With the stone, I dug chunks of clay and mounded them over the hole, then covered it with leaves. It was only then that my frozen brain started to thaw. I had buried him and covered him, but I still saw him. Crouching on all fours like an animal, panting, bleeding, I started to cry. My head hung so low it almost touched the ground."

Lester's lips continued to move in silence. "Lester speak up. I can't hear you!"

He took a slow breath then continued, "Something was

wrong. I felt it above me staring at the back of my head making no sound at all, but still somehow I knew he was there. *It's Habakkuk's ghost*, I thought, as I felt his burning glare. Terrified, I couldn't look up. I felt hot breath on my neck, panting, moving closer. Finally I gave up, rose to my knees, and found myself staring into amber eyes behind the long white fangs of a cross fox whose den I had turned into a bloody tomb. With a scream, I fell over backwards through the briars and down the embankment into the river. My mind was still half-scorched as I ran for a mile or so along the edge of the bank. Exhausted, I finally fell into a mud flat. An hour, maybe two. As I took the long walk home, the clay, heavy, drying all over my body was like a thick layer of red skin. I passed your house. You were standing at the bottom of the drive, but all I saw was Habakkuk's face still staring at me. I had to get rid of it. I grabbed you, punched, and kept punching until the face disappeared. The last thing I remember is throwing you over the fence. I don't even remember going home from there. I told my Dad everything, but never told him where the grave was. Never told anybody. I couldn't bear seeing it again. Dad sent me away. It took me a year to get it all out of my system." He stopped for a moment, then groaned, "The sonsabitches killed me. They *killed* me, but, *God...damit*, yesterday the sonsabitches saved me." He returned his glare back to the ceiling. His eyes watered over again. His voice was getting softer and he was beginning to slur his words. "Don't matter though. It took me a full year to get the poison out of my body, but it took that river only a day to stick it back in me." He continued to talk about the river but was getting less coherent. He tried to say more, but it wouldn't come out. Within minutes, his eyes no longer focused but stared blankly beyond the ceiling. His breathing became shallow and short.

Leaving his room, I took one more look back at the defenseless face behind me and struggled to find anything about it that I recognized as Lester. I couldn't. Liz watched me walk down the hall toward her office. I couldn't speak; just shook my head and waved my hand as I turned toward the exit. Even the wide corridor was suffocating. The moment I stepped into the cool outside air and felt its breath blow across my face, I deflated and slid my back down the brick wall until I sat with my chin on my knee like a homeless child. Sat there for a while, don't know how long, until I heard my name. It was one of the ambulance guys. I looked up as he said, "Stuart, you okay?"

"Yep."

"I just brought in two DOAs," he said. "The flood washed them away in their car."

"Where?"

"Upside down in the creek right below the reservoir. We think the car was at the dyke when it broke."

"Who are they?"

"Don't know yet. All I know is I brought them here after pulling them out of an old gray Studebaker."

CHAPTER THIRTY-FIVE

STUART

I had been gone three hours. My car ambled its way under the arms of the oaks lining my drive. Emily was watching through the pantry windows. I drove to the rear of the house and parked, sat there for a while—don't know how long. Emily tapped on my window. I got out of the car and put my arm around her as we walked into the carriage house. She read my face, but said nothing.

After the kitchen door closed she asked, "How did it go?"

Before answering, I pressed both palms on the bread table, took a deep breath, exhaled through puckered lips, then said, "You should have seen him."

"Was he in bad shape?"

"He was the color of raw chicken. Tubed up from all directions. Balls of sweat dangled from the end of his stiff hair and mustache. He was the opposite of himself. Weak, delicate, half-conscious and half-nightmare."

"But why did he ask for you?"

"It was a confession! It...it was a damn confession."

"Of what?"

"Bakkuk. He killed Bakkuk."

"Oh my God, how?"

"Bakkuk never went away. Lester beat his brains out with a stick. Buried him on top of Ellie's Knoll."

"Holy shit." She sat down and folded her hands in her lap for a moment, then said, "That confirms everything." Her voice was so soft she could barely be heard… "But why did he do it?"

"He didn't know why. He just wanted me to know that he did it. It may have been his last wish. They don't think he can hold on much longer."

Gaining her composure she said, "Stuart, I'm sorry."

I nodded, then walked to the little kitchen table and sat in the chair facing the window. She stood beside me. I glanced back at her for a moment then said, "You know all the years while I was growing up, even until now, I pretended Bakkuk was always somehow out there watching me. I knew he wasn't really watching, but I wanted to believe it so much that sometimes I thought I actually felt it. Now for the first time, I can't pretend. I glanced back at her and said, "Does that sound stupid coming from a grown man?"

"No. I sometimes feel like my Dad is watching me. Maybe Bakkuk is watching too."

"It gets worse," I said. "Just before I got into my car, I saw Cunningham, who had just arrived. Apparently nobody thinks Lester's going pull through. He asked me if I would hurry the portrait. I couldn't believe it. How the hell could I do it now?"

"Did you tell him what the Sheriff said?"

"No, of course not. But how can I finish the portrait knowing what I know?"

"What are you going to do?"

"He's a murderer! Do I want people to honor this guy?" I looked out the window again. A mud dauber was eagerly building her cloister of clay under a stone lintel over the window.

Emily sat in a chair close beside me and said, "Don't do anything right now. You might feel differently in a day or so."

"Don't ask me to forgive him," I snapped back.

"Wait a few days. When he's gone, you'll know just what to do." I nodded. My hands were folded on the table and she placed both her hands over mine.

"Stuart, I have some other news," she said.

I closed my eyes as she continued. "You got a call from Ceda. Joe Remington is dead."

I nodded again, but didn't tell her that the ambulance guy had already told me about finding Remington's car.

"Nettles was also in the car."

"Nettles!"

"Yes, but there's more. The little stone house at the reservoir…is gone."

"What!"

"Captain Morgan brought in an expert who told him the house was blown up. According to Ceda, they think the explosion blasted away chunks of rock at the corner of the dike, weakening the entire structure before the whole thing ruptured."

I sat down.

"One more thing," she said, "The Sheriff's deputies found dynamite, a box of fuses, and detonators in Joe's car. They think Judd and Nettles blew it up."

I closed my eyes and felt a cavernous hole opening in my mind. I started to slide inside.

I couldn't speak. Emily's chair squeaked as she stood. Her lips were warm against my neck.

"I'll be right back," I heard her say, before she went over to the Stone House.

The kitchen was quiet. The mud dauber's wings continued to buzz against the glass as she carefully sealed her nest. Somewhere in the distance, Lester's voice spoke, telling me again about killing Bakkuk.

The voice turned into pain. I didn't want to think about it, but I couldn't stop. I wanted to be alone, but I wanted Emily to come back. I wanted everything else to go away.

Emily returned with a couple of books and a bowl of leftover spaghetti. She managed to find some rolls and iced tea in the carriage house refrigerator and heated the spaghetti in the oven. I wasn't hungry, even though I hadn't eaten all day, but I managed to put down at least half of it.

She read poems to me later that night. Her voice was clear, but I didn't take in a single word. She rested her head on my pillow. Light from my table lamp shined through her hair like embers in a fire.

She was close, warm, perfectly still.

There was a light rain that night, just enough to give up a soft murmur on the copper roof above my bed. Just enough to help my mind finally close inside and go to the places it needed. She let me go, but never left my side. I fell into a long, mindless, silent sleep.

CHAPTER THIRTY-SIX

STUART

Realizing the inevitable, I waited two more days before checking on the Sheriff's condition.

"He's doing much better," said Nurse Liz.

"You're kidding!"

"Can't explain it in medical terms. For no reason, no reason at all, the night after you left, his body finally started to reject the poison and fight the infection. One by one each of his systems started to normalize. He remained unconscious for a day, then woke up, and has been conscious ever since."

"What's his prognosis?"

"It's driving the doctors crazy, but they had to admit they see no reason why he won't be sent home next week. They still predict, however, a long convalescent period of six months to a year."

"What about the Bucknell man?"

"He was released to the Sheriff's department yesterday. I understand he'll be kept in isolation until his strength returns."

The Sheriff's recovery took every bit as much time as predicted. Captain Morgan was appointed "Acting Sheriff" for the remainder of Lester Hodge's term in office, which would end the following November. The nine other inmates who were part of the Sheriff's rescue were all rewarded for their effort. The convicted misdemeanants were given a full pardon, and those who were still waiting for their trial had a complete account of the event placed in their records, to be given to the judges at their respective hearings.

As the debris began to be cleared and the red pathway cleaned, the town started talking about Ellie's Knoll and how it had blocked the water's force, diverted it, and prevented it from flooding downtown Redbriar. Also, everyone in the county knew that plans to level the knoll had been scrapped because of what they believed to be an Indian burial site. *Indian Site Saves Town* was the headline in the weekly paper. The barbershop gang and other old timers around Jefferson County swore they remembered stories told by their ancestors about great Indians who hunted, trapped animals, and helped early settlers in the area. Within weeks, the commissioners voted to erect a stone monument at the summit of Ellie's Knoll dedicated to the "Redbriar Indian."

The Sheriff's portrait was still unfinished. The portrait was a dignified pose showing the Sheriff in full uniform in the courthouse. He was turned slightly to the left so his pistol was unmistakably in view.

County officials continued to ask me when I would finish it. Two months had passed since the flood. Reluctantly I placed the canvas on my easel once again, sat on my stool, and dabbled at the painting.

I couldn't stop thinking of Bakkuk. Every minute of the years I knew my friend scrolled through my mind. I pictured Bakkuk treading his way along the river, with broad strides and a confident swagger.

I remembered a time when I was not quite ten years old. It was a day that started with a rock skipping contest with Ceda, who was barely eight. Wading ankle-deep into the river, I side armed a rock across the water. "Nine times," I shouted to Ceda who watched in amazement as the missile skipped almost to the other bank. We were waiting for Bakkuk who promised we could go with him to check his traps. Every few minutes I glanced downstream to the shallow, rocky stretches of the river. Finally I saw a dark figure silhouetted against the bright afternoon sunshine. Something was wrong. The figure walking toward us was covered in red from his head to his feet. He looked like a plastic prize from a Crackerjack box. Ceda screamed and grabbed my arm, but I knew from his gate, it was Bakkuk.

"What happened?" I asked as Bakkuk sat on a rock and started spilling his bizarre story. His family, like many people in the mountains, drew water from a private well. Lots of families couldn't afford indoor plumbing or a water heater. They kept a large, black, three legged, cast iron kettle in the yard where she boiled clothing once a week in the springtime and summer, and twice a month in the fall and winter. She let it bubble for a half hour or so before fishing the clothes out with a stick and hanging them over a line. The hot clothing in the winter sent clouds of steam down the river like they were on fire.

Bakkuk placed one foot on the rock beside him and rested both arms on his knee. He said someone had tossed a cake of red dye in the kettle the day before. When he and his aunt discovered it, they hung the clothes out to dry as usual. It didn't matter that all the clothing had turned blood red; they couldn't afford to throw anything away. He told us how he drew a bucket of red water from the kettle, cooled it in the stream, then carefully poured it over his head turning his long black hair deep crimson. Without waiting for it to dry, he tied it back with a leather cord into a ponytail. He also tossed his sneakers into the kettle long enough to turn them the same fiery color as his hair.

Ceda and I were still young enough to think that Bakkuk

possessed some kind of magic. We never thought of drawing any kind of line between reality and our active childish imaginations. We listened to his story with absorbed fascination. To us it was a typical day in my magical friend's enormously strange and fascinating life. He showed no fear, remorse, or concern about the prank that had ruined half his clothing and he never bothered to explain why he dyed his hair and shoes to match.

As soon as he finished his story, all three of us bounded off upriver to check the traps. A farmer just north of town had been paying Bakkuk for several weeks to get rid of persistent foxes around his farm. The shortest route to the farm was through the high school property and Bakkuk chose the exact time when school was letting out to cross it. After following the river past the town, we turned across an open field in front of the school. Ceda and I instinctively fell into a single file behind Bakkuk, stepping high with great pride.

Bakkuk walked with his usual long deliberate strides. As we marched with the breeze in our face, his dark red hair dried stiff and stuck straight back. In the bright afternoon sun, his sharply carved forehead, cheek bones, and nose painted dark shadows on his face. His large hands were cupped in a fist. I followed closely behind him trying to keep in step. Ceda's sandy colored pigtails swung back and forth as she marched, thinking of nothing except me, Bakkuk, and our big adventure. I remember pretending to be the middle section of a monster, carving out a path across the wide schoolyard. Students standing on the steps wanted to laugh but didn't dare. Parents picking up their kids rolled down their windows, exposing wrinkled brows. All the school busses stopped while the kids leaned out the windows. Four boys sat on a concrete wall just above the creek on the northern edge of the school property. The concrete was part of a headwall supporting a drainage pipe that dumped into the Deep Pine River. Even at a distance I recognized

Lester as one of the four boys on the wall. When they first saw our tiny parade coming toward them, the boys laughed and made jokes among themselves, but, without the slightest change in stride, Bakkuk led us in a hammering march right toward the four. By the time we were within twenty-five feet of them, Lester hopped off the wall and with his back to the rough concrete surface, eased gradually away. Turning to assure himself of the support from the other three boys, Lester found himself alone. One boy had already darted to the end of the ball field, another was sloshing his way across the shallow river, and the last had scrambled into the storm pipe as fast as he could. I knew then how much they feared Bakkuk. Marching in step with him made me feel like I was part of his power. Lester froze as our crew continued to strut toward him. I remember hearing Bakkuk saying Lester's name—not with a growl or with a shout, but simply announcing his name.

There are only two times when you can examine wild animals up close—when they are dead or when they have been trapped. There's something in the shineless faces of trapped animals. It's not fear. It's a final surrender to a power beyond themselves. Underneath Hodges' tough guy, arrogant mask was one of those faces.

I remember in complete detail the contrast between Bakkuk's fearless, stone facade and Lester's countenance with every facial muscle drawn into tight knots bulging through his thick skin. With both Bakkuk and Lester in front of me, in one snapshot, I saw two people, exact opposites. Bakkuk, born with nothing—a half breed given every possible disadvantage, but living his life believing that he had all he would ever want. His greatest ambition was to be forgotten by the world and remembered only by his few friends. The other person, Lester, trapped into a life that would never know a day of peace and despising anyone who found it.

As we stomped by Lester, his head sunk forward with

his eyes fixed on Bakkuk. Bakkuk didn't look back at him, but continued his strut as if Hodges never existed.

Over the next two years, red dye was thrown into the kettle three more times, but Bakkuk continued to wear his red clothes and continued to dye his hair blood red with the same enthusiasm and defiance. After Bakkuk was gone, I never allowed myself to think about Lester very much. Like pesky dogs, I kicked away nagging memories of him, but having been forced to do his portrait, looking deeply into his face, and remembering that day in the school yard, I finally understood him. For the first time, I pitied him and for the first time, I realized I never really had a reason to fear him.

By the next morning, the painting was finished. The final touches showed late afternoon sunlight shining through the windows of the courthouse, lighting the dark walls surrounding Hodges in a blaze of red. The portrait depicted the Sheriff, draping his left arm over the stair banister outside the superior courtroom. His right fist was placed on his hip just behind the bone handle of his forty-five. His cocky pose and dark tan skin were in sharp contrast with the frightened green eyes peering out of the canvas, painted exactly the way I remembered them from that day Bakkuk , Ceda, and I marched past him on the playground.

CHAPTER THIRTY-SEVEN

STUART

The day of the jail's grand opening finally arrived. Two years, two weeks and two days had passed since they started the project. With the windows down, Emily and I let our hair blow in the wind as we drove into town past the front of the courthouse. Low white clouds moved across the sky, creating constantly changing shadows that swept over the buildings. During construction, exposed interior concrete block and raw pre-cast concrete structural forms were, at first, in ugly contrast with the weathered dignity and beauty of the old brick courthouse. But, eventually, the town witnessed a gradual emergence of the forms, textures, and colors of the newborn buildings. The dull gray concrete block structural walls of the new jail were finally covered with a full façade of stone, carefully picked to match as closely as possible the old granite base around the courthouse. A second stone wall was built surrounding the detention facility. It was an eight-foot high security wall with concealed razor wire mounted on the back side so the ugly concertina strands would never be visible from the town. From River Street, the long, sleek windowless form of the stone jail was mirrored by the long, pure form of the stone security wall. The new two-story law enforcement office wing was tucked behind the courthouse with a stone base and brick skin, displaying double-hung windows with stone lintels and sills, resembling the style of the existing windows in the old courthouse design.

A ribbon was placed across the door of the new link connecting the courthouse to the new jail. Commissioner Moore cut the ribbon as a ceremonial symbol. The public was allowed to tour the new facility and return through the same link into the courthouse lobby, where refreshments were set up. One hundred and fifty or more people crowded the long hall and lobby. I watched Emily, in her dark gray suit and white blouse. Her hair was cut a little shorter than usual.

After stopping to look at the new portrait of Sheriff Hodges in the main corridor, I realized Lester had quietly joined me. For a few awkward moments we both stood in silence, eyes fixed on the painting. We shared a brief nod. It was strange to see his clothing hang loosely across his shoulders. His belt, tightened against his shrunken waist, buckled the top of his pants. His collar hung below his neck far enough to reveal the top of a mostly white t-shirt. After another awkward minute, Lester leaned toward me and said, with a soft, hesitant voice, "Stuart... about our conversation the night at the hospital..." His eyes dropped from the portrait to a spot on the floor just below the painting.

This was my big moment, the opportunity I thought would never happen. I finally had him in a place where I was in complete control. He was humbled, vulnerable—a gnat beneath my thumb. Yet, I heard myself saying, "Oh yeah, you were in bad shape that night...sheer gibberish."

"Gibberish?" muttered Lester, raising his eyes off the floor.

"I'm sorry, Lester. I couldn't understand anything you said that night. Something about the river, foxes, and red clay. I'm afraid nothing made sense, but I'm glad you pulled through." I then locked my elbow under the Sheriff's and led him down the corridor toward the front of the courthouse, away from the crowd. Emily watched while we spoke. With both arms crossed, Lester again stared at the floor. Without a word he turned and walked back down the hall toward Emily, but he stopped, turned around, and rejoined me. Standing about a foot from my face, he stared at my chest, avoiding my eyes. Lester opened his mouth, but couldn't bring his thoughts into words. To save him from any more embarrassment, I said, in a low and deliberate tone, "Lester, this is the absolute end of it." He nodded, glanced momentarily into my eyes, then walked past the portrait and stopped beside Emily. He looked at the entrance to the new jail then back at her and finally stretched one side of his lips slightly upward. It was the closest thing to a smile she would ever see on his face and the closest thing to a compliment he would ever give her. She answered with a full smile. Lester turned and stepped into the secure corridor leading to the jail. He looked straight forward with his head cocked slightly backward. The 14 gauge steel door slammed shut behind him. That was the last time I ever saw him.

I continued to gaze down the corridor, seeing nothing. Part of me rocked backwards in disbelief over what I had just said, while part of me exhaled in relief, as my head fell forward and my hands clutched my knees.

I had forgiven him.

It wasn't something I had planned to do. I had no choice. It didn't come from any rational thinking or reasoning. It just came over me. I don't know how long I stood there before I felt Emily's hand on my cheek. She had overheard part of my conversation with Lester. I believed she somehow understood, even if I didn't.

Officials from neighboring counties came to the open house. No jail in North Carolina had ever been built like the one in Redbriar. After inmates were moved in, there was no doubt in anyone's mind that the new design was much safer and more secure than any other jail in the state and that it would eventually save lives, including guards as well as inmates. Within a year after the opening, two other counties started plans for new jails based on the Redbriar model.

In spite of the flood and months of convalescence, Sheriff Hodges was still running for re-election. He made it a point to stay involved in his work as much as he could during working hours, but in his private life, he became more and more reclusive. After work, he avoided contact with people by staying at the law enforcement center until well after dark, then going straight home. He had groceries delivered directly to his house where he continued to live alone with his personal thoughts and twelve cats.

Exactly six weeks from the night of the jail opening Sheriff Hodges helped lead the raid called, "Operation Garbage Dump" and was killed by a high-powered bullet through his head.

CHAPTER THIRTY-EIGHT

Emily thought it odd to see Stuart sitting on the front steps of the Stone House. "Waiting for me?" she asked, as she slid out of the car and gathered her groceries. Stuart didn't answer, but gave her a slight smile.

"What's up?" She sat down beside him.

"Ceda's on her way here. She called and wanted to show me the coroner's report."

"About Lester?"

"Yes."

"Why would she think you would want to see that?"

"She didn't say, just said I needed to see it." Emily slid her groceries to the side of the step and zipped up her jacket. Even though it was ten o'clock, it took the October sun half a day to heat up the morning air. They sat quietly watching distant clouds feathering their way around the mountains. Ceda drove a little slower than usual, and parked her tan Ford directly behind Emily's car. She held a brown envelope and sat down on the other side of Stuart. Emily scooted closer to Stuart until their knees touched.

After a silent, deep breath, she pulled from the envelope a pack of official-looking papers and placed them on her lap. "These are the coroner's report and my statement."

"Why do I have a feeling I'm not supposed to see this?"

he asked.

"I need to tell you what happened at the raid. Okay?"

He nodded. "My statement and the coroner's report haven't been released officially, but I want to read them to you... to both of you." She turned to a page halfway through a pack of papers marked with a paper clip. Stuart noticed her fingers trembling slightly as she read.

" 'Coroner's Report. Death was caused by a wound to the head causing massive damage to the brain and resulting in an instantaneous failure of the heart. The wound to the head resulted in a laceration measuring 15mm in diameter at the point of penetration between the primary visual cortex and upper part of the cerebellum. The projectile moved at a high velocity through the brain and exited through the left side of the pre-motor cortex shattering the skull in that area and leaving an exit wound of 25x50mm. Traces of the skull bone from the entry wound were found throughout the path of the projectile. No other traces of the bullet were found.'" She stopped reading and looked down for a moment, then back at Stuart, waiting for him to respond.

"Ceda, that doesn't mean a thing to me except what I already know—Lester got shot and he's dead."

Sergeant Evans placed her hand on the center of his back, massaged it for a moment, then let her hand glide upward until her first three fingers were just above the intersection of his neck and the back of his head. "According to the coroner, this is the cerebellum, where the bullet entered," she said. Then lifting her hand slowly she placed it on the top of his head slightly to the left. "Pre-motor cortex. This is where the bullet exited."

"I heard he was killed while charging up the hill, right?" he asked.

"Yep."

Stuart gesturing with his hands said, "Then why does it say

he took a bullet upward through the lower back of his head that exited up here? It should have been the other way around."

"This is why the investigation was closed to the public and took so long. Let me read from *my* report"

"Who does it say was near him when it happened?"

Ceda opened her report without answering and began reading on the second page, "'We circled the base of the mountain and climbed simultaneously with twenty to thirty yards between each of us. Captain Morgan was on the sheriff's left flank.'"

"Who was on his right?" Stuart interrupted.

"I was," she said. Her eyes fixed on his for a moment. "Again, as I have written, 'It was the last minute of visibility before a blanket of clouds covered the low moon. We heard sleet bouncing off the limbs and hitting the ground around us. The sleet's constant hissing provided a cover for the crunching of our feet through the leaves. Three shots cracked from the top of the hill above us. I saw the sheriff go over the edge of a steep ravine. As I ran to check on him, gun shots and flashes of light from different locations around the mountain broke out in sporadic bursts.

I continued down into the dark gully. It was pitch black. At the bottom was a creek. I knew there was no way he had survived. After a while, the shooting around me stopped. I searched until I was numb with cold. I couldn't find my way back; I was lost. They had taken our radios for obvious reasons. The continuing sleet made the steep bank impossible to climb and any hope of seeing where I was going had long vanished. My only possible course was to follow the creek. I found my way back to Redbriar and since all available officers were still on the mountain, I called the county coroner, Bill Klontz. Klontz picked me up in his van and drove me back to the creek. We had to wait for sunrise. We followed the stream back into the mountain. We saw traces of the sheriff's blood for a hundred yards downstream before we found him on his side, draped over a rock in the water. We pulled a bag over him. It took the two of us an hour and a half to drag him down the creek bank to Klontz's van." ' Ceda tucked her papers back into the envelope and looked at Stuart.

"Ceda, why does his report imply the bullet went upward through his head?" Stuart asked again.

"Coroner had to write it the way he saw it, I told him not to leave a thing out."

"You know, it implicates either you or Captain Morgan."

"Yep, and I've spent all day answering questions about that."

"What did you tell them?"

"I told them to read my report. It would be my only statement."

Without moving, she cast her gaze back into the brown envelope, cleared her throat, then pulled something out of the bag. Concealing it in her hand, she said, "He never even missed it. I found this in the Sheriff's desk right after the flood when he was in the hospital." She held Stuart's hand and slipped the object into his grasp. He immediately recognized Bakkuk's leather pouch with the deer figure sewn with beads. After stroking it for a minute with his thumb, Stuart looked down and placed it on his chest just below his chin. The leather cord hung to his lap.

Finally realizing what she was trying to say, he moved toward her. Her green eyes blurred with tears. "Are you okay?" he asked.

"Yes," she said softly.

"Ceda, I have to tell you what he said to me."

"When?"

"In the hospital."

"You already knew?"

"I suspected it as soon as they found the relics on the knoll and Lester covered up the evidence. You know Bakkuk loved to sit up there and look down the river."

"You suspected?"

"Well, I did then, but…there's more. In the hospital, I thought he was dying. He thought he was dying too, and he told me all about it."

"Why didn't you tell me?"

Emily sat down.

"I told nobody," he said with a flick of his eye toward Emily.

"But why couldn't you say something to me?" Ceda asked.

"I didn't know what you would do."

"Yeah you did. You knew *exactly* what I would do."

She lifted the pouch from his hand and slid it back into the envelope

"What will the final report say?" he asked.

"That he was killed in the line of duty, possibly by the criminal who also was killed that night."

"But, what will it say about the bullet?"

"They said it couldn't be explained, unless he was running away. The SBI and the Feds had no choice but to accept it, there's no other evidence." She was interrupted by the sound of tires rumbling across driveway pavers as Captain Morgan pulled in front of them.

"Sergeant Evans, stand by your vehicle." The Captain's expressionless voice hammered at her, a little deeper than usual. He walked straight to Stuart placing his hands on his hips. "Well, Stuart," he paused. I have a few questions to ask you."

"Okay," Stuart said, looking at Ceda for a clue.

"Have you been to the Jenkins' farm in the last year?"

"Yes."

"What were you doing there?"

"Why are you asking these questions?"

"Just answer me."

"I went there to pick up my daughter. Tell me why you're asking?"

"Do you own a thirty-two caliber pistol?"

"Will you tell me why you want to know?"

"Sure, you have a right to know that. You've also got a right to remain silent."

"What are you talking about?"

"We searched the farm this morning. A thirty-two pistol was found under the seat in a truck parked by the barn. We believe the truck was used by Daggett and his gang."

"So what?"

"The gun had your fingerprints on it."

Stuart looked back at Emily. They both realized then that Tad had left the gun in the truck and somehow she was involved in the crime.

"Morgan, why are you doing this?" asked Stuart.

"You have a right to remain silent," Captain Morgan repeated. "Everything you say's gonna to be used against you in court. You have a right to as many high-powered attorneys that your stinking money can buy, but we got a right to put your ass in a place where who you are don't mean shit."

"What the hell are you talking about, Morgan?" Stuart stood up and ran his fingers through his hair. Emily stood behind him. Ceda put her hands over her mouth.

"What are you accusing me of?"

"We believe that truck may be evidence in a crime investigation. The pistol bears the finger prints of a convicted felon—that would be you—and you know it's against the law in this state for a felon to own a gun. You can't believe that I'm really arresting you, can you?" Emily put her hand in the middle of Stuart's back and patted him lightly. Ceda started shivering as she tucked her left thumb under her belt and draped her right wrist over the butt end of her forty-five.

"Captain Morgan!" Ceda cried out.

"Back off, Sergeant," the captain snapped.

As he reached out to touch the captain's arm, Stuart said, "Morgan you know me... " but Captain Morgan spun him around, wrestled him across the drive, and rammed his chest into the car door.

"You're goddamned right I know you, and you still can't believe that I'm arresting your ass, can you?"

As Morgan cuffed him, opened the back door, and placed his hand on top of his head, Stuart cast his eyes toward Emily and said, "Call my...." Before he could finish, the captain shoved him into the car.

"Rusty!" Ceda screamed. The captain jerked his head at her. Nobody had called him that for decades. She tried to regain her composure as she marched across the drive toward him. Her face was blazing and she yelled through her teeth, "Have you lost your mind?"

"I said, back off, Sergeant." He pointed at her with two fingers squeezed together. "I don't wanta even see you at work for the rest of the week, got it?"

Ceda and Emily remained stunned as the car drove away. Emily put both arms around her and squeezed while Ceda continued to tremble. "I'm going to call his attorneys right now," said Emily.

Both women stood in silence for several more minutes, then Ceda turned toward her car. "He's gonna be all right," Emily whispered.

"If we get him out..." Ceda didn't finish. That was the last thing she said. She had already been holding in too much and needed to be alone.

Emily stroked Ceda's shoulder with her hand. Both women looked down for a moment. "Ceda," Emily said, "I ... I can't even imagine what's going to happen, but I know we need to stay close now—okay?"

Ceda nodded.

"Are you sure?" asked Emily.

Ceda nodded again. As she tilted forward, long strands on each side of her head escaped the rubber band holding back her stiff weedy hair. Her pink complexion turned red again. She said good-by with a kiss on Emily's cheek and drove away.

.

CHAPTER THIRTY-NINE

TAD

My Dad was sentenced to a year in prison for owning a gun—the gun I left in Daggett's truck. Jefferson County had already decided to house state inmates in the new county jail, so it wasn't difficult for Dad's lawyers to get him assigned there for his full sentence. At least he felt close to home even if he couldn't see it.

The time had finally come for me to move back to the Stone House. Emily was there and I still didn't trust her, but Dad did. He put everything in her hands—power of attorney over his estate and investments, everything. I left a note to her on the front door. Didn't say much just that I needed to come home. As soon as Emily read it, she came to get me.

It was awkward. In the first few months, we seldom talked. Emily tried. God knows she tried, but I guess I wasn't ready. Like everything else I did, it took me a long time to figure out what I was supposed to do. Our lives were still completely out of sync. Emily was on her way to Asheville each morning long before I crawled out of bed and since I painted late at night, I didn't get up or eat breakfast until the afternoon. We seldom ate together at night.

I could only imagine how she must have felt visiting my

Dad in jail—the jail she designed. She went every Saturday morning and told me about each visit. Even though I pretended not to be interested in what she was saying, I was as worried about him as she was. There was no way I would ever get around the fact that he was there because of me, and every day that went by I was killing him.

I was told he managed to get a job working in the jail kitchen. At least part of each day, he would be out of the dayroom and away from most of the other inmates. Ceda made sure he had plenty of charcoal pencils and drawing paper. He spent his extra time sketching the other prisoners. He gave a lot of the drawings to the men in his dayroom and they sent the portraits of their tough, stubbled faces to their girlfriends. I understand why he did it. Like me, he had to keep drawing to stay healthy, and also the sketches were a kind of peace offering to the other prisoners.

Through Emily, Dad sent a message asking me to round up his finished paintings in the carriage house and in his studio, package them, and send them to Pierce in Charlotte. I got to know Pierce that year and she talked to me about my own paintings and asked for photos of my work. She said she loved them and that someday she would help me put together a showing of my own. She said my work would sell, not just because I was the daughter of Stuart Burns, but because she thought my paintings were *good*.

With my permission, Emily took her own photos of the paintings as I finished them and showed them to Dad through the visitation window. I hate to admit how long it took, but I finally began to see how much Emily cared for him. I still couldn't picture them together, as a couple. I couldn't believe they had been so close, so long and still claimed to live in separate houses.

It wasn't just another winter, another spring, and another summer. Emily put a calendar on the front of the refrigerator to cross off the days as they inched by—otherwise it seemed like time had stopped altogether. I continued to assist Pierce in deciding where Dad's paintings should be exhibited. By the end of the summer, I had a contract with Pierce to promote my own work. I painted endlessly to prepare for an exhibit she was planning for some time the following year.

Emily zipped up her jacket as she walked through the studio. "About an hour," she said, opening the door to the deck. Saturday afternoon was her time to walk.

"Okay, see ya," I answered. She never looked like she needed the exercise and I always felt like I did. Not that I wasn't a good walker. Since I didn't have a car, I walked everywhere, but mostly I spent long hours at my easel or bent over a sketch pad.

Emily's weekly routine was to circle the entire base of Mount Tsula starting along the river and returning from the back side of the mountain, about three miles.

I was transferring some drawings to a canvas from sketches I made earlier. The day blew by before I knew it. Natural light was fading so fast I had to stop. It was only then that I realized Emily had not returned.

The mountains and earth had turned black against a dull gray sky. Emily was always home hours before that. I walked to the end of the deck. Within minutes, the glow behind the western mountains disappeared into a starless night.

I grabbed a lantern from the pantry and slowly shuffled down the ravine and across the flat rock. The lantern gave just enough light for me to see the narrow trail that followed the river. Occasionally I stopped to listen, but I was afraid to call out. A dog barked in the distance. The night, the mountain, the trees, and the shrubs covered me like a black wool blanket. The cold air made everything feel heavy, wet, and slick. I stayed as far back from the river's edge as I could. In some places the trail disappeared completely and I had to push my way through solid brush until the path reappeared, only to disappear again. I recognized the place where the river straightened out and became shallow and stony. Even with my lamp, I couldn't see the rocks in the river well enough to cross it. I sat on the bank to rest and listen. The barking started again, much closer this time. The sound was definitely on my side of the river and I knew there were no farms or houses near there. The only option left was to bore through the brush along the river as far as I could. Briars pulled at my jeans and scratched my ankles. I was still too afraid to call out. I reached a place where there was a little clearing beside an inlet. My dim lamplight reflected off a figure sitting on a rock and a small dog standing guard. "Emily?" I said, but all I heard was the puppy's brave protest. Finally, I heard a voice as frightened as mine say, "Tad is that you?"

"Emily, what happened?" She reached to the ground and picked up a long stick and leaned on it to help her stand.

"Thank God you came."

"Are you okay?"

"I'm afraid I hurt my ankle." She leaned on her stick and hobbled a few steps toward me, then picked up the dog who was peering at me between Emily's legs. "I found this little gal stranded on a rock in the river. Not more than ten feet from the bank, but after I waded out to get her, I turned my ankle on a stone in the water."

"Oh, my God!"

"I fell in face first, but managed to hold on to the puppy and crawl to the bank. Inched my way back up river until I ran out of light. This is as far as I could go."

" Are you in pain?"

"I'll live, but I'm going to need your help to get home."

We slowly made our way through the bushes and along the trail. The hardest part was climbing the rocky ravine. When we finally got home, I put her on the couch in the sunroom. "Your clothes are soaked, you must be freezing!" I said. Emily didn't answer. I pulled her legs onto the couch, then pushed a pillow under her head. "I'm going to your room to get some dry clothes and blankets." When I returned the little dog had managed to jump onto the couch and bury herself against Emily's back.

"I don't know how long this little girl was stranded on the rock," Emily said, "but she was cold and very scared. When I waded out to her, she practically jumped into my arms."

"It was her barking that lead me to you."

"We'll have to find out where she came from. She has no tags or anything, but she's so friendly I know she's not just a wild dog. I mean, she obviously grew up around people."

"Wherever she came from, I know she's glad you found her." After firmly securing a wrap around Emily's foot I said, "You need to stay right here tonight. I'll be down first thing in the morning."

I sat with her until about midnight, and returned at seven the next morning with eggs, bacon, toast, and hot coffee. I even found a can of dog food in the pantry for Emily's new friend.

Emily spent three nights and days on the couch before she could climb the stairs. Except for trips to the store, the dog and I never left her alone until she could walk by herself. Wednesday night, Emily had recovered enough to cook fried chicken, rice, and beans and set the dining room table.

"What's the occasion?" I asked.

"I'm celebrating being back on my feet, even if I still have to use this old cane you loaned me."

"It's an antique. It was my grandmother's; I found it stashed away it in the attic,"

"I'll bet you've got lot of interesting things in that attic."

"Oh yes."

"Well, the cane still works," she said as we sat down to dinner. "This is one of Stuart's favorite meals."

I nodded realizing I had no idea what his favorite food was or favorite anything outside art stuff, but Emily was obviously so close to him she described his favorite dish as naturally as if she were talking about herself—as naturally as if she and Dad had been married for years.

"Do you love him?" The words shot out of my mouth. She was surprised at my question, but only half as surprised as I was.

"Tad, why do you ask?" she said. "I've never met anybody like your Dad. I don't know exactly what it is and I can't begin to explain it. All the time I've lived here, it seems he and I have been carefully watching and circling each other with no idea where to stop or what to do next, but why did you ask?"

"*You* know," I fired back because I didn't have any idea what else to say, and I wanted to hear her answer.

She looked away from me with an embarrassed smile long enough to collect her thoughts, then quietly spoke straight at me.

"Do I love him? Of course I do."

I still had no reply, not because of my awkward question, but because of her honest answer. All I could think to say was, "So…fried chicken is his favorite meal."

"Yes, but with rice and beans."

A minute of silence passed while we dug into our dinner, then we talked about nothing but her little dog and the weather.

I carried most of the dishes back to the kitchen and Emily managed a few while leaning on the cane. After mixing a few scraps with dry dog food I gave it to the eager puppy, who was dancing around my feet.

"Are you going to keep her?"

"I'd like to keep her. We've needed a dog around here and you've already seen that she's a good watch dog."

"Have you thought about a name?"

"I'm going to call her Bessie. "

298

"Bessie!"

"Yes."

"Bessie?"

"Why not?"

"Bessie's a cow name!"

"It's also my grandmother's name. I swear the dog's coat is the same color as my grandmother's long red hair."

"It's a nice color."

"My grandmother died without a gray hair. Kept that same beautiful color to the end."

"Are you going to be able to see my Dad on Saturday?"

"I'm planning to. I just can't walk very far yet, but if I can't make it, could you go and tell him what happened?" I was leaning over the sink and turned on the water and watched it pour over the pile of dishes. Emily asked again, "If I can't go, could you..."

"Emily, please don't ask me that," I said, " I can't face him or look at him now, not yet." Emily put away the leftovers, and didn't attempt to talk about it again.

Jack Hemphill

CHAPTER FORTY

By Saturday, Emily managed to hobble alone to the Jefferson County Jail. She was already waiting for him when he found his place in the visitation booth. They looked at each other through the thick glass and talked into the black telephone receivers. Stuart had a wide bandage over the right side of his forehead and a denim-colored knot under his left eye.

"Stuart!" she cried.

"I'm okay."

"What happened?"

"I was beaten up."

"When?"

"Two days ago."

"Who did it?"

"A guy named Pursy."

"Why?"

"I didn't really know him and still don't know why he did it. I was sitting at the little writing table in my cell. Pursy was my new roommate. I didn't know anything about him, other than the fact that he was weird. It was still early in the evening; he just walked up behind me and kicked me in the head. Knocked me to the concrete floor so hard I was half stunned. I barely remember being dragged across the floor. He yanked me to the side of the steel toilet and tried to stuff my head inside."

Emily put her hands over her face and peered between her fingers trying to hide the emotion flushing through her cheeks.

"I think I went foggy for a little while. From the bruises on my back and beside my ribs, he kicked me like he was stomping out a fire. Three guards appeared over us, grabbed him and threw him on the floor—nose first. By the time I pushed myself up on an elbow, the guards had Pursy on his feet, hands behind his back, plowing him out the door. I never saw him again."

"What did they do with him?"

"Isolation. That's where he'll probably be for the remainder of his time here."

"Are you sure you are all right?"

"Yes, but Emily, some of the guys told me I was lucky. They said if I had been in the regular state prison in Raleigh, the guards wouldn't have known anything about it until they made their rounds and I would have been dead in less than a minute."

"Oh, my God!"

"Fifteen seconds. It took only fifteen seconds for the guards up in the Control Room to see what was going on in my cell, get down the stairs, and put Pursy on the floor."

"But, why did he do it?"

"Nobody knows. He never talked to anybody—maybe just because it was Thursday." Stuart smoothed out the bandage with his hand.

"Are you *sure* you're okay?"

"I'm fine—really. But, how are *you*? How's everything at home?" Since she had arrived at the visitation area before he did, he didn't see her hobbling in and she never mentioned anything about her ankle.

Emily gave him the usual update on Tad, work at her office, and the things around the farm. She didn't tell him how thin he looked and how much softer his voice had become.

With a thin smile, he said, "You know what I thought about this morning?" He looked down at the painted shelf below the visitation window and drew little circles with his finger. "I thought about the night you slept by the fire wrapped in your red quilt."

"I wasn't the only one by the fire that night," she replied.

"I know, but you were the only one I could see."

"What made you think about that?"

"I don't know, maybe because I was cold." She was at first disappointed that his answer wasn't more personal, but convinced herself it was his way of saying he missed her.

"It won't be long now. I have plenty of wood and I still have that red silk blanket," she said softly.

"How's Tad doing?"

"She's doing great. I brought some pictures of her new work." One by one she held up six pictures against the glass. He studied them carefully.

"When I'm finished here, will you come get me?"

"You know I will."

"Just you."

"Of course."

Jack Hemphill

CHAPTER FORTY-ONE

STUART

Sunlight flickered through the trees as we made our way around the curved drive. After twelve months in jail, I had almost forgotten how bright the morning sun can be. When she stopped the car, I opened the door and pushed my way to my feet. As I turned toward the house I saw the curtains moved in Tad's room. I thought I saw her face in the window, but when I looked closer, it was just white clouds reflected across the panes.

Emily walked with me to the top step. "Wait here for a moment. I have something to show you." She darted into the house and in less than a moment a red dog bounced through the half-opened door. With its long legs and auburn coat I thought for a second it was Sergeant.

The dog ran around her and sniffed my leg. "Bessie, sit!" Emily said with authority.

"Good girl." Emily said. "Bessie this is Stuart." That was my cue to extend my hand, palm down, so Bessie could give me another sniff.

"Where did she come from?"

"I found her on a rock in the river."

"Why didn't you tell me?"

"I thought it would be kind of a surprise."

"She's got Sergeant's color," I said. As I rubbed the dog behind her ear, she tilted her head toward my hand and gave me a little moan just the way Sergeant used to do. We all entered the house together.

"I moved some of your things from the carriage house into your mother's room for you. Is that okay?"

"Sure, and to tell you the truth, the first thing I want to do is take a long shower and put on blue jeans and normal clothes."

"Of course, whatever you want."

"Tad's in her room. I'm sure she'll come out when she's ready."

Bessie walked beside us up the stairs and down the long south hall toward my mother's room. I paused for a moment in front of Tad's door. There was no sound, so we continued down the hall.

Bessie instinctively walked close to Emily but kept her eye on me. Emily kissed me lightly on my cheek. "I'll be downstairs whenever you want to come down." I watched her walk away with her dog. I wanted to say something, but couldn't. She was wearing a white blouse and green skirt. Her hair had grown longer in the back and bounced when she walked. She looked like she belonged there and I felt like an invited guest.

Inside my mother's room, I walked to the south window and looked over the trees toward the duck pond. Slowly I ran my eyes back and forth across the landscape which perfectly matched the picture in my mind. As I watched, I listened to the silence that filled the house. My ears had become so used to the constant clamor echoed off hard jail walls that silence seemed like a strange, solid presence. Silence is rare and personal. It's one of those things you don't think about until it's gone, but when you get it back, it's like re-uniting with a part of you that you can't live without.

A small glass vase was on the mantel with a cluster of blue violets. Emily had set a wooden easel beside the fireplace and placed on it my unfinished portrait of Tad. I held it in my hands and walked to the window for more light. Stroked my fingers over her face. Once again I vowed to finish it. After removing my coat and placing it over the rail at the foot of the bed, I took off my shoes and sat down. I noticed a small watercolor painting and a brown envelope with a letter on my pillow. I looked at the watercolor first; it was Tad's work. A picture of a boy wading in the river. His jeans were wet up to his thighs while blue sky bounced off the water around him. It was good. I opened the brown envelope and a pack of papers clipped together fell out. I picked up the handwritten letter. It was from Tad. I spent the next half hour reading.

My fingers trembled as I finished the last page. I let it fall to the floor. I lay back on the bed motionless, then threw the pages across the room.

I picked up my portrait of Tad. Couldn't look at it…at her. For the first time the painting made no sense. Holding it in both hands, I hurled it with all the strength I had left. With a loud crack it bounced off the brick fireplace. The tightly stretched canvas twisted and ripped into a hopelessly deformed knot. I pounded my fist on the bed before I buried my face in my hands. I couldn't cry, stand, or lie down. I couldn't speak or think. I walked over to the clump of broken wood and cloth on the hearth. It had ripped right through Tad's face. Her eyes lay on top of the heap. They were the eyes of a child. A child who, at the time she was being painted, had no idea that everything she loved was about to disappear and everything she believed in was about to shatter into dust. I walked back into the hall. Her door was open, but she was gone. I knew she went down to the sunroom.

Emily saw me descend the stair, cross the foyer, and tiptoe into the living room. The sound of the boards under my feet reminded how long I had been away.

I stopped, retraced my steps, and walked back under the stair into the storage room. I found what I was looking for and walked to the sunroom.

CHAPTER FORTY-TWO

The tips of Tad's fingers shook as she stroked the lining of her curtains watching for Emily's light green car to turn into the driveway. It was the day of Stuart's homecoming and Tad looked forward to it as much as she feared it. The last time she saw her Dad he was peering in her window; he had snow caked in his eyebrows and beard.

Sunlight flashed off Emily's windshield as she entered the drive, and tires rumbled over stone pavers. The car door opened and a man with stubby gray hair stepped out. Stuart's beard had been shaved and hair cut short. The first thing he did was glance up at Tad's window hoping for a glimpse of his daughter. Fearful of being seen, Tad jerked her head back behind the curtain, then peeped out from the other side. The gray suit given him by the state was draped over his thin frame. A hollow shadow lay lightly over his cheeks and eyes. She stumbled to her bed and fell face down between two pillows where she stayed while sounds of her Dad and Emily entering the house filled the foyer and drifted into her room.

Two sets of footsteps and the tapping of Bessie's claws ascended the stairs and walked to her door, paused in silence, then moved to her grandmother's room. One set of footsteps returned, stopped again outside her door, then faded away down the stairs.

On Stuart's bed, she had placed a neatly folded letter just below his pillow. Beside the letter she had placed a brown envelope and a watercolor painting. Even though she never wrote to him while he was in prison, she spent months composing the note, saying all the things she thought needed to be said.

Dad,

You need to read this note before you see me. There are some things I want you to know. I'm not sure I can say everything I want to, but please read all that I'm writing and try to understand.

This time three years ago I was in jail, the old one. One morning a guard banged on the bars outside my cell and told me an attorney wanted to see me. She escorted me from the secure portion of the jail to the office area and then into a small meeting room. The guard waited with me for a few minutes until the Sheriff arrived. He dismissed the officer, closed and locked the door. I asked where the attorney was. He said he couldn't come. He was lying, but I wasn't surprised. He sat down across from me, at a small table, and started asking questions. At first he wanted to know what I knew about my cell mate, Novie, and what I knew about her brother, Daggett. I told him I didn't know anything about either one of them, but he continued asking. Finally I told him flat out he was wasting his time, that Novie kept to herself, pretty much, and she never mentioned her brother. I was lying. I didn't know how to say it more plainly but it still seemed to take a while to sink into his thick mushy brain. When it finally did, he started asking questions about <u>me</u>. I couldn't believe it. I didn't want to tell him anything about me. I didn't trust him, I didn't like him. Sheriff Hodges is probably the least likely person on earth that I would have shared <u>anything</u> with. I could tell he was on a fishing expedition, looking for a way to get to me, to get me to do something, but I didn't know what. He asked about you and Mom and what I knew about other people in Jefferson County. Everything I said seemed to be wrong. As he continued, a shiver rippled through me while my head pounded. Frightened over what I imagined he was trying to do to me, I covered my face. He stood and pressed his knuckles on the table, stared at me while he hammered a series of questions pounding *like he was trying to bust open a walnut. After an hour, maybe longer, I grew smaller, he grew larger. I felt captured, condemned, exposed.*

There are some things that we can't hold inside forever. I started to cry. My sobs shook the table I was leaning on. After a while, I said little things that pleased him. I felt better. Eventually things I never wanted to say to anybody started coming out of me easy as my breath. He spoke to me in a completely different tone, softer, lower, more personal and private. I poured out my fears. All of them. To my surprise, he comforted me, told me I had nothing to be frightened about and he would take care of me. Eventually, I told him. I told him my one real secret. No one knew it but me. I had promised myself many times that I would die before telling anyone, but I blurted it out like something inside me that needed to be coughed up.

He squinted at me, got out of his chair, walked to the window, and opened the blinds far enough for me to peek out. I could see trees in front of the building and cars gliding by on River Street. He just gazed at the sky for a while, then sat down again, and rapped his knuckles on the desk. He said that if I was telling the truth, he would help me.

Leaning back in his chair, he said that he wouldn't tell anybody about my secret, but that he knew someone who could help me and all I had to do was assist him in getting information about Daggett.

I told him again that I didn't know anything about Daggett and very little about his sister. He said that I was with her twenty-four hours a day and all he asked was for me to try. 'Just pour out your emotions; make up a story,' he said. Sooner or later she would open up. I told him I would see what I could do. Again, he said all I had to do was give it a try and he would help me.

Once a week for the next month, I told him trivial stuff that I had learned. But he acted as if everything I said was big news. He constantly wanted more, and constantly promised he was getting help for me. He even said he had discussed it in total privacy with a judge who might help me, but only after he was finished with Daggett. I never really knew if I could believe him, but I wanted it to be true and I was beginning to feel I was doing something worthwhile, a feeling I had forgotten. He promised me he would never discuss what I was doing with anyone else and for me not to discuss it with anyone either.

The Sheriff routinely interviewed inmates so Novie never suspected what I was doing. I told Novie the Sheriff was asking me questions about my cousins. After I got out of jail and stayed with Ceda, I kept in touch with Novie and finally met Daggett. He started coming around to see me. He was tall, fairly well-dressed, loaded with money, and probably the biggest slime-ball I've ever known, but I continued to see him and talk with him and eventually I found out how to get secret notes to the Sheriff. It was Novie who asked me to come live with them at the Jenkins Farm.

I was scared. Really scared. I kept telling myself that I was insane for doing it, but Sheriff Hodges continued to make promises and so I found ways to deal with it. I made up stories about me and I made up some stories about you, too. But, it was a kind of self-defense; I didn't trust any of those guys at the farm. They seemed to trust me probably because Novie did. I don't know why she did. Most of the guys got high several times a week, usually at night. That's when I tried to get away from them. I stayed in my room most nights. Usually I went to bed early. A couple of times I got drunk—by myself—but I guess you figured that out.

You remember I love to get up early in the morning. From the window in my room I could see the first early glow in the sky. I took long morning walks down the river all the way to town and back. Hidden by the high banks on each side of the river, no one saw me. I felt safe and invisible.

I never understood anything about those guys or exactly what they did. Mostly I think they were freeloaders. They did odd jobs for Daggett whenever he asked, but I don't think he really trusted them to do anything important. It was like a fraternity there and I was like a mascot or something. They never tired of making jokes about me, crude jokes mostly.

We had one telephone in the house. It was below the staircase in the lower hall. Almost nobody ever got calls but Daggett. Whenever I heard the phone ring, I scooted from my room into the upstairs hall and pretended to look out the window. I heard every word except when he whispered, and sometimes

I heard that too. He wasn't just your run-of-the-mill slime-ball, he was a truly stupid one. I wrote down on my drawing pad the dates and times he got calls, and information or names I heard, and I wrote down the dates and times he was gone.

I continued to find scraps and tidbits about Daggett. Early each Sunday morning, I slipped up the river to the Sheriff's house and slid my latest notes under his door. It all stopped for a while after I moved off the Jenkins farm back to my cousins' place, but one day Novie came to see me. She was working for her brother. Each week she had to drive a truck from the western part of the state back into Jefferson County. She asked me to help her but never said what we were hauling. Of course I knew. Each week we drove in her car to Cherokee County where we met some other people in a truck. I drove the truck back while she followed in her car. I did it for over eight months every week except for the three weeks after the flood and Redbriar was filled with outsiders. When we got to Cherokee, Daggett was always there, but he was never alone. At different times there were other guys with him. A total of six others. I never talked to any of them but I studied them and memorized every angle, wrinkle, and wart in their scaly faces. Each night after a trip, I drew pictures of them. I did lots of sketches of their faces from different angles. All in soft pencil on drawing paper with notes about color of eyes, hair, height and so forth. I resumed my early morning weekly visits to the Sheriff's house. Each time a drawing was finished I slid it under his door along with my other notes. At the Sheriff's request, my name never appeared on anything I gave him.

One Sunday morning several months after the flood, the fog was so thick it was almost impossible to walk the river bank safely. After an hour the sun rose into a dull glow. I made my way upriver to a spot near the Sheriff's house. No one could see me and I could barely make out the shapes of the houses. As I bent over to deliver my notes, the back door opened. From the dark kitchen, the Sheriff's big hand beckoned me in. When he closed the door behind me, I saw the silhouette of a cat on the counter staring out a window into the gray mist. The Sheriff flipped on the light. Over a year had passed since I last saw him. He was thinner, much thinner. Older. Somehow less intimidating.

313

Those weeks at the jail, he always seemed so arrogant, like every part of him was swollen. Now, he seemed timid—deflated. He spoke with a soft voice. I handed him my papers which he took, opened a drawer, pulled out a large brown envelope, and placed the stack into the drawer. He said that would be the last time I would have to do it and that it was almost over. He actually thanked me for what I had done, then opened another envelope and placed its contents on the table. He pulled a stack of papers from the pile and waved them in the air. He explained that they were copies of everything I had given him so far, along with reports from his detectives on what they thought the notes meant and how they were able to piece them together into a solid case against Daggett and the others. My drawings gave them what they needed to identify all the men he was working with. He said the only thing left was to catch them and that was about to happen. He placed the papers back into the envelope, then pulled up a cassette tape from the drawer. The tape had a handwritten label on the side that I couldn't read, but he said all our conversations back at the jail had been recorded and that tape in his hand was the only copy. Everything I had told him about Novie and Daggett and everything I told him about me and you and Mom was recorded on that tape. He said he wanted me to have it, then placed it into the envelope. With both hands he slid the envelope on the table beside me.

He tried to speak but stopped. He picked up an orange cat and sat down. "I don't have anybody that can help you with your problem."

"What about the judge!" I asked, and he said he didn't have one and never did. I was too stunned to speak, too stunned to think. I just stood there. Then he said he knew of someone who could help and he said he wanted me to give the envelope to that person.

"Who?" I asked.

"The only person who can help you and the last one you want to see." I knew immediately who he meant.

"Sheriff, you know I can't do that!" I shouted.

"You need to give these to your Dad and tell him everything."

"I can't do that!" I said again. Then I cried. I didn't want to cry—I

thought I had stopped doing that a long time ago. I never wanted any of this shit to happen to any of us.

"Tad," he said again, "Take it to your father—that's all I can say to you now."

Stuart dropped the paper in his lap and laid his head against the pillow trying to take in the last sentence. He sat up and read it twice again, *"Take it to your father— that's all I can say to you now."* He walked to the window. The view of the river from his mother's room looked upstream toward Redbriar, toward the knoll with Habakkuk's grave under the Redbriar Indian monument, and toward Sheriff Hodge's grave on the knoll beside Habakkuk with a tall granite obelisk engraved with the words, *Lester D. Hodges, Jefferson County's Sheriff.* Stuart returned to the bed and continued reading the remainder of the note.

He thanked me again while he petted his cat. That was it and the last time I saw him. This was not the same Sheriff Hodges that I met at the jail before. I think that man died in the flood. Maybe he turned into a better man, I don't know, but I do know that everything I had trusted and everything I had hoped he could do for me was gone. I was empty. No emotions were left in me.

Instead of returning along the river bank, I walked back through town. The buildings were faint ghosts in the thick fog. I never returned to my cousins' house, but found my way back to Ceda's. The moment she saw me she knew something was wrong. Her warm arms felt so good around me. She listened. I told her everything. She understood. The strongest, toughest woman I ever knew fought back tears as she insisted I had to find a way to explain it all to you. I said I would, but I also pleaded with her not to say anything before I found a way to do it. Then, she said something really odd. She said that she promised me I would never have to worry about the Sheriff again—like she already knew he would die, or something bad was going to happen to him that night.

By noon, the fog lifted, but heavy clouds hung low around the mountains. Later, a black and cold night rolled in. It started to sleet. I stayed at Ceda's alone while she went with the Sheriff on his last raid.

The next day I learned that Daggett had been captured and the Sheriff had been killed. I was afraid for a while that I would be called to testify against Daggett, but apparently the Sheriff was true to his word about not revealing his source. They had enough on all of them by then to put them away and apparently wouldn't have needed me anyway.

The envelope with my papers and the tape is on your pillow. I want you to have them. I want you to believe me. I think my art has kept me going. I love my art, but I want you to know, I love you. Before I write anything else, I need for you to know that, but now I have to tell you about my problem—my secret. I've never told anybody but the Sheriff and Ceda and I realize now that if I hadn't told him and if he hadn't made me do what I did, I probably wouldn't have the courage to write this letter today.

Along with this letter you have found a watercolor sketch of a boy my age. I painted it at the end of the last summer we spent together here. He lived close by and we hung out and swam together near the flat rock. He didn't mind the fact that I continually sketched and did watercolors of him.

As much as I loved Mom—and I still do—I was so mad at her that summer. She was angry at you and I heard her picking at you every day. I wanted you guys so much to get along and I don't know why she was so heated up all the time. By August, she was beginning to snap at me for no reason. If I didn't take my shoes off at the back door, or didn't clean up my mess in the utility room sink, or whatever—she seemed to stay in some kind of snit. She was fussy about washing her vegetables from the garden. It seemed she took hours doing it. A colander of blueberries sat on the utility sink drain board. She had been picking and canning that day and hadn't paid much attention to anyone else. I placed my sketches and paint box on the counter and started to pour out my paint water and wash my brushes when she walked through. With a sharp point in her voice she told me my paint box was muddy and I was to get it out of there. I put my paint brushes back into the jar of paint water, left the jar there and carried the paint box to the sunroom. When I returned, she was busy in the kitchen. I was mad and hurt and generally pissed off. After washing each of the brushes I started to pour out the paint jar when I noticed the color of the water matched the blueberries in the colander. Out of nothing but pure spite I poured the blue paint water over the berries and watched the colored water seep through her precious berries, onto the drain board, and into the sink. I laughed because I realized if she knew it, she would be really mad, but she would never know. After peeking at her again through the pantry door, I felt better. Returning to the sink, I ran a little water over the berries and placed them again on the drain board. I thought that was all I needed to do. I returned to my room and forgot all about it.

The colors in that painting I left on your bed are Tatum white, burnt sienna, cerulean blue, olive green, and two other shades of green with names written in French. They were water colors. Even children paint with watercolors. They were supposed to be harmless, but I was using your paint. I had no idea what they contained and never thought about it– not once until the trial. I listened to the testimony—the experts—about how that green poison doesn't dissolve in water and doesn't easily wash away and all that stuff. I didn't want to believe I had anything to do with it. I didn't mean to hurt her. I wanted to die, right then. I did my stupid prank because I was a kid and I was mad, but I didn't mean to hurt her. I was so frightened, but I knew—I thought—they would find you innocent, or thought they would let you go or something, and they sort of did. I was just fourteen and didn't know what they would do to me if they knew. I thought they would put me in jail or a reform school or whatever they do to stupid kids. So, I didn't say anything. I should have said something, but I just sat there frozen—scared to death. I should have told somebody. The man with the pink face and tiny glasses—that poison expert at the trial—looked right at me when he gave his testimony, or at least it felt like he did. I was ashamed. Still am. I couldn't even look at you, and couldn't bear for you to look at me. I finally buried my face in Granma's arms.

When Granma died I was seventeen, just a year to go before they would let you come for me. I knew you wouldn't wait and you would come, in spite of what the court said, so I ran away. My cousins took me in. Still ashamed. The little cabin was cold as hell but had a view of the river. I watched the river. Three times that year I saw you walk along the bank. I wanted to talk to you, but I couldn't do it. One week after my eighteenth birthday, everyone in the cabin was arrested. You know the rest.

The Sheriff told me he knew of cases where verdicts have been overturned years later because of new evidence and he told me he knew a judge that could help overturn your conviction. That was the only shred of comfort I had heard since I was fourteen. It made me feel better. I needed it and he knew just how much to dangle in front of me to keep me going. I was willing to do anything.

Daddy, I know it's impossible to understand all this. I can't tell you how I felt then. I can't tell you how I feel now. I couldn't control anything. Everything crushed me, everything, and I was alone.

Emily has a dog named Bessie. She found her stranded on a rock in the middle of the river with the water roaring around her feet. Bessie had no choices, nothing she could do except try to dig in her claws, shiver in fear, and hope for someone to come. I know how that little dog felt.

One more thing, I told you I was always scared when I was with Novie's people. You know I took your gun. At first I kept it under my pillow at the cousins' house, still in its sack. Wasn't even loaded but it made me feel better. After Novie asked me to start hauling stuff in her brother's truck with her, I hid the gun in the truck, under the seat, not on the floor but up under the lining of the seat, still in its cloth bag. I didn't think anybody would ever find it. It seems like no matter what I did or how hard I tried I always made things worse for you. I know how much I have hurt you.

I'm working on a painting I want you to see, if you can still talk to me after this letter. If you can't talk to me, I wouldn't blame you. Please come.

Tad

Managing to push off her bed, Tad walked slowly into the hall. Her Dad's room was quiet. In the sunroom, she settled onto her stool in front of the easel, then uncovered a wet palette and freshly cleaned brushes. Using a narrow sable brush and tiny strokes, she dabbled at her painting. It was a portrait of a man sitting in the middle of cattails and high grass beside a pond watching the sunrise. She had spent weeks on the figure, which she painted completely from memory of her Dad.

She thought she heard footsteps lightly tapping across the foyer. She froze, leaned her head to the side, and listened. Hearing nothing more, she picked up the brush again, but occasionally tilted her head to listen. Again, the old wood on the living room floor broadcast a careful rhythm walking toward the sunroom. The sound stopped for a moment, then groaned its way back into the foyer. Cast iron hinges squeaked on the door to the storage room under the stairs. A minute later, the footsteps were again making their way across the living room, then the study. She placed her brush along the edge of her palette, and closed her eyes until she heard her name.

She turned. Stuart stood in the doorway, as if he needed permission to come in. Under his right arm he clutched a large sketch pad. In his left hand he had his wooden pencil box. "Dad," she heard herself say.

He entered the room.

She never knew him to look so thin and tired, and he never knew her to look so beautiful.

Emily, who had been sitting at the dining room table, listened to his footsteps, anxiously anticipating the sounds of their reunion. Startled by the crash of his pencil box striking the tile floor she flew through the house clutching the neck of her sweater. Bessie ran by her side. From the sunroom doorway she saw Stuart's pencils scattered around his feet and his sketch pad sprawled on the floor beside Tad. Their faces were buried silently in each other's arms. Their emotions so far exceeded their stilted vocabulary neither one dared spoil the moment with clumsy conversation.

As Stuart kissed the side of Tad's head, he noticed the

painting on the easel, the tubes lined in a row, and dabs of paint in a circle on her palette arranged exactly the way he taught her. He kissed her again. She buried her face deeper into his shirt.

It took Tad three days to finish the portrait of her Dad and it took Stuart the same three days to finish new sketches of Tad. Two weeks later, he completed the full painting. It was a portrait of a fully mature woman wearing her mother's red sweater. She had her father's long thin frame. Her left hand was resting gently on the frame of the window. She was looking up at the rocky summit of Mt. Tsula where she and her Dad once climbed all the way to the top. The deep blue sky reflected off her eyes while the mountain glowed green with the innocence of new spring.

CHAPTER FORTY-THREE

STUART

What's purer, what's more beautiful, and what's more peaceful than the first dry snow of the season? Like death, everything is silenced by it. What quiets the heart more than attending a funeral during that snow?

An early winter morning found Possum frozen to his tractor's seat. Like a worn -out clock, he simply stopped, Hands still on the rusty wheel. He looked as if he had become a piece of the old machinery. Nothing was left of his last cigarette but a small black spot burned into the corner of his mouth. The Weavertown Baptist Church agreed to let me bury him in their cemetery near his family.

The air was perfectly still as snowflakes floated straight to the ground. The hills, the trees, the church, everything was covered in soft white. The dark, red-clay walls of Possum's deep grave was the only color we saw. Even the top of the black coffin had turned white. I wore my charcoal gray suit, no coat. Emily and Tad wore black coats. Caldwell, Mayor Kinkle, three commissioners, and Ceda were there.

The entire Remington clan arrived together and stood on the opposite side of the grave facing Tad, Emily, and me. We never spoke to the Remington's before or after the ceremony.

As white snowflakes drifted into the open grave, the preacher's white breath rose to the sky. His clear voice was the only sound throughout the short service. I don't think he knew quite what to say about Possum except that he had been a humble man who had been faithful to the few people he knew in his short seventy-five year life. I'm not sure if Possum ever believed in God, but I saw to it he was given a Christian burial.

When it was over, Tad and I walked to Sarah's grave. The gray polished stone stood in sharp contrast with the snow. Tad's hand slipped into mine. We stood in silence while most of the crowd left.

In the foyer of the Stone House, Tad's luggage was waiting next to Emily's and mine. She had only a minute to say goodbye before she was off to Atlanta for her first exhibition. As she picked up her bags, she kissed Emily, who returned the affection with a double-armed rocking hug and said, "We're both so proud of you. I know it will go well. I wish we could be there."

"What time is your flight?" Tad asked.

"Not 'till five," Emily replied.

Tad kissed my cheek. "We'll be back in a few months," I said as I touched her hair. She hugged Ceda, who was there to say goodbye and to take Bessie home with her until Tad returned from Atlanta.

After helping Tad put her bags in the car, and after one more long hug, she was off. I wrapped my arms around Emily to keep her warm. One last look as Tad's car curved its way down the drive. Emily turned in my arms towards me. She slid her hands around my back as my face caressed her thick red hair. "Are we ready to go?" I asked.

"Almost. Three bags packed and one still on our bed."

I looked up to see Tad's taillights disappear in the dry swirling snow. She would be back in two weeks, but Emily and

I had decided to take at least two months for our honeymoon. We started in Inverness where her grandmother lived. With no itinerary, we traveled wherever we felt like going. Two months later we ended up in Rome.

For years after that, the river, the farm, and Redbriar continued to give both Tad and me endless material for our paintings.

After Tad's first exhibit, I never again let my paintings go to gallery exhibitions. I only showed my work privately at the Stone House, and even then, only to selected people. I had to expand my store room because of the growing stock of finished paintings. Tad continued to show in Atlanta, Charlotte, Asheville, and eventually in Washington and New York. In Asheville, she met a talented potter named Harland—she called him Harley. They married on the flat rock and moved into the carriage house. We converted part of the carriage house into a potter's workshop. Tad and I still shared the sunroom studio. She put her easel in a corner where she could see the river and I kept my easel in its usual spot in the middle of the room, but a little closer to the fireplace.

Emily's office in Asheville grew to ten employees. She was eventually named Principal in Charge, but turned it down. Instead, she took an early retirement to help raise Tad's three children and be with me.

Eventually Tad would become so well known that the art world would all but forget about me and my paintings and I would be remembered only by a title I had earned...and one that I loved—Father of Kathleen Remington Burns.

"Forgiveness is the fragrance that the violet sprays on the heel that has crushed it."
Mark Twain

www.ingramcontent.com/pod-product-compliance
Lightning Source LLC
Chambersburg PA
CBHW062036170626
46813CB00001B/349